Recent Books by Mignon G. Eberhart

Three Days for Emeralds

Three Days for Emeralds

Mignon G. Eberhart

Random House · New York

Library of Congress Cataloging-in-Publication Data
Eberhart, Mignon Good, 1899–
Three days for emeralds.
I. Title.
PS3509.B453T47 1988   813'.52   87-42668
ISBN 0-394-56108-2

Manufactured in the United States of America
24689753 23456789 98765432
First Edition

To Janet Gregg Howell in gratitude
for a very long and good friendship

Author's Note

This novel is entirely fiction, and all the persons and events are completely imaginary. However, I have taken a few liberties. Actually there are four, not merely two, gates to Gramercy Park, which in the beginning was a gift of land that is maintained by those who are permitted to use it. There are sets of keys that go to each user of the park; these are paid for, and the funds go toward the maintenance of the area.

I have enjoyed pleasant hours as a guest in the park and have my own respect and affection for it. I must say truthfully that nothing that occurs in this novel has ever taken place in Gramercy Park and, in my opinion, ever could happen there.

Three Days for Emeralds

One

Gramercy Park is a beautiful and quiet bit of old New York. Even the insistent throb of traffic settles into a kind of muted city pulse with only the occasional squawk of a brake to be heard along the streets outlining the park and bordered by its fence.

It was past nine when the couple entered Gramercy Park. By then, the soft summer twilight had settled all over the small but cherished park. Globe lights shone gently through the darkness, and a few wisps of fog had drifted over from the East River. Hiram smiled a little when Lacy dug into her handbag and drew out a key to the tall Lexington Avenue gate to the park. It didn't even rasp as she turned the lock, and Hiram Bascom, anticipating her move, swung back half the gate. "Wow," he said softly.

"Yes," she said. "It is nice. You wanted someplace where nobody was likely to overhear us. There's an empty bench over there." No one else would hear Hiram's reaction to the letter she had given him to read. She hoped that her temerity had not made him decide to dispose of her hard-earned secretarial skills; that would be tragic from her viewpoint: Boss Fires Secretary While Sitting on Bench in Gramercy Park. Still she had had a strong feeling that she must show him the letter. Rose was an old friend and needed help.

No, he would not have invited her to dinner to let her down gently and then, because the men's club to which he had taken her had so many tables closely wedged together, decided that it was not the opportune time to tell her whatever decision he had made.

He slapped at a mosquito. "I see they can't keep bugs out of the park," he said with a laugh that was not quite a laugh, for he had been very sober all evening. Indeed, during dinner, he had only helped make polite conversation in an absent way.

She glanced at the insects whirling around the light on the nearest lamppost. He said, "I'd better get to the point. This letter—I don't really know what would be best to do."

He turned to her and she admired the strong yet pleasant lines of his face, even the nose, which had probably been broken in some schoolboy game and was not quite straight; now she actually saw his whole face quite clearly.

"Do you really know this Rose Murphy Mendez? She says you do, that you were—at least, had been before her marriage—good friends. That is why she sent you the letter?"

"Yes. It sounds so—so desperate. She must need help."

"You feel sorry for her. I can see why. By the way, why do the other girls in the office call you Lacy? In the personnel file your name is Alicia. Alicia Wales."

If he meant to fire her, yes, she supposed he would look up her file. She replied briefly, "My mother's name was Alice. So I was christened Alicia. After she died I think my father really couldn't bear to hear anybody called Alice, or anything like it, even his daughter. Somehow, in a baby way, I suppose, I must have pronounced it Lacy or something close to it. In any event that's what most people have always called me. The girls I went to school with and my stepmother and my father. He adopted it gratefully, I thought. It's Alicia, if anyone insists."

"I don't insist. Lacy's rather nice. In the office I've been saying Miss Wales. After all, we're both newcomers there."

"It's been nearly six months now," Lacy reminded him soberly. If he intended to fire her for her boldness in foisting the problem of the letter on him, she might remind him at least of the time (and she hoped the satisfactory time) of her employment as his private secretary. Indeed, she had devoted herself to his interests and the hideously involved legal briefs she had to decipher.

He still seemed diverted from Rose's letter. He said, "You mentioned a stepmother?"

"Inez? Oh, yes. But she is not the wicked kind. She's been great."

"To get back to the letter—this woman reminds you of your friendship. I see that she signed it Rose Mendez, nee Murphy."

"It is a very—very troubled letter, isn't it?"

"Yes, I saw that, too." First thing in the morning, she had daringly placed the letter on his desk; she could do nothing less. There was something very urgent and frightening in Rose's words.

He dug out the letter from an inside pocket, unfolded it and peered at it through the pale light. "Let's go over it together. Shall we?"

"Yes. Oh, yes. But I can't help thinking she means every word."

"Scared you, huh? I don't blame you. It does sound a bit hysterical."

"She says she must have legal help. She insists that I tell no one but a lawyer."

"How did she know that you work for Bascom, Fitterling and Bascom?"

"Oh, we both attended a drama school. They keep a file there on all their students."

"In the hope that one of them will blossom in the theater? Good publicity for the school. But this letter—your friend is either hysterical or in real terror."

Lacy swallowed hard. "I'm afraid it is real terror."

"Sounds like it, yes. Let's read what she says again." Apparently the letter she had nerved herself to place on his desk had clung to his memory; he couldn't have seen clearly enough in the dim light to read it for the first time so easily, yet he seemed to know it as she did, word for word.

"She begins 'Dear Lacy.' " He glanced at her. "That is why I asked about your name. Well, I'll go on. 'Dear Lacy. I am in dreadful trouble. I am so frightened, Lacy! Perhaps a lawyer can help. I got your place of work from the school. You are my only friend. Will you please, *please* give this letter to the member of the firm you work for? Remember our friendship. Lacy, I am in fear of my life. That is the truth. Surely you can persuade your boss to listen to me at least. I'm sure you will want to do that after you have talked to me. Oh, Lacy, please, please, I beg you, come to see me. Let me tell you why I am so afraid. It will be easy to find me. Remember that little place where you went to school? Fairview. I remembered your talking of it so I took a little place here on Winding Lane. Very near your old school. You are so sensible and kind. But I must beg you, I mean *beg, not to tell anyone* but your lawyer of this. Do not tell *anyone else.*' " He paused. "She underlines 'anyone' quite heavily."

"I'm sure she means that."

He finished the letter. "I've got to have help. That or—oh, Lacy, please come. Rose.' It does sound hysterical," he said slowly. "And yet—"

"Yes. It is not exactly hysterical. I guess she means that somebody is threatening her."

He looked off into the shadows and slapped at a mosquito. "She seems to think that somebody—somebody might—

good God—kill her!" He folded up the letter and put it back in his pocket.

"I think so, too. Although—oh, I don't know what it is all about. But she is my friend, still, and she does need help."

He said thoughtfully, "Do you know her husband?"

"Yes, I've met him."

"When?"

"Oh, before their marriage. That is," she said, remembering, "just before."

"Mind telling me about it?"

"I don't remember much. Rose and I—we were both in a drama school play that was about to be professionally produced, so potential backers were assembled to hear the play and, as a matter of fact, to see the proposed cast. The producers hoped this man, Carlos Mendez, would help back the play. It's important, you know—"

"Oh, yes," he said rather wearily. "I know. The costs now are . . . well, so what happened?"

"A short story. Carlos Mendez took one look at Rose and in a month they were married. She got a part in the play that folded, sadly. I didn't even get a part, which was sad, too. I could see that I wasn't going to set the world on fire with my dramatic talent, so I took a secretarial course, and your firm hired me, and—"

"Now you are my valued and helpful and altogether splendid secretary," Hiram said, but formally. "The problem here is this Rose, who thinks she is in danger and wants to see you because you are sensible. And her friend." Hiram Bascom turned toward her. "I can't say that you look particularly sensible. I mean, that is not what springs to mind when anybody looks at you. Pretty, yes—beautiful. . ."

"What?" Lacy was startled but certainly appreciative.

He drew back a little, as if to view her from a distance. "Yes. Yes, I think, beautiful. Blue eyes, black hair, fine— Well, yes, very nice-looking indeed. You look surprised.

Don't you ever try a mirror? But I always see you, you know, bending over a typewriter or a word processor and, I rather think, swearing under your breath but—yes, keeping at it. It's a good thing the partners don't see you as often as I do. Not," he said rather crossly, "that any of them is a judge, my father included. None of them approves of pretty girls in the office. But your work is very good, you know."

"Oh! Thank you." So no firing for imposing a private affair upon him, at least, not yet.

"Sure. I'm your boss, remember? Well, I suppose the whole firm is your boss in a way. But what I mean . . . oh, the hell with it. This woman, I mean this Rose, does seem scared, and she expects you to find her a lawyer."

"Yes. I'm sorry, but I had to try."

"So you tried me."

A couple who had been sitting on the nearest bench rose and strolled toward the exit; the man turned the key in the lock and opened the gate; they both went out, their figures dimly outlined against the streetlights. The man turned and relocked the gate.

Hiram said, surprised, "Are we locked in?"

"Not really. My key will unlock the gate. Besides, there are still people here and there."

"Yes, I see." He glanced around the small, lovely park. There were only one or two couples on scattered benches. Lacy looked on as another couple started toward the Lexington Avenue gate; there was again the business of unlocking and then relocking the gate.

Hiram watched, dug the toe of his shoe into the velvet sod and said, "So you want to go to see her?"

"I . . . why, yes. I feel I must go. But you are my boss. If you'll just give me a day off—" She fished for an argument. "It might be a case for the firm."

"I'm not so sure. I tried my father and Old Fitterling with this letter and got nowhere. Too busy with this Frankson affair. Hysterical woman, they said. But I can see that you feel you must try to help her. I'm not sure I can take on her case, whatever it is. But perhaps when I know the facts I can try."

Her heart warmed toward him. "I know that you will if it *is* a case. Haven't I read your briefs and typed them up, too? Or word-processed them!"

"And I'll bet they needed some processing. My spelling— But we're getting off the subject." Again he turned directly to her. "I don't really want you to go to see her even though something in her letter does sound—true. I can't help thinking that she may have reason to feel that she is in some kind of danger . . . real danger. Yet, it may be nothing at all. She only wants desperately to see you. I believe that. If she can talk to you, she may tell you the whole story."

"I'll go, then." An untimely giggle threatened her. "I wonder if she is thin or fat?"

"Thin or—What has that to do with it?"

"Rose, as I remember her. She loved sweets, especially candy. She was always trying to resist it and failing. She never was exactly slim but sometimes less chunky. Then she'd go off the wagon, so to speak, and munch away at candy."

"I just can't help feeling that, humanly speaking, something has got to be done for her." He sounded genuinely troubled.

She sighed. "Do you think it could be her husband she is afraid of?"

She could see his frown in the pale light. "Look here," he said abruptly. "You and I could be making a really dangerous mistake, sending you off into the blue simply because this woman wants to see you."

"Oh, I'm not afraid of Rose."

"I didn't mean that. I mean"—he turned to her again—"I know you don't have a husband. It was in your file. I know your age and where you live. . . ." He nodded across the misty park in the right direction for the Wales house.

9

"You see"—he thrust a hand across his face worriedly—
"You may be all wrong about your Rose's cry for help. You
could be getting into some real danger. I may be encouraging
you to go on a stupid kind of chore. Old Fitterling and my
father could be right. Yet if there's a question of saving
somebody's life, one's instinct is to act. But you and I could
be so wrong about your Rose."

"I'll go to see her."

In the half dark she could see that he was still uncertain.
He said with a kind of reluctance, "I'll get a rental car for
you and cover for you at the office."

"I have my own car," she said proudly. "I can drive there
easily. I'll find out whatever it is she wants to talk to me
about."

"Then . . . let me know. Or just use your own judgment
about her. It might be a good idea, if she's living alone in the
wilds, to get her to come to a hotel in New York."

"Fairview is not in the wilds," she said with dignity. "If
it's all right with you, I'll go in the morning."

"Good," he said, and added morosely, "I guess."

They rose. All at once they noticed that the park had
become completely deserted except for them. At the gate,
Lacy fumbled in her handbag for the key. Hiram stopped her
abruptly, with a hand hard on her arm. "No! I've changed
my mind! You can't go!"

"But . . . you said . . ."

"Never mind what I said! You are not to go and see this
fool woman!" He took the key from her hand and unlocked
the gate, and they moved out of the park. He carefully closed
and relocked the gate.

"But you said—" she began again.

"I take it back. You are *not* to go!"

He shoved the key back into her hand, looked down at her
for a second, said, "You little idiot! I can't let you go!"
Suddenly, he bent over her and kissed her, then lifted his

head, looked at her and kissed her again, holding her in his arms for what seemed a very long time.

"No!" She pushed herself back, away from him, took a long breath and steadied herself. There was a light streaming from the entrance of the Gramercy Park Hotel.

His eyes were laughing, yet very intent too. "I know you're not married."

"No. But I am engaged."

The doorman at the hotel blew a piercingly sharp whistle for a cab. It broke an oddly shared, vastly quiet moment, except perhaps for the pounding of her heart. Then Hiram turned her in the direction of the Wales house. They walked a few paces together, slowly. Finally he said rather crossly, "You don't wear a ring."

"No. That is, I did wear one. I lost it."

He gave her a sharp glance. "How careless of you. I suppose it was an enormous diamond."

"No. It was an emerald."

"I'm sure it was the best. . . . Tell me about him. Where did he come from? Where did he go to school—not that it really matters, of course. But how did he get rich enough to buy you what is undoubtedly a superb stone?"

"He inherited money from a rich uncle who died. He was left without a father and mother, but the uncle took him in, helped educate him—a school in Colorado, I think."

"Kind of the uncle—to die, I mean. Well, of course, to take him in and educate him. Costs plenty these days. Where—that is, how did you happen to know him?"

What an inquisition, she thought crossly. Yet she couldn't ignore a small sense of being taken care of. She replied, "It just happened. Inez and I were looking at a Fabergé collection at the Metropolitan Museum. He was there, too. Somehow he and Inez fell into conversation. When we came out, so many people were leaving at once that there was a cab shortage. He got a cab and took us home and—oh, then Inez happened to meet him again. That's all. Except that I am now engaged to marry him and"—she could feel a flush rising in her face—"I shouldn't have let you kiss me and— Oh, here is where I live."

The lighted doorway of her home lay ahead as they turned the corner.

After a moment Hiram said, "Well, then, I needn't save to buy you a rajah's ruby. Not that there seem to be many rajahs left. Here we are." They stopped at white steps. "When are you to be married?"

"I don't know exactly. You see, Richard's work takes him away often. So the wedding date depends upon his time at home. It is that kind of job." She reminded herself that this bordered upon a forbidden description. She compromised. "I mean it's—it's confidential."

"I see." He paused. The constant pulse and beat of Manhattan—taxis, people, everything—now seemed louder, pounding in her ears. At the same time there was an extraordinary sense of electric silence between them.

A light in the doorway sprang into a fullness, and Inez stood looking down at them.

"Thank you," Hiram said politely. "A pleasant evening. But I do mean it, you know. You are to forget Rose and . . . everything. Good night."

He turned and swung away into the dimly lighted street. Inez gazed after him sharply. "Where have you been, Lacy? We have been waiting for you."

We? Inez and *Richard!* This time her heart really did skip a beat or two, a guilty beat.

"You mean Richard? But he's gone. He's not in the city!"

Inez moved a little to one side and Richard appeared beside her. "My trip was postponed," he said. "Come on in, Lacy. You can't stand out there on the doorstep."

He came down a step or two and took her hand, drawing her up and into the house. Inez rustled a rather shabby but once elegant silk dressing gown and disappeared. Inez was always tactful, especially with Richard Blake, of whom she approved.

Richard held Lacy's hand and reached out to close the door to the street.

Lacy felt absurdly embarrassed, like a child caught at a cake box, she thought oddly. Because of a kiss? Well, two kisses and—Never mind all that. She led the way into the long, narrow living room. He and Inez had obviously been having a companionable night cap together. Richard's quick glance caught her own look at the decanter and two glasses. He smiled, "Waiting for you. Where in the world have you been?"

Richard Blake was very elegant, handsome, slim and yet actually quite athletic; his clothing was always carefully tailored—she knew that this was certainly desirable for one in his position. "I'm only a cog," he often said. "A small cog. But sometimes I tell myself a necessary cog in all this diplomatic and varied kind of career I've had—that is, that I chose for myself."

Lacy was sure that he understated his own contribution to that almost unseen, very quiet and carefully secret world. He had tact; he could be, indeed always was, gracious, charming—anything he felt the circumstances required. Usually the parties they attended together were stately and dignified (that was thanks to Inez and possibly also to Richard) and Richard was never an awkward or difficult guest. Indeed, they had met again at one dinner party, a large one given by a brokerage firm that was one of the Bascom company's clients. After that, he had taken her out many times, but these times were interspersed by absences, sometimes quite long.

However, he had always come back and always, he had assured her, heart-whole; he had implied that in the beginning but then, later, had spoken very directly. He had said flatly that he couldn't keep away from her, he ought not even to talk of marriage but couldn't help it. So they had been engaged, somehow, for over a month.

She had liked everything about him. Inez was satisfied, indeed very pleased. Lacy now secretly reproached herself for, well, a couple of kisses—especially at a time when she thought he had been at least well out over the Atlantic.

He gave her a glass and smiled; he sat down and swung one neatly polished handmade shoe so glittering that he might have been attending some very important embassy function. "Glad I waited? Where in the world have you been?"

Two

"Just having dinner. Then sitting in the park. It's a beautiful evening."

"Night, I'd say. By now. One of your admirers?" It was said with a laugh, but there was no laugh in his hazy brown eyes.

He waited.

"Only—" She swallowed hard. "Only somebody from the firm. Just wanted to talk."

He really smiled now, a little condescendingly. "Some old fogy, I expect." She intended to nod or say something; instead she was caught by a gigantic yawn. She felt oddly that she was blushing. Richard saw that, too.

"Dear me!" he said. "Such pink cheeks! You look so lovely, darling. Quite as if you had just come home from a particularly thrilling"—he paused for a second—"dance. Or something."

Lacy said shortly. "What do you mean by 'or something'?"

"My darling! I meant nothing at all." He put down his own glass and leaned toward her, smiling. It was a very warm

15

smile; Richard was in love with her and she was in love with him and she had no business letting herself be kissed by somebody else.

Richard rose. "I've got to be off soon." He glanced down at his handsome watch and said, "At once, I'm afraid. I only wanted to see you before I must leave."

"May I ask you how long you will be gone?"

"I don't know, Lacy. I'm going to Washington tonight. Might meet some colleagues in the morning. Depends. I'll try to phone you before I go wherever I'm slated to go. Darling, are you sure you can put up with this unsatisfactory kind of domestic life I'm promising you?"

"Why, yes. Inez is already planning our wedding."

He glanced at his watch again. "I've got to get to Kennedy. Good-bye, for now." He drew her to her feet, put his arms around her and unexpectedly held her tightly, almost brutally, and kissed her over and over, her lips, her face, her throat.

He was a different Richard. He was indeed rather like an actor in a scene of terrifically ardent love and desire, so much like a carefully rehearsed, dramatic scene that she almost expected a wave of applause from the audience.

She couldn't quite respond to this kind of caress from Richard, of all people. He had been polite, kind, always rather distant—nothing at all like this! In a moment he put her down hard in a chair.

"There," he said with a kind of triumph, "you see. You're my wife-to-be." He wasn't even ruffled by all this display of ferocious emotion. He was completely untouched, again like an actor ready to make his exit.

She heard the street door close hard, as if he had also been somehow triumphant: Curtain! While the audience applauded, she thought wildly.

Luckily his forceful exit had not knocked over the precious Baccarat vase that stood on the hall table, waiting to be packed very carefully, lugged to the nearest post office branch and mailed, with suitable thanks but regrets, to Buddha.

Buddha, otherwise Mr. Burden Smith. She and Inez called him Buddha privately. He had been a longtime friend of Lacy's father, he was always kind and calm, and had been attentive and helpful since her father's death. But Inez, she suspected, had always refused any kind of help in the way of a loan of money. They would get along, she and Lacy. But Buddha rallied with pleasant friendliness, and the vase still stood on the hall table because he had remembered Inez's birthday and sent two dozen (two dozen!) roses in the vase. Inez had accepted the roses, but the vase, she knew was too valuable to accept even from a close friend like Buddha. In the meantime, until Inez wrote him a note thanking him for the roses—which she kept putting off because it was a most difficult letter to compose, for Buddha liked making absurdly expensive gifts—the vase stood there waiting for either Lacy or Inez to wrap it with the utmost care and get it mailed. They had rather hoped that Buddha would chance to call and take it back himself.

Lacy put her hand on the vase, which was quivering slightly, almost as if it had been insulted. She really ought not to have such treacherous feelings about Richard.

That was wrong. Richard was sedate perhaps, very cool and polite but proper and sincere. Otherwise he'd never have asked her to marry him. Not that he had made a great point of it. She had rather suspected sometimes that Inez had contrived their engagement. That was not fair, however, to either Inez or Richard.

But whatever had come over him? She felt a guilty kind of stirring. Richard's touch hadn't even given her an extra heartbeat.

Naturally he had had to hurry to get to the airport. No time for anything but swift, dramatic embraces and kisses, which were totally unlike him.

Also, in a shocking way she still seemed to feel not Rich-

17

ard's hard and furious kisses but Hiram's lips on hers. This was really shocking. This she could not permit. She must take a firm grip upon such wayward notions. Blame sitting in the warm dusk with another man who— Oh, never mind all that!

Inez rustled in from the hall. "So, he's gone. Lacy, how can you treat him like that? Keeping him waiting so long! A man like Richard!"

"I was out," Lacy said feebly.

"Don't you suppose I know that? When I got home it was after seven and you were not here, so, of course, I thought you had gone to dinner with Richard. . . ." She eyed suspiciously the dress Lacy was wearing. "You did at least change from office clothing."

Again Lacy felt guilty, for no good reason. She had hurried home from the office, showered and put on her only rather dressy dress (black and sleek and impressively becoming), brushed her black hair, thanked heaven that it was in an obedient mood, snatched up gloves and a handbag and gone to meet Hiram.

"Yes," Inez went on. "I knew you must have gone out to dinner. But I thought with Richard. I never dreamed that you had gone out with some other man." Inez's eyes sharpened. "Whoever it was has been kissing you! Don't say he hasn't. I could tell from the way you looked when you came home!"

"I didn't look anything!" Lacy tried to rally.

But Inez had very lively blue eyes that missed nothing. "See here, Lacy. You are engaged to Richard. He is the most interesting and best-looking young man of all the young men that I have seen buzzing around you."

"Oh, Inez, I am so tired."

Inez sat down firmly. "Who took you out to dinner?"

"Somebody from the firm. It was—it was business."

Inez looked at her thoughtfully. "Which member of the firm?"

"If you must know, it was Hiram Bascom."

Inez eyed her sternly now. "Where did you have dinner?"

"At his club."

Inez's face cleared. She had an almost encyclopedic knowledge of New York club life. "That's all right, then. Plying you with food and drink but most decorously. Firm business?"

"Yes," Lacy said flatly.

"Hiram Bascom. Dear me! But he did kiss you. Rather thoroughly? He is a very eligible bachelor."

"Oh, Inez, how can you think—"

Inez laughed. "The way you looked when you came in. Bright eyes. A little—oh, something."

"You are seeing too much. It really was business—in its way. And I can't tell you what." There was Rose's anguished plea for secrecy. "I was—told to tell no one, dear Inez."

"Why did he kiss you?"

Lacy did fumble a little there but brought it out. "Conscience, I expect."

Inez sat up. "Conscience! What *do* you *mean*?"

Sometimes Lacy could read Inez's mind. She giggled. "Not that kind. He had told me something that is professional. Something"—she did grope there for a moment, but told the truth—"connected with business."

"Sure it was professional?"

"Oh, yes."

Inez let a few seconds pass before she said with finality, "There's more to this than you want to tell me." She meant to scold, but her mischievous lips betrayed her. "It was something a little more than professional, wasn't it? Well, that might be a good thing. This young Bascom. A junior in his father's, yes, and grandfather's firm. Glad you work there. When will he see you again?"

19

"I don't know," Lacy said slowly.

"But he'll have to see you in the office. Or doesn't His Highness ever talk to his special private secretary? Does he dictate by sign language?"

"Oh, no more questions. Please." She had made up her mind. "I am driving up to Connecticut tomorrow."

"So you will not tell me the facts." Inez rose. "If you're driving tomorrow, be sure your car is oiled and gassed, and don't forget your identity cards." Inez meant Social Security and insurance cards.

"Dear Inez, I'll be very careful." Lacy's voice was unsteady. Inez's love for her was often disguised under seeming nonchalance. She was saying this time, I've got to be sure that if anything at all goes wrong I'll be told so I can help.

"I always count on you, Inez."

"Why not!" Inez picked up her skirts. "Time for bed." She swished into the hall. She ascended the stairs as lightly as a girl and at the top she turned back. "Richard has gone, I gather. When does he expect to be home?"

"I don't know. He never can say."

"Doesn't he ever tell you?"

"Of course not. He is not to tell anyone, ever."

Inez thought for a moment. Finally she said slowly, "You know I like Richard. He is so—so suitable. You must be really very serious about him and your engagement, Alicia."

She called Lacy Alicia only when she was very serious herself. Richard was her choice for a husband. He had to be rather reserved about his career; that was certainly a sine qua non. Inez had more to say. "You can't fool me, Lacy. There's something bothering you. But tell me only when you can." She smiled and said good night.

Oddly, Inez seemed to have no family of her own, no sisters, brothers—no close blood relations at all. This had not struck Lacy earlier; it was only after her father died and they went through a period of worrying about money that it occurred to her that perhaps—just perhaps—Inez might be related to somebody who could give them a hand. She never spoke of this to Inez, and as time went on never thought of it again. They made out somehow.

Lacy saw that the street door was locked, glanced rather guiltily at Buddha's vase and went up the stairs, her hand trailing along a bannister that was smooth and worn from the pressure of many hands over the years.

She closed the door of her bedroom; it was narrow and long and had been her own all her life. Even now, tucked away in a closet, were a favorite toy or two, such things as roller skates, even a toy piano with eight keys, much used and scarred and all but forgotten. The room surrounded her with comfort. The cupboard was locked, only because the once-a-week cleaning woman was extremely thorough and would certainly have thrown out such survivals that she would have classified, relentlessly, as rubbish.

She went to the window and looked down at the soft lights, dimmed by the fog that had crept silently from the East River. She could discern the neatly railed outlines of Gramercy Park and also the Lexington Avenue gate and, very near, the light of the Gramercy Park Hotel.

She and Hiram Bascom had stood there—well, that was only a moment. An old song she had once heard asserted itself, so she even sang in a low voice, " 'A kiss is just a kiss—' " She cut off that teasing unimportant memory.

It was her home that was important. Her grandfather had bought it many years ago, paying what by current standards seemed an absurdly small price. The sum paid for it was practically the equivalent of cab fare—if that, she thought. Her father had held on to the house. During his long period of prosperity that had been easy, and indeed, the house was almost a refuge against the rapid whirl of the present New York City.

Inez had made changes during Tom Wales's lifetime. A dark basement kitchen had been converted to a storeroom. A large pantry, dedicated to an almost vanished breed, a butler, had become a modern, shining, extremely convenient kitchen. A glass-lined cabinet had been provided to protect what Inez called "Lacy's wedding china," thin, fragile and not to be used by anybody until Lacy married and took it to her own home.

Thanks to Inez, also, there were now many long windows overlooking the park, and there were handsomely equipped bathrooms. All these had been rather costly, as prices were rising even before Tom Wales's death.

Tom had owned a small but respected brokerage firm. Lacy always remembered his slowly decreasing confidence in his own opinions (and advice to his clients) on the course of the stock market. Prices were too low, he had insisted; they had to rise. So in that belief he had continued to buy and advise buying, but as it turned out, he was wrong. The bear market continued its decline, and in consequence of Tom Wales's stubborn beliefs his own money and that of his thinning number of clients shrank and shrank.

He had been at the height of his prosperity when he met and married Inez. Lacy could barely remember her own mother, so she was startled and really puzzled when her father told her of his coming marriage.

He had brought Inez to dinner a time or two; Lacy was a twelve-year-old, in school at Fairview and consequently away from home most of the time. Several years later, when Tom Wales decided to marry, he took Lacy out of school; he said that now home was the right place for his daughter. Tom Wales had been very wise about people; he did not say that Inez would be a mother to her; he merely said in a casual way that he hoped Lacy would like Inez.

She was still puzzled and a little nervous when her father and Inez arrived home from their honeymoon. Her new stepmother said only "Hello" to her and nothing more (this to Lacy had been a very kind omission), and about then, with no effort or problems at all, she had simply swept her way into Lacy's heart.

Now that Lacy was older and had seen something of the world, she could piece together some of the events that had contributed to Tom Wales's death. In his last hours he was still desperately trying to provide for his wife and his daughter.

Inez had helped then and ever since. She had refrained from weeping publicly and clasping Lacy in her arms; that was not Inez's way. She had gone directly to the task of handling the sobering business details after Tom Wales was gone. Buddha helped them with steady advice. Eventually, of course, with the recession that was to grip the entire country, indeed the world, the supply of Tom Wales's money had dwindled further. There had been at last barely enough money for Lacy's drama class. Later she realized (she must have had a suspicion at the time) that this expenditure was a terrific gamble when they could not afford it. She had soon realized its futility; she was simply not an actress and could never earn a living in the theater.

Again Inez had advised her as best she could, and somehow the money had been scraped up to pay for a demanding course at Katie Gibbs; secretaries were almost always assured of an adequate salary. Lacy had worked hard; she had to, but Inez looked far ahead.

Although they had never really been poor, both Lacy and Inez had had a taste of what poverty might be like and neither wanted it as a permanent diet. So if one can be said to have one preeminent aim in life, Inez's was to secure a suitable marriage for Lacy. This would be beneficial for Inez, too, and she did not pretend otherwise. Luckily for this project, Inez was innately sociable. She was scarcely in her forties, very New Englandish in an elegant way, with attractive blue eyes, little makeup, enticing lips (when not tightened in disapproval), and brown wavy hair that loosely framed her almost beautiful if somewhat austere face. She had the figure of a girl. It was not difficult for her to look up some of the kind if reserved people Lacy's mother had once known, the type of people she wished Lacy to marry among—quiet, dignified people, who were also rich.

Inez could be skeptical. "Don't hunt for a rich husband. Just go where the rich are," she had once advised Lacy.

For Inez herself another marriage would be nothing short of bigamy; she felt herself still married to Tom Wales and still in love with him. Inez was strong. Not for her were efforts to be youthful, she *was* youthful.

She was also extremely practical about money. When she saw that Lacy must have a car of some kind (she considered subways to be too often dangerous and cabs too expensive), she had somehow managed again to scrape up the money for Lacy's car. Lacy would have taken the subway, but did not out of respect for Inez's wishes. She had even found a kind of garage. Real garage rentals were shockingly high, but with Yankee ingenuity and her own determination, Inez had discovered a small, forsaken factory up for sale but possibly, just for a while, usable as a garage. She had had doors put on it and a sound lock installed. As she always said, "Carpe diem." Enjoy the day as it comes.

Parking was almost impossible in the Wall Street district, but somehow—this time Lacy suspected that Inez had accepted help from Buddha, who always knew somebody who knew somebody—had found a probably temporary, rented parking place not far from Fraunces Tavern and from Trinity Church. In the summer Lacy discovered that the churchyard was a shady, roomy place where a few secretaries and clerks could munch on their cafeteria lunches.

At first she rather resented the freedom with which a handful of her peers sat on the tombstones or grass and ate, but was pleased that they left not a single scrap of their brief repast to litter the place. It always tickled her fancy to realize that the windows of the American Stock Exchange looked down on the churchyard and its tombs, one of which was that of Alexander Hamilton, whose spirit must have enjoyed the proximity to finance. She could never permit herself to perch on the magnificent slab that protected Albert Gallatin, secretary of the treasury in the early 1800s.

Somewhere in Tom Wales's family line there had been a great-great-somebody who not only had been a neighbor of Albert Gallatin but had helped carry Lafayette off the field when he was wounded. Tom was always modest about the family history; but he revered it and had taken a teenaged Lacy several times to lunch at Fraunces Tavern, where, he reminded her, General Washington had said farewell to his troops.

In any event, she guessed it was Buddha who had somehow arranged a parking place for her modest car where it was generally supposed there was none. Her own peers arrived by subway; the higher-echelon personages arrived by chauffeured limousine.

Her little car was nothing like Tom Wales's elegant town car; Inez had disposed of that earlier (advantageously, as a matter of fact). And Lacy had noted about that time that many of the diamonds Tom Wales had given Inez had begun to disappear, but she thought it wiser to say nothing. Later, Inez explained frankly to Lacy that she wanted to mortgage the house. Lacy, as co-owner, had had to sign the papers. There was a very small income from what money Tom Wales had left; this was hoarded and spent, dollar by dollar or, sometimes, penny by penny. Lacy's practical new job was therefore very helpful to both of them.

Lacy still smiled when she recalled Tom Wales's courtship; Lacy's father had described it many times. Inez and he had happened to sit beside each other on a horrifically turbulent plane trip from either Caracas or Tampa—Lacy was too young to pay much attention to that detail, but her youthful imagination was caught by the story. Most of the passengers on the plane got off at its first stop, hoping to avoid more turbulence; Inez and Tom Wales had remained. When they did at last land at Kennedy, he had turned to Inez and said, "You're wonderful. Will you marry me?" They had both laughed, and since Tom's car and chauffeur were waiting at the airport, he invited Inez to ride into the city with him. A few weeks later they were married; it was the happy ending.

Inez felt herself still and always Tom's wife. Now a good marriage for Lacy was Inez's goal. Yes, Lacy had every reason to be grateful to her stepmother.

She wished that she could have felt free to tell Inez of Rose's letter and of Hiram Bascom and his counsel. Yet she could not dismiss Rose's strong plea for secrecy from everybody except a lawyer. Later, when she knew more, maybe she could confide in Inez.

The lights in and about the park were comforting and reassuring in their staid, established way. There were the lighted entrances of the Players Club, the National Arts Club, and the Gramercy Park Hotel. She could even see a certain gate quite clearly. And that was enough of that, she told herself firmly.

Remember, she told herself, Rose was my friend. She simply knew that she must try to help, as quickly and efficiently as she could. There was no possibility of danger to herself, as Hiram had suddenly seemed to fear. No, she would go to see Rose. Now to bed, she told herself: sleep.

She did eventually sleep but kept waking drowsily, remembering the lights of the park and a bench and the rajah's rubies. It was a jumble, but a rather pleasant jumble, and she drifted back into sleep every time. It was early when she fully awoke with the urgent realization that the trip to see Rose lay ahead of her. She wished that she could recall more about Rose and also the directions for Fairview. She dressed hurriedly, remembered as always to put the tiny case that held her contact lenses into her pocket, after first adroitly sliding the lenses into her eyes. This had become a routine on the advice of the ophthalmologist Inez had sought out. He explained that Lacy had a not uncommon trouble: she could see perfectly anything close at hand and reading was no problem at all, but distances blurred and confused her. So if she intended to drive at all, she must wear either big, not very flattering spectacles, or these lenses. Inez had sewn convenient little pockets in every dress and skirt Lacy had. Any object, ten or fifteen feet away, too often led her drastically astray.

She managed to go downstairs without waking Inez and opened the big street door as quietly as she could. Just then, near the door she saw the vase, glittering rather reproachfully, it seemed to her. She would have to pass Buddha's apartment house on the way out of the city. Why not simply take the vase and leave it there? Much easier and, indeed, safer. Inez could apologize politely later. She scooped up the vase, managed to shut the door very softly and clutch the shining and valuable vase closely hoping that no unlucky step would make her trip and break it as she made her way over to Second Avenue and the makeshift but welcome shelter for her car.

It was later than she had thought; a crowded coffee shop tempted her, yet it was already late enough for it to be losing some of its early morning patrons. Anyway, she was afraid to take the vase into any shop; she could get some breakfast on the way to Fairview.

As she started the car, the vase wedged carefully into the seat beside her, she was thankful as always for the distance lenses.

It occurred to her, not for the first time, that they made her eyes look very big and bright. Too bad she hadn't worn them the previous night! Oddly, Hiram's kiss seemed to linger on her lips. Oh, forget it, she thought, and eased her car into the traffic, which was light at that fairly early hour. After she saw Rose she would report to Hiram and, released from the secrecy Rose had insisted on, tell Inez about it; that would be the end of that. She followed Lexington Avenue and finally shifted over to Park Avenue to the handsome apartment building where Buddha kept his luxurious abode. Sometimes she wondered what Buddha would say if he knew the name by which Inez and Lacy referred to him. It had no religious significance; it was simply that he looked like the photographs of a Buddha image and was always serene under any pressure.

The doorman recognized her and said he'd see to her car; he bowed her in. She knew which elevator to take to the right floor. The door was opened by Buddha himself, clad in a gorgeous kind of lounge robe. "Why, Lacy! Good morning! Come in."

"What's happened to Spook?"

Spook was the name Buddha had given to his houseboy, a kind of man-of-all-work, including cooking. He was a small, dark Oriental or Spaniard or Mexican—Lacy was never sure which. Buddha had said he couldn't possibly pronounce the little man's name, so he called him Spook. "Have you had breakfast?" Buddha asked politely, ushering her into the living room. "You don't look it. So early. Stay right here. I'll fix something for you. I'm not a bad cook. You'll see."

"Where *is* Spook?" She deposited the vase on a nearby table.

Buddha smiled and said comfortably, "Dear Inez! I see the vase is back. . . . Oh, it was Spook's day off yesterday. Seems to have prolonged it— Wait here." As Lacy made a movement to help—indeed she did want breakfast, at least a cup of coffee—he said, "No, I don't need help."

Buddha, naturally, would know something, perhaps a great deal, about the fine art of cooking, for he was enormous. He moved as gracefully as a ballet dancer, but layers of fat seemed to have stealthily asserted themselves; he had chins and a vast stomach. He still walked lightly, but when he sat down, he either had to choose a very substantial chair or lower himself cautiously even into the great leather-covered chair in his own living room. Inez and Lacy had managed to discover such a chair—in a thrift shop, actually; they had tried to restore it to some semblance of comfort, and it stood in their living room to accommodate Buddha and his increasing bulk.

He often puffed a little and had a rather disconcerting little breathy chuckle, but neither of these was noticeable as he brought in a handsome breakfast tray and deposited it on a small table beside her. The food smelled delicious. Buddha watched her dive into the thin slice of ham and the eggs; she drank two cups of coffee, felt better and sat back.

"All right now." Buddha arranged himself comfortably. "You have a day off, too?"

"No, not really. That is, my—my boss said I could visit—that is, undertake to see somebody who might become a client. Nobody important," she added hurriedly.

"That's interesting." Buddha smiled. "You must be rising in the ranks. Where does this possible client live?"

"Oh, nowhere you would know."

"Try me."

"It's only a little place. Where I went to school. Long ago."

"At your age, my dear, nothing can be long ago. Let me see now. I remember when your father married and brought you home to Inez. Dear Inez," he said again, glancing toward the table where she had placed the vase. "She is so very determined never to be—oh, dependent, or rather, in debt even to an old friend. After all, it was just the slightest token of old friendship."

"It is a very valuable vase."

He lifted his shoulders. "It gives me pleasure, since I can afford to give anything I like. I enjoy a little birthday gift."

"Oh, she loved the roses. It was only the vase—"

"I know. I know Inez. I certainly did not mean to offend her."

"Oh, we know that. You've always been so kind and helpful—"

"You see, I made money while your father was losing it. I felt sure that the market would go down, so I sold. Your father was sure it would go up and thus advised his clients. Past history."

"Inez was very touched and pleased about the roses."

"How did it happen that you brought the vase to me?"

"Well, honestly, we left it on the table in the hall, thinking you just might call, and I really dreaded packing it as it should be packed—"

"So you brought it. Good for you. Actually I had a slight qualm about Inez's reception of it when I took it to the florist for the roses. Now, tell me how you happened to be passing my place. Surely it's out of your way."

"Oh no. I'm going up to Connecticut. My school was there."

"Of course, I remember. Something like Happy View— No, I've got it—Fairview. Anyone you knew in school?"

She sipped more coffee and said, "I've got to get on. Thanks for breakfast."

"But that is quite a drive, isn't it? Luckily, it is now so late that incoming traffic would be a bother, but look out for trucks. They rampage along at all times."

Lacy rose. "You are always so helpful. And—and understanding, I don't know what Inez and I would have done without you."

"Oh, nonsense." He escorted her to the elevator. The doorman had parked her automobile beside a very impressive Rolls, but he assisted her into her own car with as much care as he would have given, say, the president's lady.

The incoming traffic had lessened, and soon she was fairly clear of the early cars; so late in the morning, she had a quiet drive. Years ago she had traveled this way often. Now, however, once she had turned onto Route I-95, she found herself confused by the growth of manufacturing plants, stores, motels. She was thankful for her distance lenses; she could easily read the various highway signs and knew the precise turnoff that would lead to Fairview. It was by then after twelve— much later than she had meant to be.

Once there, she found that Fairview, too, had changed; she hadn't the least idea where Winding Lane might be. Eventually she found a filling station and stopped. "I'm afraid I am lost," she told the cheerful young attendant. "Things have changed so much around here."

"Sure," he said happily. "Fairview is quite a town, now. Gas?"

"No. . . . That is, I'm simply trying to find Winding Lane. Is this it?"

"Three streets to your left. You are looking for anybody in particular?"

"Yes, please. Mrs. Mendez."

"Oh!" His face grew as secretive as that of a ten-year-old who has been caught stealing cookies. "Sure. She's had some other company today, asking for directions to her place. It's hard to find."

She wanted to say: Who? Yet it seemed unfair to question this boy. But the boy, who couldn't have been more than sixteen, said briskly, "She's supposed to have a husband, too. I've never seen him. I'm here only during daytimes. Not very busy then."

"But you—"

He had quick wits. "Oh, it's vacation. If you're thinking I ought to be in school. But today's been busy for Mrs. Mendez. This morning early there was a couple—big car, chauffeur. Handsome guy, thin, looked sort of Spanish. Bony face but, oh, kind of elegant."

"Spanish-looking?" Lacy said, puzzled.

"Sure. I know. I'm in high school. Whole class went into New York City to visit the big art museum there. Saw a lot of Spanish faces—painted, that is. Portraits. Thin, long faces, light blue eyes, very high-hat-looking. Wouldn't have voted for one of them!"

Lacy couldn't help laughing a little. "When are you going to vote?"

"Soon as I can," the boy said severely. "My civic duty.

Now this Spanish-looking guy had a lady with him. I guess she looked kind of Spanish too, but I didn't get much of a look at her—she was just kind of dark and fat. Luscious!" He grinned at his own word. "But they didn't stay long. Came right back. Oh, yes, and even earlier before they came there was another guy. Young, veddy, veddy British. Had a cat with him—or something. Talked as if he had a mouthful of mush. At least he bought some gas. Had a rental car. I can tell by the number on the license. He didn't stay long either." Looking curious, he asked, "You a friend of Mrs. Mendez? Nice lady but— Oh, nice lady," he said hurriedly, as if embarrassed. "Well, you go that way. Just follow the yellow-brick—that is, the road. Can't miss Mrs. Mendez's house. Has the name on the post office box outside, on the road."

Of course, she thought crossly, whenever anybody says you can't miss it, you do miss it. However, she thanked the boy, who gave her a rather inquisitive look but also a cheerful grin. She started up her car again and soon found a signpost that said WINDING LANE. Probably Rose's house would be large and luxurious; she could envision a tennis court, a swimming pool, a fine blue-stoned approach. At last, around a curve she came to a mailbox with the name "Mendez" printed in black letters upon it. A house loomed up among crowding shrubbery and trees.

Yet as she turned in and came nearer to the house she felt that there must be some mistake. This house could not have been taken by Rose, who had a love of wealth and luxury. Lacy could soon see it clearly, and while it had a certain charm, it was by no means a vast and rich dwelling. It was instead a long, low house with wide French windows along a terrace in front. There was a door between the second and third set of French windows—certainly the main entrance to the house—but it was closed. It was a heavy door, painted green and oddly forbidding as if it said, Strangers, keep out.

She was certainly a stranger. But this house could not have been selected by Rose. Oh, well, then, ask for further directions. She got out of her car, shaking down her linen skirt and pulling her blouse straight. The jacket for the skirt lay next to the driver's seat; no use putting it on. Certainly some stranger would not care. There was no doorbell. It occurred to her with irritation that she still wore her distance lenses; she eased them out carefully as the ophthalmologist had cautioned, shoved them in their tiny case and the case into her skirt pocket and was then able to see the doorbell or, rather, a large knocker of tarnished brass. She raised it and dropped it with such a resounding thud that it seemed to echo in the woods nearby.

There were two narrow slits of windows on the sides of the door. They had curtains, one of which twitched slightly. Suddenly Rose threw the door open and flung herself into Lacy's arms. More accurately, in her haste she stumbled over the doorsill and Lacy caught her and helped her to right herself. Rose cried unevenly, "Lacy! Oh, Lacy, I knew you'd come!"

Rose couldn't be drunk; she was too careful of her looks to do anything excessive in the way of drinking. Unless she had changed.

And indeed she had changed. She drew Lacy into the house, cast an oddly watchful look over Lacy's shoulder and cried shakily, "Sure you are alone?"

"Oh, yes, yes! For heaven's sake, Rose, tell me what is wrong."

Rose steadied herself against a table that stood in the small hall. "Somebody may kill me! Are you sure nobody else is out there?"

Three

"Oh, Rose! You must be mistaken. You must— Here, let's sit down somewhere and talk about this." She straightened her cotton blouse where Rose's clutching hands had dragged it askew and closed the door.

There was a living room just off the hall. Rose led the way, staggering a little.

She took Lacy's hands; her own hands were clammy. "There. . . ." she said vaguely and pointed to a rather shabby chair. She waved a flabby hand and sank into a sofa. She wore a curious garment, loose and varicolored—red, yellow, green—and, Lacy was astonished to see, not very clean. Rose who had always been well dressed, finically fastidious about herself, perfectly manicured and coiffed, with only light touches of makeup on her face! Now Lacy was shocked to see her face was as flabby as her hands and a pasty white.

The room itself was not attractive. The furniture must have been a part of Rose's purchase or rental of the house because it was so different from what one might expect from her own luxurious tastes. The sofa had tattered patches, and the rug was stained here and there. Nothing about the room indicated that Rose had the slightest interest in it. Rose had plumped down into the sofa as if her legs had given way.

"Now then, Rose." Lacy did her best to assume a brisk, no-nonsense manner and to hide her dismay that the once beautiful and charming Rose was now too fat and sloppy-looking and living in such uncharming disorder.

Or, she wondered suddenly, was it a hiding place? The filling station boy had said that Mrs. Mendez had apparently refused visitors.

Rose put shaky hands to her face and then awkwardly tried to smooth her hair. A moment of reason seemed to return to her fleshy white face. Her eyes were heavy, almost dreamy, and red-rimmed. Her lips had no color at all, which gave Lacy another shock. Rose had always used a certain lipstick, which, she had once told Lacy, her admirers had said was exactly right for her name, Rose.

"Now then," Lacy said firmly. "Why did you want to see me?"

"You know why. I found out where you work from the file they keep at the drama school. I had to reach you. I wanted your lawyer. Your boss. Did you show him my letter?"

"Yes. I gave it to him. He read it and told me to take the day off to come here and see you. Now, Rose, he'll listen to your problem if you tell me what is wrong so I can tell him."

"He didn't think I was out of my head?"

"Well, he thought you just might be a little hysterical—"

Rose's voice rose in a thin and unnerving scream.

"Now, Rose, take it easy! He sent me to see you and I'm to report to him. If he feels he can take you on as a client, then—well, that's what you want, isn't it?"

"I want help! I want something—I'm so frightened—I don't know—" She seemed irrational, but she said with a gleam of reason in her eyes, "You are my friend. My only friend really."

Rose had always claimed that her eyes were the color of topaz and perhaps they were when she was happy, but now they were dull and almost colorless. "I tell you I must have help. Now—"

"I only know what Mr. Bascom told me. How can I be of help?"

"He means what he said!"

"He—?"

"Carlos. Who else?"

"But Carlos is your husband."

"No, no." Rose shook her head vaguely but then clutched at her forehead as if she had a blinding headache. "Not my husband anymore. Divorced. That's the trouble."

"Why? What's the trouble? Why are you afraid of him?"

"Because he is Carlos. He has cut off my money. He's never forgiven me. I don't know what to do. I'm afraid." Her words tumbled out in shuddering phrases.

Lacy snatched at what seemed a sensible reason for Rose's incoherence. "You aren't yourself, Rose. Have you had a—a drink? Or anything?"

"Oh, no! I only feel—*so cold—so cold!* I think I'd better have some whiskey. In the kitchen."

Lacy thought rapidly. Perhaps some whiskey might help. Rose had always struggled to care for her own body, but her battle with candy or whatever else was obviously a losing one now.

"I thought *you* might believe me!" Rose caught her breath and cried sobbing, "Nobody would believe— Now even you don't believe me! Just leave me here and wait for him to kill me—"

Breathing deeply to calm herself, Lacy noticed for the first time that the house had an unpleasant odor, as if it had not been opened for some time. "Wait, I'll get you a drink. Where's the kitchen?"

Rose waved a hand. "That way—"

The kitchen was surprising, too. A few dishes had been left in the sink. A table held a coffee pot and a cup next to a plate with bits of nibbled toast and cold egg along with an open box of candy. So that was it! Too much candy! Lacy debated for a moment. There couldn't be any risk in giving Rose a drink; it might restore her to some kind of sensible speech. On the counter, she found the whiskey. Luckily the bottle had been opened and some of the contents used, but not enough to account for Rose's incoherence. Still her terror was real. Lacy did not question that.

All at once Lacy looked nervously around the kitchen; she felt almost under observation, as if somebody were there, hiding perhaps, keeping very quiet. She even thought that something somewhere creaked just slightly. That was silly! Rose would have told her if someone was there. Besides, there was only the small littered kitchen, a tiny pantry, and an even smaller entry to a back door. So Lacy found a clean glass in another cupboard and rather tartly congratulated herself on finding anything clean. However, she rinsed the glass in a stream of brown tinted water that flowed from the tap at the sink. When it finally ran clear, she put some of it in the glass and added whiskey. But now, ice.

She might have guessed; the refrigerator yielded scraps of dry or moldy bits of food on saucers and two or three dried-looking pieces of candy. A damp package of something or other was wedged into a shelf. The refrigerator itself was adamantly and dismally silent. No ice, naturally.

She took the glass to the sitting room, where Rose still sat in a kind of huddled lump. Rose took it in both hands as if she might spill it.

"It's all right," Lacy said. "Whiskey and water. I remember that you don't drink—" But there was the bottle, obviously opened and partially used!

Rose mumbled. "It helps. Sometimes. Oh, you don't know. Carlos is a fiend when he's angry. He's never forgiven me for leaving him, you know. He wasn't so fond of me really—not really, only at first. But I told him, I was angry about—about that woman he had lived with for years and said I was going to leave him. He asked who the man was.

Oh, I don't *remember* all he said! He's—" She took another gulp of whiskey, shivered a little, stared at nothing and said, "You don't know Carlos. His pride—he'd sooner kill anybody as look at her. He guessed I wanted to go with another man—so he threatened me—Carlos is a bad enemy—"

"Well, he's not here now—" That was not very comforting. Rose gave her a glazed look that held fear.

"You never know what Carlos can do or—or when. But he never forgets what he calls pride. Besides, now he knows."

"What does he know?"

"Why, I—naturally, I remarried!" She shoved out a shaky hand showing a new and very plain wedding ring.

"Well, but—you divorced Carlos—"

"No, no. He divorced me. Now I have no money at all."

"Well, I—" She thought rapidly; there was her own small savings account. "I can help you a bit."

"No, no. This has got to be— Oh, Lacy, I don't know what to do."

Her hand shook, splashing the drink on the already stained sofa. "Need it—so cold—" Rose mumbled again.

"You'll be all right. Just perhaps, well, too much candy!"

Lacy got down to brass tacks again, or tried to. "Why do you think Carlos means to kill you? You say that he divorced you. But, Rose, surely Carlos gave you some sort of settlement. He was—is—very rich, isn't he?"

Rose seemed to peer at her from some unseen cloud. She shrugged, sloppily. "Carlos? Oh, yes. But not my new husband. You don't understand." She was getting more and more muddled. Lacy measured the glass with her eyes. Rose had taken almost all of it and it had certainly hit her very hard. Too hard. It had been a mistake to give it to her.

Rose said jerkily, "Carlos married again. A Spanish slut who had her eye on him—seems he had lived with her long before he married me, and she clung to him and at last caught him, but she had to get rid of me first. She or Carlos had me watched. Yes, I'm sure. The point is I married again, too. So—" She put down the empty glass with a crash. It didn't break the glass but it was a near thing. Rose leaned forward, her eyes blurred and yet glassy. "That's the point. That bastard Carlos gave me a fine allowance, I will admit. But then he got hold of the fact that I had remarried."

"Wait, Rose. Who told him that? You?"

"Me! Oh, never. That friend of his or somebody anyway from Logonda had been acting as Carlos's emissary. And I discovered not a friend but a spy. I was told that since I had married again, the allowance Carlos had given me was to be cut off. It was in our divorce settlement. Now I have no money at all. So"—she gave something like a sob—"so I took this ghastly little place—really, oh, Lacy, really to hide in. And hope for help. But my new husband likes money. The plain fact is, Lacy—I can tell you—I think he has some debts he expects me to take care of for him. I am afraid he wouldn't have married me at all if he didn't think I still had all that money. I could live in luxury and I did, for a while. I can't bring myself to tell him the truth—the truth. Better just to hide—" Rose sobbed, leaned over like a soggy cushion and collapsed into an untidy heap.

Moving like a machine, Lacy tried to massage the flabby body, she tried to bring air into the lungs. She moved the rib cage up and down. There was not the faintest flicker of a pulse in Rose's wrist. Even when Lacy put her head down over Rose's heart, she could feel not even a flutter.

She was dead!

Lacy had to accept the unbelievable fact. Actually only a few moments had passed—ten, perhaps fifteen at most. Finally she looked helplessly at the crumpled-up mass that was Rose. A doctor, of course! How could she get a doctor? She looked at her watch and wondered frantically how long it would take to get a doctor. It was impossible to accept the fact of Rose's death right there, before her eyes. It couldn't be. But it was.

She lifted her tired arms and cramped body. A telephone.

Certainly there had to be a telephone somewhere in the house. She got a handkerchief from her handbag and wiped her own lips hard before she stumbled her way into the hall. She felt like an old, old woman, utterly exhausted. Rose couldn't have died, just like that while she was talking!

There was a telephone in the kitchen. What did one dial? She tried the famous danger-help-help number and got nothing at first, but after a long, long moment a faraway voice advised her to try another number. "Please note the number," said the voice.

She had no way to write it down. She'd remember it. She couldn't remember it. But there was a kind of mental click and the telephone buzzed—she had remembered the number. "Doctor Steane's office," said another voice in her ear; it seemed near and more human.

"There's been a terrible accident—can the doctor come? Please—oh, please—"

"Where are you?" the pleasant voice said distinctly.

She gave as accurate a description of the road to the house on Winding Lane as she could. She gave Rose's name as Mrs. Mendez, for that name was on the post office box. According to Rose it was no longer her name. Yet she continued to use it. Lacy thanked the pleasant voice at the end of the telephone. The voice was concerned. "Yes, I know Fellows filling station. His boy, Hobie, helps him. A mile or two further along Winding Lane? The doctor doesn't have a patient there, I'm sure."

"She's not a patient. She just died," Lacy said with dreadful bluntness.

"Oh!" The voice wavered but resumed with kindness. "I see. I'll let the doctor know. I'm sure he'll come to help you if he can. As soon as he can."

But he didn't come soon enough.

It seemed wrong to leave Rose lying on the sofa slack and unlovely. After a moment Lacy went up the narrow stairs and found a bedroom that must be the one Rose used, for there were crumpled pillows on the bed and a dressing table laden with cosmetics. Lacy thought first of a sheet. She looked around vaguely, wondering where or if there was some kind of linen chest or closet, and found herself looking at the face of Richard Blake.

It was a photograph, a snapshot really, taken with the sun in his smiling eyes, but it certainly was Richard, in shorts and a loose shirt, laughing.

She looked for a frozen moment before she saw the inscription scrawled across it that said, unbelievably, "For my loving wife."

Four

This could not be!

The snapshot, the inscription and Richard's laughing face! It was not possible. The unframed photograph was standing propped up by a jar of something or other—talcum powder, she remembered later. But the man *was* Richard. She picked up the picture and took it to the window to peer more closely at it. There was no mistake. Her mind, like a mad runaway horse, leaped to every explanation. Richard's brother? Twin? He had no brother. His cousin? If he had a cousin who resembled him so closely, surely he'd have mentioned it. No, she remembered clearly, Richard had told her that he had no family. Well, a joke of some kind, then? A meeting on some tropical island, or in some tropical country, for there were palm trees in the background. And wasn't that a swimming pool in the corner beside him? It had to be a joke. She could see it far too clearly.

Just then, she had the feeling that a fluttering motion on the lawn below had attracted her attention without her actually being aware of it. Closely edging the house itself was a sparse scrap of lawn, a thick hedge and then woodland. It seemed to her that perhaps there had been some motion of some shrub, some shadow, something. . . . Instinctively she groped in her pocket for her distance lenses, and slid them into her eyes. But in that instant everything became perfectly still. There was simply nothing moving. The wind? There was no wind. A creature? A deer? Even a dog? No. The shrubs were still; nothing dodged among the trees. There was simply nothing at all. A figment of the imagination, she told herself firmly; it had nothing to do with her stunning discovery.

She looked at the snapshot of Richard again, but with her distance lenses she couldn't see his face clearly. She didn't need to see it. Richard could not possibly be married to Rose while Lacy and Richard were planning their own marriage.

Even a fantastic speculation about bigamy on Richard's part touched her utterly confused thoughts. That was as unbelievable as Rose's dying as she had. This is a nightmare, Lacy told herself. But it was no nightmare; it had happened.

She tried again to make herself believe—at least half believe—that the inscription on the picture was a joke of some kind. Just at that moment the huge knocker thundered through the house. Automatically she shoved the snapshot into her convenient pocket along with her distance lenses, and ran down the stairs. The front door was opening and a man came in, nodded in a kind but sober way and said, "I'm Dr. Steane. Trouble here?"

"Oh, yes. Yes. She's in here—"

She led him into the living room. She had not found a sheet with which to cover poor Rose. It didn't matter now. Nothing mattered just now but the doctor's careful scrutiny of Rose. The sudden death had appalled Lacy: the totally unreal discovery of Richard's picture had frozen her senses as she watched the doctor swiftly test Rose's vital signs.

He looked at Lacy and asked gravely, "You are a relative?"

"No, a friend—"

"What is your name, please?"

"Lacy—I mean Alicia Wales."

He nodded. "She's gone, you know."

"Oh yes, I know. While she was talking. I was here—"

He glanced at the whiskey bottle and glass. "You gave her something to drink?"

"Yes." Lacy must pull herself together as best she could. "Yes, that." She nodded at the bottle and glass.

The doctor didn't touch either, but he leaned over, sniffed and shook his head. He replaced a stethoscope, which Lacy had not noticed, in a little black bag, shoved his hands in his pockets and said again very gravely, "I'm afraid that was the wrong thing to do."

"Wrong? But she asked me for it. I thought she needed it."

"You thought wrong. Didn't you know that she was already heavily sedated with something? There are many drugs that shouldn't be mixed with alcohol. I'll have a look at her medicine cabinet."

"But she had only had sugar! That is, candy. She always wanted sweets and tried to fight it and—hasn't succeeded, I think, lately. Anyway, she seemed so dazed and cold. I thought she would be better for a drink."

He said abruptly, "You are as white as a sheet."

A sheet, she thought; if it hadn't been for trying to find a sheet, I wouldn't have seen the picture of Richard. The doctor put a hand on her shoulder.

"I think she may have been accustomed to a certain amount of drinking—moderate perhaps. If it is any comfort to you, her dying like this is far preferable to living in a comatose state perhaps for years. These things are difficult, sometimes impossible to judge with accuracy. But that is what I am inclined to think."

"But Rose drank only, I suppose, recently. She was lonely. She never took drugs. Never."

"You live here with her?"

"Oh, no. But I knew her once. She sent me a letter asking

me to give it to a lawyer in the firm where she found out I work. She said she was in trouble."

"Do you have the letter here?"

"No, no, Hiram—Mr. Bascom—has it. She begged me to come to see her."

The doctor waited a moment. Then he said, "I'll have to call the police, you know. But they would have called me anyway. I'm the medical examiner for this district. You go out in the hall or somewhere and wait. I'll phone first. Then I'll take a look at her room. I'm sure I can find it. She probably kept whatever she was taking in her room, or in a medicine cabinet in the bathroom. Come with me."

He led her—almost carried her, in fact—to the hall and then into a small dining room, which looked curiously unused. He put her down in a chair. He found the kitchen telephone. She could hear him talking slowly and carefully to someone who knew him and whom he knew.

He came back to her. "Don't worry now. The police will be here soon. I'll tell them—"

She found speech. "But Rose never took drugs before or not even much alcohol! Everybody knows how very dangerous that combination is!"

The doctor shook his head. "Not everybody. At least, sometimes people get so heavily sedated that they don't know what they are doing, don't even remember, what they have just done. Actually I think you might do with a little"— he gave her the barest flicker of a grin—"a little spiritus frumenti." He added rather boyishly, "How do you like my Latin?"

"Yes. All right, I mean. But not from that bottle—" She could see herself pouring a glass of whiskey for Rose and holding it to her flaccid hand. "No!" She cried.

His brief glimmer of youthfulness disappeared. He looked out the window behind her. Finally he said, "Nobody else here?"

"No. That is—" What about her momentary notion that

someone else was hiding in the house? What about that vague impression of movement into the shrubbery? "She lived alone. Except for her—" But Richard could not be her present husband.

"Her husband?" the doctor said. "Where is he?"

She could tell the truth here. "I don't know." Could she possibly be talking about Richard?

The doctor's gaze shot to her own face and sharpened. "Do you know him?"

She got out a word. "No!" But she was sure of that picture. She was thankful that she had thrust it into her pocket.

He sounded like a lawyer, not a doctor. Yet every doctor had to be a kind of lawyer, or detective, using knowledge plus intuition in investigating.

"I was alone with Rose when she—she died. But when I was upstairs looking for a sheet, I thought there was some kind of movement toward the woods. Out there—" She motioned with her hand. "I did put my distance contact lenses in, but there was nothing. Not even a moving blur."

"I see. Will you let me look at your lenses?"

"Certainly." She slid them out of her pocket, cautiously as always.

He took them carefully, eyed the two small disks and said, "I'm not an ophthalmologist. Here, take them back. This blurred figure you saw. Could it have been a man?"

"No. I really think I only imagined it. I couldn't possibly know. . . . There's somebody coming."

"The police!" the doctor said and started for the narrow hall as an automobile zipped up the driveway and stopped with a squeal of brakes. The outside street door was thrust open, feet came pounding into the house and a voice shouted, "Lacy! Are you here?"

It was Hiram Bascom; she had taken too many letters at his dictation not to recognize his voice at once. She flung herself toward the hall, after the doctor.

Hiram shouted again, "Lacy! Oh, there you are! I knew

you'd be here. I kept phoning you and your mother—and phoning and— What in hell is the matter?"

She flung herself against him, and he held her close in his arms. "Oh, Hiram, you don't know! She was talking to me—in there—she was talking—"

"What is all this? Who are you?" Hiram demanded in a furious voice, speaking to the doctor, who calmly replied, "Dr. Steane. You are a friend or a relative of Mrs. Mendez perhaps—"

"No! There, there, Lacy, don't cry! I'm here—" He was promising her protection from the shocking world she had insisted upon venturing into.

The doctor said, "She is all right. If you are not a relative—"

Hiram burst in, "I'm not! *What has happened?*"

Lacy sobbed into his shoulder and got words out. "In there—she died—talking—"

There was an instant or two of a kind of packed silence. Lacy lifted her head while continuing to sob; the doctor and Hiram were exchanging a serious yet somehow sympathetic look. Why, she thought vaguely, it's as if they were old friends. The doctor said quietly, "If you'll come in here. Miss Wales is quite upset—" (What a word for it, Lacy thought wildly. Miss Wales is having a fine fit of hysterics.)

She drew herself up a little at that, but not too far from Hiram. She mopped her eyes with the back of her hands. Hiram looked down at her, drew out a handkerchief and gently wiped her face.

"Yes, Doctor," he said. "Tell me."

The doctor told him quietly, stressing nothing, merely the facts as he had found them. Hiram listened. His face was completely devoid of any expression; yet because he was there, in an odd way Lacy began to feel more like herself, more in control, more as if she had not strayed into a nightmare that had turned into tragic reality.

Hiram said at last to the doctor, "I see. That is—no, I

47

don't see. But I sent Miss Wales here. She works in our office. Bascom, Fitterling and Bascom—"

"I know the name of the firm," the doctor said quietly. "You are—"

"Bascom the third. Mrs. Rose Mendez wrote a note to Miss Wales, asking her to give it to one of the lawyers in our firm. She said she needed help and so urgently asked to see Miss Wales that I consented to Miss Wales's wish to come out here and talk to her friend."

"Do you happen to have the note with you?"

Hiram, the lawyer, did not hesitate. He pulled it out of an inner pocket. "Here it is. Mrs. Mendez does sound a bit hysterical—but here it is."

The doctor took poor Rose's letter, read it carefully and turned to Lacy. "So then—"

Lacy said, "She was a friend. She sounded so frightened and—of course, I came." Lacy mopped at her eyes again. "I had to come."

Hiram said crisply, again the lawyer, "After Miss Wales and I had talked it over, I began to think that if there was something to the letter, then Miss Wales just might find herself in trouble—"

"Ah," said the doctor.

"So," Hiram went on, "I changed my mind and advised her not to come. I told her to forget it." He gave Lacy a look that was both angry and, oddly, proud. "I might have known she'd come anyway. This morning I started phoning and phoning and couldn't even reach her mother, and—well, I guessed she had come here. So I followed. I couldn't have been more than an hour or so behind her. What killed Rose Mendez? I'm assuming that something killed her, she didn't die of natural causes."

"Yes," the doctor said calmly. "I'm very much afraid something like that happened. In a peculiar way—that is, I regret to say, Miss Wales here gave her the final touch—"

Hiram's face hardened. "You must explain."

"But I didn't mean to," Lacy began. "I didn't know."

"Let the doctor explain, Lacy." Hiram's voice was firm.

"Perhaps we'd better go into the dining room. Miss Wales looks—Yes, this way."

It wasn't far, but Lacy clutched Hiram's arm. He put her into a chair; it was near the dining room table; she put her arms down on the cold, unpolished wood.

The doctor explained. He couldn't explain much. But he did emphasize his view that it was better for Rose to have died so swiftly, rather than to linger in a comatose state for perhaps years.

"But I killed her—" Lacy's voice wavered.

"You did no such thing," Hiram said. "If I had dreamed— But I did hope you wouldn't come. However"—he turned to the doctor— "have you found anything—drugs, anything that could have made a little drink of whiskey so lethal, and so very quick."

"No, Mr. Bascom. I was about to go upstairs and look through the medicine chest, or wherever she kept her medicines. I may get an idea then of what she must have taken. And I may not," he added morosely. "About that movement that Miss Wales thinks she may have seen going toward the woods—"

"I didn't really see anything!" Lacy said.

"Certainly." The doctor was a little flustered. "But she couldn't be sure. Couldn't—" the doctor added rather dubiously, "or wouldn't."

Hiram turned to her. "Were your contacts in?"

Now, how did Hiram know that she wore those lenses? He must have seen her at some time adjusting them surreptitiously; it was her notion that nobody would employ a girl who couldn't see beyond a few feet. Hiram saw more than she had known he did.

She shook her head. "Not then. I dug them out and put them in my eyes, but by that time if there was anything at all it had disappeared."

A long wail like a low moan was rising in the distance. The doctor said, "Here are the police!" He went into the hall. Hiram sprang up, came to her and took her hands. "Now, pull yourself together. You had no reason to hurt Rose. If the doctor is right, somebody had to have a reason. And," he added grimly, "Rose was afraid. Let me see to this. Just keep quiet and—" He looked around. "No place to lie down or—well, anyway, just keep quiet. But tell the police anything they ask if you really know the answers. Take my advice now."

He went out into the hall. She leaned on the dinner table. She had had too many shocks too quickly to reason out anything at all, much less reply sensibly to any inquiry.

First, Rose had died as she had died. Clearly, the doctor viewed it as homicide. Yet the doctor said that Lacy herself had unknowingly given the final blow. It was all unbelievable!

The other deep shock was the picture of Richard and its inscription. That *could* not be the truth. Richard had met Rose somewhere, there must have been a party with some kind of silly jokes, photographs. All the same she would keep the photograph safely in her pocket and tell nobody of it.

Certainly Richard was not available to be questioned. She had no idea when he would return.

She could only wait and try to restore some inner well of self-confidence, which not only had been threatened, but seemed to have vanished completely.

Five

It did return a little, although not entirely, when Hiram came to summon her to talk to the police. Two or three hours later she and Hiram started for home.

Hiram at first insisted upon leaving her own car there to be picked up later. She couldn't, at least wouldn't do that, not the car that had been purchased with so much saving by Inez. Hiram at last gave in but followed her closely in his own automobile.

Hiram had stood between her and the hall when an ambulance had drawn up outside at last and in a very short time had departed. Hiram had helped with the police: he gave Rose's letter to the captain in charge, who read it slowly and asked Lacy how recently she had seen Rose. Several years? But they must have been very close friends. Yes, she supposed they had been. But then Rose had married and she had taken secretarial training and gotten a job. She had given the letter to Mr. Hiram Bascom for whom she worked.

Hiram explained again the course the letter had taken. The captain nodded gravely and asked again if Rose Mendez had been a very special friend of Lacy's. Well, not exactly, but they had been friends. "Good enough friends for her to appeal to you?" The captain asked.

"Why, yes. You see, in drama school we entered at the same time and and we shared chocolate malteds and worries and stage fright and all that. Rose was beautiful," Lacy added sadly.

So Rose had married, then been divorced by her husband, was that it?

Lacy had to say, yes, that was what Rose had said.

She repeated as best she could the all too brief and inconclusive talk she had had with Rose. No, Rose had not seemed herself, she said she was cold and needed a drink.

Hiram said, "So she must have had some real and tangible cause to turn to Miss Wales for help. And so to me. Miss Wales intended to try to get a lawyer—me—to do what I could for her friend."

The captain, O'Leary proved to be his name, asked Lacy, "What else did she tell you?"

Lacy hesitated for a second; the captain's eyes seemed to drill into her hesitation as if he might guess the reason for it. But then Richard simply could not be the new husband Rose had so despaired of. Lacy went on again hurriedly. "She was very confused. That is, I thought she was afraid of her former husband. She said—" Lacy gulped but went on, "She said that in the divorce settlement, there was a clause saying that he would supply her with a very generous allowance as long as she remained unmarried. But if she remarried at any time, the allowance would be cut off. So she didn't tell him of her new marriage. But he found out, and so she had no more money from Carlos Mendez. And she—" This was hard to get out; yet that new husband could not possibly be Richard. She went on, "She felt that her new husband *might* have married her in the belief that she was a rich woman and she was afraid of losing him. I'm not making much sense of this. But she was very confused, mumbling, talking wildly, I thought."

"Do you know who this new husband is?"

"No!" she said promptly, definitely. "No! She didn't tell me."

"I take it she still used the name of her first husband, though?"

"Yes," Lacy replied.

"Ah," Captain O'Leary said and continued with his inquiries. The doctor helped when he could offer any fact.

Yet even with Hiram's good sense and firm support, as well as some sympathetic help from the doctor, it had been a very hard time, especially when Captain O'Leary got out what looked like a schoolchild's notebook and began making notes of everything Lacy said. He caught Hiram's look of surprise and said agreeably, "We are old-fashioned here. Not much money for fancy modern gadgets."

The whiskey bottle was carefully wrapped in what looked like cellophane. Lacy knew her fingerprints were on it.

She did recount—several times, as a matter of fact— Rose's demand for whiskey because she was cold. It would have been, she told them, quite unlike the Rose she had once known to drink at all. But considering the half-empty bottle, she could only suppose that perhaps it was only an occasional lonely drink.

Much of it was repetition.

There had been, it developed soon, no sign of any household help. Not even a maid or cook, keeping out of sight in the tiny pantry merely to avoid Rose—or Lacy or anything in the way of problems with Rose.

The police captain questioned Lacy about the hint of motion she thought she had seen out toward the woods, and the doctor put another oar in then, explaining about her contact lenses. She had in fact seen nothing, certainly nothing identifiable. Pressed, she said if anything at all had moved, it had to be very small.

At last Hiram quietly but very firmly suggested that Miss Wales had had a terrible shock and that she might be permitted to go home. The doctor, in that quick, tacit friendship with Hiram, agreed that Miss Wales had had a dreadful experience; they could question her again at any time; she would leave her address and telephone number.

Finally, O'Leary had permitted her departure with Hiram, first asking if he could retain the letter. Hiram said, certainly, if Miss Wales agreed; Lacy said feebly, "Oh, yes. Yes." O'Leary added a quick word that they would be questioned again and tucked away the letter and paper on which Lacy had written her address and phone number.

The doctor went with her and Hiram to their two cars in the shabby driveway. The doctor became very serious when Lacy insisted upon driving and, with a glance at Hiram, said that it might be better if she rode with Mr. Bascom, and he would see that her car was sent to her. But Lacy stubbornly said no and crawled into her own car. Nothing to be done about it, she heard Hiram say to the doctor, who shook his hand and said something like "Girl couldn't help Mrs. Mendez."

Hiram said, "Thank you, Doctor. We'll be in touch."

So the procession of two started out. Oddly, the moment Lacy got behind the wheel of her shabby but beloved automobile, a measure of normalcy returned to her. At least, here was something she could do and knew how to do. She led Hiram along Winding Lane. She stopped only when they reached the filling station and the boy stepped out into the road and hailed her. "Hey, miss—"

She braked automatically and looked at the fuel gauge; she had enough gas for her return to the city. But by that time the boy was leaning in at the door beside her, his freckled face alive with curiosity. She knew that Hiram had stopped, too, behind her own car.

"Say," the boy said. "I saw the doctor's car and then the police and then an ambulance and— Say, what was going on at Mrs. Mendez's place?"

"You'll hear later."

"Who died?" he asked.

"Mrs.—Mrs. Mendez."

"The lady that lived there. Sure. Who killed her?"

She replied, stumbling over the words. "She just—that is—nobody killed her!"

"Oh, come on. They don't turn out like that for anything but murder. I think—"

"I've got to go."

"Hey, wait a minute!" He turned to yell at Hiram, "Hold on!" And quickly back to Lacy: "I don't know. I've got to go. Well, my name is Hobie, Hobie Fellows. Everybody knows me. I only thought," he said, eyeing her significantly, "that somebody might want some information. That is, if she was killed. So, miss—"

"Thank you," Lacy said and put the car into gear.

"All right, then," he called after her. "But I'll likely be seeing you. . . . Okay, mister. Gas?"

After a rather long five minutes Hiram's car loomed up again in her mirror. She remembered the way to Route 95, although she didn't actually remember any of the signposts or directions as such; she seemed to be going home, she thought, like a cat finding its way back. She was very careful about traffic. At a certain point she thought she would never reach Gramercy Park, but eventually she did, and thankfully, almost with a sob in her throat, she parked her car in front of her own doorstep. Hiram, following her closely now, stopped just behind her. Another car was parked nearby, too; a long luxurious town car of a distinguished make. She paid no attention to it; her only thought was that now she would see Inez, now she was home, but she was thankful for Hiram's presence. He would explain anything at all more concisely and better than she could.

She was suddenly enormously hungry. She glanced at her watch and was vaguely surprised to find that it was only five o'clock, yet so much, so dreadfully much, had happened.

Hiram was beside her when she thrust her hand into her handbag and took out the key to the house door.

Inez was in the living room.

A tall, bony, very elegant man who looked vaguely familiar to Lacy rose from a chair and looked over Inez's shoulder. Even in her exhausted state, Lacy was conscious of his appearance, so tall, so graceful; he had a very long, thin face and pale blue eyes, and even his clothes exuded a kind of authority. Spanish, the boy Hobie had said. His chin and lower lip actually suggested some long ago and certainly impossible connection with the Hapsburgs; this notion struck Lacy as a result of the young Hobie's erudite description. But a neat mustache, pointed beard and Elizabethan ruff would not have looked out of place on him.

Inez cried, "Lacy! Where have you been? Are you ill? You look terrible."

Hiram came quietly to Lacy and put a hand on her arm. The strange man came gracefully forward. "Allow me. This young lady is about to faint—"

Hiram was ahead of him and half lifted Lacy into a chair. "Get her something to drink, Mrs. Wales. She's had a bad time. I'll tell you about it later, but just now—"

Inez turned pale; she went swiftly toward the liquor cabinet in the dining room. Lacy sat back.

"You don't know me," said a cool, rather condescending voice near her. The tall, elegant man stood beside Lacy, eyeing her with cold but watchful eyes. "I am Inez's brother. That is, her stepbrother. My name is Carlos Mendez. Oh, there you are, Inez. Miss Wales, I suggest you drink this."

Lacy stared at him. Did he say Mendez? Mendez? Inez's stepbrother? Why, then, Rose's husband! This was the Carlos who had terrified Rose! Hiram, rather oddly, took the glass and actually tasted it before he held it out to Lacy. She tried to drink, gulped, tried again and Inez said, "Haven't you eaten anything all day? You'd better get some food into you before—"

Hiram said shortly, "She hasn't had time to eat."

Lacy continued to look with astonishment at Inez's self-proclaimed stepbrother.

Carlos said icily, "I see that it is news to her that you have a family of any kind."

"Never mind that now, Carlos," Inez said in an equally cold, clear voice, which Lacy had never heard from her before. It could have cut granite at that moment. She said, "I'll get the child some food. How about you, Mr.—Mr. Bascom, is it?"

"Hi," said Hiram unexpectedly, and added in a bored way as if he'd heard the comment too often, "I'll answer to hi or any loud cry." He looked hard at Lacy and then turned to Inez. "Let me help you. Don't drink too much of that, Lacy. Just sit back and don't think." He didn't say, "Don't talk" but an odd notion that that was what he meant drifted into Lacy's mind.

Carlos Mendez, Rose's onetime husband, here in the city, so close, too close, to Rose's murder! Carlos Mendez, who was probably seen by the boy Hobie on his way to Rose's house! Lacy felt that the drink she had taken had gone to her head with alarming rapidity. But Rose was afraid of him; she was a little anxious about the new husband—who was not, couldn't be Richard—but afraid of Carlos.

Carlos smiled; it was a rather tight smile, which made one think of a cat that had seen its prey. "You didn't know that Inez had a brother?"

She shook her head.

"Or a sister-in-law—"

Why, yes, Rose, she nearly said, but Carlos continued, "My wife. I should say my present wife, Yolanda. Although"— he paused thoughtfully— "Inez has another brother, too. Rafael. Quite a family," said Carlos, smiling tightly again.

Six

Lacy simply sat; she turned and turned the now empty glass in her hand and tried to recall anything Inez had ever said about a family; there was nothing.

Carlos went to the fireplace and stood in a graceful way, one elbow on the pinkish marble mantel. "We all live in Logonda, in South America. A small country. Some might call it just a good-sized farm, but it's more than that." His handsome yet chilly face moved slightly. "It is very rich. You didn't know anything about me? Or Rafael? Or my wife, Yolanda?"

"Only that Rose Mendez was—had been—your wife! Rose and I were friends in drama school."

Carlos did not appear to notice the change of tenses in the verb. He said nothing, but his icy, pale blue eyes surveyed her minutely. From the kitchen came the sound of voices, low; Inez and Hiram were talking and also clattering dishes and silver. A smell of something very good drifted into the living room. Oh, I'm so hungry; how can I be so hungry, Lacy thought, and watched the elegant tiger—Inez's brother. No, only stepbrother. That seemed to make a difference. Like an old-time movie scene, a kind of biography of Inez flashed across her mind. Certainly, Inez had never mentioned Carlos or the name Mendez. It seemed an incredible coincidence, but this Carlos must be the first husband who had cut off Rose's allowance, and the man Rose had feared.

Sometime or other in the past, Lacy had seen Inez's passport or some official document; her name there had been Susan Timpson, a good old New Englandish-sounding name. She was sure that Inez had never mentioned the name Mendez, so she must have had some reason for cutting herself off from this member of the family.

She would have stopped Lacy if she had known that Lacy intended to visit Carlos's former wife, Inez's former sister-in-law. Hiram must be telling her about it now, in the kitchen. Lacy closed her eyes and leaned back. The entire day had proved so eventful in a dreadful way that somehow another surprise didn't seem remarkable.

Suddenly someone rang the doorbell violently and persistently and then must have given a hard thrust to the door itself, which evidently neither Lacy nor Inez had locked because it banged open against the wall. It was closed hard, and there was the sound of footsteps as someone crossed the hall, seemed to pause for a second to take bearings and then approached the living room. A tall, handsome woman appeared in the doorway, staring at Carlos Mendez with wide and very angry black eyes.

"Yolanda, darling," said Carlos. His pale blue eyes had a wicked gleam.

The woman's black eyes flashed. "Don't darling me! You've been trying again to see that bitch—"

"Stop it!"

"She can't get you back. I'll never let her get you again." For the first time the newcomer seemed to be aware of Lacy's presence. There was another angry flash of her black eyes. "Don't tell me you've got another one! I'll not have it! I tell you, I'll not—"

"This is my sister's stepdaughter. Her name is Alicia Wales. They seem to call her something else—" He shot a demanding pale gaze at Lacy, who had to reply: "Lacy. Inez is in the kitchen—"

"Ah!" Yolanda gave Lacy another sweeping, and doubtful, glance. "But what are you doing here anyway, Carlos?"

Carlos was still unperturbed. "You've done some shopping, haven't you? Expensive shopping, I'm afraid! That bracelet—"

"Naturally, I'm not going to sit around in a hotel most of the afternoon while you chase women. It's a nice bracelet. Not," she said as if hurling an insult at Carlos, "with any emeralds in it!"

Carlos moved; an emperor could scarcely have moved more confidently. He caught Yolanda's wrist, held it up, peered at the sparkle of a large band of gems on her wrist, got out a curious kind of glass, which he fastened neatly in one eye, peered again and said, "You've been cheated. Whatever you paid—or expect me to pay—for this bauble, you've been cheated!"

"I was not cheated! I'll show you the box—a most reputable shop!"

Carlos eyed the box she pulled from a handbag and thrust at him. Of course, Carlos's present wife also lived in the South American place he had named, a place Lacy was perfectly sure was as rich as Carlos had said.

He shoved the box back into Yolanda's hand. "When you buy jewels, you really must take my advice."

Yolanda gave Lacy another suspicious glance.

"Where is Inez?"

"In the kitchen. This girl, Inez's stepdaughter, has not had time," said Carlos carefully, "to eat today. So Inez is arranging some kind of food for her. She'll be here in a moment. Something very unpleasant seems to have happened. You'll hear—"

Yolanda seemed to mull this over but stormily. Then she

hissed, "Emeralds," an impossible word to hiss but Yolanda managed it.

"Sit down," Carlos said in what seemed his usual voice of command. He might as well have added, "and shut up." Lacy rested her head against the chair back.

Hiram returned, carrying a tray that clattered musically and sent forth an aroma of Inez's special and delicious soup. Inez followed him, rolling down the sleeves of her pale green cotton dress.

"Rose—" she began. "Rose Mendez! Oh, Lacy, why didn't you tell me where you were going today and why? I ought not to have let you go. Rose! This is terrible—" Then she saw Yolanda and stopped with an odd kind of gasp. "You—here!" she cried.

Carlos showed no emotion. He took the tray from Hiram and deposited it on a table beside Lacy. "This is my wife, Inez. You remember Yolanda. She's a little upset. I have been here longer than I intended."

"Not more than fifteen minutes," Inez said and took a long breath. "How do you do, Yolanda?"

"Oh," Yolanda said. "You can't pretend to have forgotten me, Inez."

"No," Inez said, as coolly as Carlos. "I have not forgotten. I suppose I only thought that you might not wish to be reminded of how well I know you."

This was an attack; Lacy dimly recognized it as such, and Hiram stood near her almost as if he wished to provide a kind of barrier. He must have told Inez the whole story about Rose while they were in the kitchen. Inez was not one to let any emotion show if she could help it. She said, "Do sit down, Yolanda. How are the children?"

This seemed to be another quiet but telling thrust, which was out of character for Inez, who was never malicious. Yolanda's dark face flushed. Her black eyebrows lowered over angry dark eyes. Madame De Farge, Lacy thought wildly, taking one quick glance at her.

Yolanda's eyes glittered with rage. "They are quite well. All of them," she added as if daring Inez to speak again, possibly to name the children, one by one. Lacy gulped her soup and decided that the ties between Carlos and Yolanda must have been long and close. The children? How many, and where were they?

Yolanda herself took the initiative. She sat down, in a composed way now, but it was the composure of a brooding volcano. "How kind of you to think of them, Inez! César and young Emilio are enrolled in school in England. No need for a governess! Little Maretta is still at home with us." She sat down, neat feet close together. But her legs? Lacy peered over her soup; Yolanda's legs were more than a trifle plump; so was a double chin below an extremely firm face with full and fully painted lips. Her dress, however, was beautiful, the kind of street dress that Lacy and Inez admired and must have set Carlos back at least six or seven hundred dollars. She ate more soup and was thankful for the warm and natural kind of glow that began to spread through her; thankful for that and for Hiram's gravely (and carefully, she was sure) listening ears.

"Another spoonful," he said in her own ear.

Inez sat down and stared at nothing. Her face was so drawn and pale that Lacy was sure that Hiram had given her a full résumé of the facts.

Hiram now turned to Carlos. "I'm afraid we have brought dreadful news for you, sir."

Carlos's thinly arched dark eyebrows drew together. "You mean?" An iceberg couldn't have given off more coldness.

"Your wife—" Inez began, then stopped as if she could not force herself to go on, and gave Lacy an anguished look.

Yolanda uttered a small hiss like a coiled serpent's. There might not be much flora around at the moment, but a wicked little voice suggested to Lacy that just then in the sitting room there was plenty of ferocious fauna.

Carlos took one dignified step toward Hiram. "What is actually wrong?"

"Your wife—I mean your former wife—Rose, is dead."

There was a sudden, heavy silence. Then Yolanda gave a pleased kind of chuckle. It was hideously shocking.

Hiram turned to her. "I am sorry to say that the police believe she was murdered."

At that the heavy silence deepened. It was as if everyone in the room had been suddenly paralyzed except for Lacy, who lifted the bowl and drank the last of the soup. Even that sound seemed very loud and normal in a world which had, that afternoon, become unreal.

Yolanda got her breath back. "*Rose! Did you say murdered?*"

Carlos advanced on Hiram, who, however, stood his ground so firmly that Carlos was obliged to stop dead. "Go on! How do you know that?"

The doorbell pealed again; and as Inez turned toward the hall, the street door was flung back again too abruptly and Inez ran out of sight.

Lacy heard her exclaim, "*Raf!* My dear Raf!"

"Oh, God," said Carlos, but resumed his graceful pose at the mantel.

Yolanda stared at him. "He is following you!"

Inez appeared in the doorway clinging to a tall, dark, very handsome young man. Inez was almost crying. "Raf! You've changed. My dear, Raf, you've grown up—"

"How long have *you* been in New York?" Carlos demanded in an authoritative way.

The young man barely looked at him but gave a very graceful shrug.

"Long enough. I had to see Inez."

"Then," Carlos said, "you don't know—"

Yolanda cut in. "She's been killed. That witch. That Rose! No real wife—but—"

"But a legal spouse," Inez said. Lacy realized that, unusual as it was for her stepmother, Inez was again wielding a wicked kind of dagger and Lacy could guess now what that dagger was. Three children, of an age where the two boys could be sent to England to school! Oh, Yolanda might have considered herself Carlos's wife; indeed she might even have been legally his wife and Rose—poor Rose—the illegal interloper. However that was not exactly a likely notion. Remembering Rose's onetime shrewdness, Lacy could not accept it. And in any event, Rose was dead.

Carlos spoke icily to Hiram. "You were about to explain this—this extraordinary statement about Rose."

Inez left Raf and went swiftly over to Hiram. She said, "Buddha, I mean Mr. Burden Smith. He is a friend."

Hiram stared for a second and then appeared to see some sense in her few words. "A good idea. Might help. The telephone?"

"In the hall. Under the stairs."

Hiram walked quickly into the hall.

Carlos's eyebrows lowered. "Who—what—what is Buddha? I didn't know that you had taken up a religion, Inez."

Inez tried to give a little laugh but it came out as a sigh. "Oh, no. It's only a name—a kind of nickname Lacy and I have given him. I mean Mr. Smith. His name is Burden Smith. He doesn't know that we call him Buddha. It's only because he—"

There was a listening silence in the room. Raf alone looked puzzled but also troubled. Yolanda fussed with her glittering new bracelet. Lacy leaned back again.

They could hear snatches of Hiram's words from the Hall. ". . . Yes, Mr. Smith. This is Hiram Bascom. Well, we are at Mrs. Wales's—she hopes you can come. Yes, here. . . . Why, yes, yes, very urgent I'm afraid. . . . Thank you."

The telephone clicked and Hiram came back. "He's coming, Mrs. Wales. As soon as he can get his car out—or his chauffeur can get it, I suppose. Anyway he's coming."

He caught the fire of Carlos's pale eyes. "He is an old friend of Mrs. Wales."

Carlos was clearly offended. "Can you mean that our family affairs are about to be thrust upon this man, whoever he is?"

"Oh yes," Hiram replied lightly. "Seems indicated." He looked at Raf. "You really are Mrs. Wales's brother?"

Inez was still capable of producing a kind of laugh, though not a very merry one. "Why, of course! My own brother! That is, half brother. Much younger, of course. Carlos is"—her voice hardened again—"a stepbrother to both of us."

The tension in the room became almost palpable. A family quarrel, Lacy knew, was impending and she had to be part of the family because she owed it to Inez. Her stepmother linked her arm through Raf's, and he looked down at her lovingly. Clearly Raf was on Inez's side, whatever the quarrel was about. Strangely—and indeed sadly—nobody seemed really concerned about Rose. But Lacy was deeply concerned; at the thought of Rose she seemed again to lose contact with the real world. She was brought back to it when suddenly the street door was pushed back with another crash. A yellow creature darted into the room and gave a rapid look around with very bright eyes. Wagging a plumy yellow tail, it flung itself toward Raf, who gave a low chuckle. Inez cried, "What is it, Raf?"

Yolanda drew up her plump legs as if the creature might attack her. Hiram went over to take a closer look and said, with a little chuckle, too, "Why, it's a dog! Of course!"

"She's a dog," Raf said. "Name's Jessica—" There was a strong accent upon the last syllable. Hearing her name, Jessica jumped into Raf's arms.

Yolanda shrieked. "That's a dog? It's a rat! It's a ferret—"

"Now, now, Yolanda," Carlos interposed but looked glacial with anger at the same time. "Where did you get that creature, Raf? Why on earth did you bring it here with you?"

Raf scratched the back of the dog's ears. Not being a cat,

65

it couldn't purr but looked as if it wanted to. "Couldn't help myself," Raf said.

"Oh, come on, boy. Of course you could help it. Where did you get her?"

"She got me," Raf said pleasantly.

"Explain that!" Carlos ordered.

Raf did not take offense. "But that is what happened. Nobody knows how. It was on the plane from London." Lacy thought there was a teasing light in his dark eyes.

"Dogs," said Carlos icily, "do not ride in planes."

"This one did," Raf said, still with a wicked sparkle in his eyes.

Inez swiftly tried to intervene. "Tell us how, Raf. She looks a darling—"

"Odd," said Raf. "A very odd little thing! But I like her. And she likes me. I couldn't possibly get rid of her. Could I, Jessica?"

Jessica wriggled and thumped her tail, but by now she was lifting a shiny black nose and sniffing; her black eyes were on the soup dish Lacy had placed on the table beside her.

"Don't act so stupid," Carlos said sharply. "You don't mean she simply came on the plane. She couldn't—"

"She did," Raf said. He paused. Lacy had a suspicion that he was rapidly inventing. "Nobody knew quite how. The only reasonable guess was that some previous passenger had smuggled her in with a carrying bag or something, and nobody realized the dog was there, and then, well, we—the pilots and the steward and the girls—all decided that she had hidden under a seat somewhere until the latest batch of passengers arrived and then crawled out and got on my lap. Of course, there was an alternate theory that she had crawled up the passenger gangway only to explore and then hidden, but that's all any of us could think of. And as she wouldn't leave me, I had to bring her along. Simple," he concluded, his eyes dancing.

There was a longish pause, but then Jessica signified her

intention to get down from Raf's arms, made it with a wild leap and darted, a flash of furry yellow, to the table beside Lacy, where she shoved her tiny black nose over the table toward the empty soup bowl. It gave Lacy a welcome feeling that the world as she had known it up to that visit to Rose still existed. She got up. "She's hungry. I'll feed her. Come on, Jessica," she called to the dog, who followed her, tail wagging, knowing perfectly well what Lacy meant.

Hiram said to Raf, "Stay here. I'll go with her."

He went with Lacy and the frisking dog to the kitchen. There was plenty of Inez's excellent soup, which included meat and vegetables and gave off a most enticing odor. It was now lukewarm. Jessica got up on very tiny hind legs, but her tail still wagged wildly as she sniffed and watched Lacy pour soup into a flat dish and put it on the floor. Jessica showed good manners by giving Lacy's ankle a lick before she started in on the soup noisily and hungrily.

Hiram said, "Well! This family affair does grow complicated."

"I didn't even know that Inez had brothers or—or anything. She never talked of them."

"Must be a sound reason," Hiram said.

"But—but, Hiram, they don't show much interest in Rose."

"Oh, they're interested all right. Very interested indeed, I should say. They just don't want to talk about it. At least," he added thoughtfully, "they don't want us to hear their talk. So we'll give them a chance. Until Burden Smith arrives."

Lacy sat down on a straight-backed kitchen chair. "Hiram, I keep thinking of what the filling station boy said. I mean, that Mrs. Mendez had had company this morning."

"That boy who stopped you and talked and talked. What exactly did he say? What company?"

"He said that a big handsome man, who looked Spanish, came in a big rental car, he could tell by the license and chauffeur. Had a dark—he said luscious—woman with him.

But before that, quite early he said, another man had come. He said veddy, veddy British, talked as if he had a mouthful of mush. This young man didn't stay long, stopped to get gas. He had a rental car, too, and a cat. But he wasn't exactly sure it was a cat—"

"Jessica," said Hiram.

"It could have been. The young man—"

"Raf, I suppose."

"—was driving himself. On the way back, as you saw, the boy at the filling station stopped me and asked what had happened. He had seen the doctor's car, and the police, and the ambulance, and—and then he asked who killed her. He guessed it was a murder—I expect from the expression on my face, and everything else—anyway, that's what he guessed and I said I had to go and you were waiting and he sort of yelled and said somebody might want some information and told me his name."

"A forward-looking boy," said Hiram soberly.

"His name is Hobie something. Then he said he'd be seeing me."

Hiram nodded. "Sure. Of course, he just might have seen enough to identify these visitors. He looked like a smart kid. Well, I expect the police ought to be told. Don't look like that, Lacy. We've got to go through with this as sensibly as we can."

"Oh, I know." The little touch of normality to which Raf and his doggy friend had contributed drifted away as a great wave of harsh reality swept over her again.

"I can't—I can't believe it happened just like that—"

Hiram put his arm around her. "Easy, now. We'll get through it."

"But I was there!"

Jessica cleaned up the bowl and sat down to lick her paws. The doorbell rang, stabbing in short bursts. It was Buddha's way of ringing.

"It's Buddha," Lacy said. "We've got to tell him—"

"Certainly. That's why we called him."

Buddha's hearty voice came from the hall. "Thank you, Inez. What's all this about?"

"We'll tell you," Inez said. "This way—"

"Come on, Lacy." Hiram put a steadying and comforting arm around her. But it was terrible, unbelievable, part of a nightmare to have to admit that she not only had been there beside Rose when she died but also had actually helped bring about her death.

Seven

It was not quite as bad as she had felt it would be, but it was not easy either. Buddha somehow seemed to take it all in stride. He acknowledged introductions; he did say that he had not known that Inez had two brothers and a sister-in-law. Yolanda pulled down her skirt and allowed a pleasant but momentary gleam to come into her black eyes.

Buddha shook hands with Carlos. He leaned over to kiss Inez lightly on the cheek. He shook hands with Raf, too, giving him a swiftly appraising look, shook hands with Hiram, advised Lacy to sit down for heaven's sake before she fell down and established himself comfortably in the enormous chair that only he was big enough to fill.

"Now then," Buddha said calmly, his shrewd eyes almost hidden by his fat cheeks. "Now then, Mr. Bascom. You told me some things over the phone. I believe you said—"

"Yes," said Hiram. "I'll tell you everything we know."

Hiram went to stand by the mantel. Carlos had seated himself, choosing a very stiff straight-backed chair and looking so much like old paintings of Spanish grandees that he

70

needed only the tiny mustache, beard and white ruff to qualify entirely for the boy Hobie's description.

Raf appeared simply puzzled, but his bright eyes shone. Yolanda leaned forward, eyes greedy and intent. Only Buddha looked thoroughly comfortable, but his eyes were mere slits above his large cheeks. Lacy had no doubt that he was absorbing every word Hiram said. She also knew, after following Hiram's words too, that he had omitted at least one item.

"And that's all," Hiram had said firmly at last.

Yet it was not quite all. Lacy was tired and confused; she hated coming back into a nightmare world. In the kitchen, with the hungry dog, somehow everything had assumed a more natural and comforting tone. Now she felt herself back in Rose's house and being forced to believe the unbelievable. She was sure Hiram had not told quite everything, but she was too desperately weary to weed out just what he had not revealed.

Buddha stirred and heaved himself a little further upright. "So that is all," he said softly.

"Yes," Hiram replied shortly. "I mean, that's all we know now."

"Now," Buddha said.

"Oh, my God!" Inez took a long breath. "You can't mean—Why, Lacy wouldn't, she couldn't!"

"There now, Inez!" Buddha said. "Don't get ahead of yourself. Why didn't you tell me you had a family before?"

"I couldn't!" said Inez, biting off the words. "I couldn't brag about them—except Raf here. And I hadn't seen Raf since I left what was called my home."

"Didn't you know the first Mrs. Mendez, Inez?"

Yolanda bristled at that but kept quiet. Inez said clearly, "Never. Carlos married her after I came here and married. This is my home. I'm Mrs. Thomas Wales."

"Yes, Inez! I know. But there must have been some family differences."

Carlos could keep his majestic silence no longer. "If she tells it, you'll not understand—"

Inez interrupted. "He *will* understand. The fact is my kind and loving stepbrother took every cent he could get his hands on of my father's property, including what was legally left to me. I don't know how he did it, but I know he did it. That's the main reason why I left home. I came to New York. I thought I could get a job somewhere. Also I had to get away from his—that—" She looked so pointedly at Yolanda that that lady sat up and cried, "That is a terrible thing for you to say! And hint at—"

"Nonsense," Inez said icily. "They had—have—three children. I knew I had to make my own living. I didn't intend to continue to act as nursemaid or— But it didn't matter, after all. It was on the plane from Caracas that I met Tom Wales and he asked me to marry him."

Buddha's eyes flickered toward Lacy. "The child is very tired, Inez. She has had a terrible experience. Shouldn't she—"

"Yes." Inez took Lacy's hand. "Come on, Lacy. What you need is a good sleep."

Sleep, Lacy thought vaguely. How could she sleep?

Yet moments later, after Inez had propelled her up into her own room, she fell asleep at once. She was dimly aware of the talking downstairs, and of doors closing and cars starting up in the street below. She did rouse when somebody tiptoed into her room and stood above her. She knew, too, who it was, and struggled to gain some degree of consciousness. "Hiram—"

"Sure. Lacy, they've all gone. Except that half brother of Inez's. He's still here and also"—there was the faintest touch of amusement, not in his face, which she couldn't quite see, but in his voice. "Jessica is with him. What a dog! I really cannot believe he acquired her as he said he did."

She worked hard to hold on to a hazy sort of understanding. "I thought he made it up. Just to annoy Carlos—"

"Perhaps. But—can you hear me, Lacy? I mean, can you understand me?"

"Certainly."

"All right." He leaned over and put his hands around her face. "Listen. You are not to say a word about the movement or anything at all you saw, but didn't really see, vanishing in the woods. Understand me?"

"Why not?"

Hiram said flatly, "Because somebody somewhere might not believe you couldn't see anything identifiable. Go back to sleep, but remember that."

She knew that he leaned over her; she thought vaguely that he had kissed her very lightly.

Then he was gone. She dropped back into a world where murders couldn't happen. Yet somehow in the dream Inez came, too, leaned over Lacy, pushed her hair back from her face and told her to listen. Lacy roused again and listened.

"It's a short story," Inez said. "My mother was married very young to a man who was a civil engineer. They were in that small place in South America, Logonda. It's more like an enormous ranch, but it's rich. My own father died. My mother married Carlos's father, who was a widower. He liked Inez for my name—so I became Inez Mendez. Rafael, my half brother, was born when I was about fifteen. He's older than he looks, but by the time he reached his twenties, Carlos had a stranglehold on his property and on mine. So Raf left home, too. Somehow, I think, he got a job in England and now has come back. You hear me, don't you, Lacy?"

Lacy knew that she heard every word.

"So that's all there is to it. Except that neither Raf nor I can trust Carlos about anything. Oh, my poor child, go back to sleep."

Lacy's eyes closed heavily before Inez had even left the

room. She was only dimly aware of a window being opened and a second later the door closing softly.

It explained the family struggle; she could understand that, even half asleep and drugged with the shocks of the day. She thought again of the snapshot showing Richard. Richard himself was too far away to consult or even to explain the existence of the photograph.

But when she became thoroughly awake in the morning, she roused herself, took the crumpled snapshot from her skirt pocket and tucked it in the zipper compartment of her handbag. Then she crawled back into bed and slept again.

In the early afternoon, Fairview's Captain O'Leary came, accompanied by one of New York's finest, both in such discreet plain clothes that that alone all but proclaimed: Police! The extra man had been sent obligingly—and no doubt, also legally—by the nearest precinct captain. Captain O'Leary brought with him an envelope of odds and ends, among them Lacy's own engagement ring.

Eight

It had been, up to then, a peculiar, gloomy day in spite of summer sun and a light breeze. Inez had busied herself feverishly about the house. Raf had taken Jessica for a short run in the narrow garden back of the house and then gone over to Third Avenue and bought a collar and leash, which the dog didn't like and tried to remove by rolling and biting at the leash and clawing at the collar.

Inez had told Raf that he must bring his baggage to the house and stay with them, but only after she had glanced at Lacy for Lacy's approval as she always did in any matter concerning their home. Lacy had nodded as she glanced at the newspapers that Raf had found at a newsstand.

It was at this point that the doorbell rang announcing the police. Raf opened the door and the two men came soberly into the room. Lacy had a terrifying notion that they had come to arrest her on a murder charge. But when she introduced Inez and Raff, the captain gave Raf a sharp look. The city policeman politely gave precedence to O'Leary. "Mr.— Mendez?" O'Leary began.

Raf nodded pleasantly but with a wary look in his dark

eyes. Inez explained that he was her brother, her half brother.

The captain thought for a moment; then, holding out a big envelope, said to Inez, "Then you must have known Mrs. Rose Mendez. You must be, in a way, next of kin."

"I didn't know her." Inez gazed at the envelope as if it were a venomous snake.

"Is Carlos Mendez your brother? Is he here, too?"

Raf replied. "No, sir. He is in New York City, yes. I don't know where he is staying. I'm not in his confidence. I do know that his present wife is with him."

The captain waited another moment. Then he said slowly, "Seems to me you people are not, well, not what I'd call a close family."

"That's right" Raf agreed good-naturedly.

Again O'Leary seemed to pause for thought. The others waited. Finally O'Leary said, "Well, I was bringing these things for Miss Wales to look at. But perhaps you, Mrs. Wales, are the person who might give us some information." As he spoke he put the envelope in Inez's lap. "Also," he continued, "perhaps Rose Mendez's former husband should be notified of her murder."

So there it was, a dreadful word.

"And Miss Wales"—he turned to Lacy—"since you did know Rose Mendez, perhaps you also know of some near connection of hers, or even where she was born. Anything at all."

"Murphy was her family name. I do remember that her home had been in Chicago. Then she married Carlos Mendez."

"Now, will you both just take a look at the contents of that envelope and advise us if you can—"

Inez tumbled out the various objects, including a few papers, not many, but the first thing Lacy saw was her own beautiful engagement ring, an emerald.

"But that—" she began before she could stop herself.

It brought the sparkling green-eyed gaze of O'Leary in her direction and a subtly increased attention on the part of the other policeman. "So you recognize that ring, Miss Wales."

"Why yes, that is—" She swallowed hard. "It is—is like one that I had. It can't be the same ring, of course!"

"You're sure of that?" O'Leary said.

"Oh, yes." She told herself that Richard could not have simply taken her ring and given it to Rose. Rose happened to have one like it.

"Well, then, take a look at the other things in the envelope, please, Miss Wales. You and Mrs. Wales together just might recognize something. Please look, both of you."

Inez spread the remaining contents of the envelope on the table next to her chair and both women bent over them. There were bills—unpaid; Rose had had little if any money. But then came a folded official-looking paper, stiff and rustling as Inez opened it. Lacy and Inez both looked. Inez made some kind of sound, which she tried to stifle, but O'Leary's sharp ears had caught it.

"Recognize that, either of you?" He waited a little and added, "Something wrong?"

Everything was wrong, Lacy thought; she felt rather dizzy. But the ring ought to have warned her. The snapshot she had found and hidden away ought to have warned her. The official-looking paper was official indeed. It was a certificate of marriage between Rose Mendez and Richard Blake.

It was an oddly foreign-looking certificate, mainly printed in Spanish and highly decorated. For anybody who wished to examine it, there was a neat translation of the Spanish into English. She looked at the place and date; the place was Acapulco and the date was barely over three months ago.

The man's signature appeared on it, but it was not Richard's handwriting. Lacy couldn't remember ever having seen

77

an American marriage certificate, but somehow this one seemed unusual. Anyway it was unthinkable that the Richard Blake to whom—and to Rose—it had been issued, could be the Richard Blake she knew!

Inez had regained some of her composure. She said firmly, "We know a Richard Blake. Not—not this one."

"Oh?" said O'Leary politely. "Perhaps we'd better see the Blake you know. Wouldn't hurt, now, would it?"

Inez was very steady, "You can't see him now. He is not here. That is, he is unavailable."

"You can't mean he's in the hospital or something like that. What do you mean?"

Inez was still very steady. "I'll have to tell you. I shouldn't but this is a special situation. The Richard Blake we know is with a government bureau. He went to Washington to meet somebody the night before last. But he never can tell me or Lacy just what or where his mission may be. I ought not to say this, but he is a member of— I can't tell you the department, but I know that it is very secret. He can't even tell us where he goes or what he is told to do. But the name on that marriage certificate cannot belong to the man we know. Why, he—he is engaged to marry my stepdaughter."

Lacy thrust away ring and papers. The ring shot green lights as it fell to the floor. My ring, Lacy thought. That snapshot! Now this marriage certificate!

O'Leary said, "Can't you help us, Miss Wales?"

"No," Lacy said firmly.

"Nevertheless. I think we'll have to question him. If either of you *could* tell us where to find him. Mrs. Wales?"

Inez replied. "I told you, I don't know! Lacy doesn't know. He was to go to Washington first. For orders."

O'Leary paused for a moment, then reached over, slid all the papers back in the envelope and did not appear to see the ring on the floor.

"Very well." He straightened up. "We'll get in touch with

our colleagues in Washington. I'm flattering myself when I say colleagues. Those we'll have to question are very high up. But we can try. Now, about this whiskey. You took it to her, didn't you say, Miss Wales?"

"Yes."

"Why?"

"I told you yesterday. She always tried to diet but then she would slip and eat all the candy or sweets she could hold. I thought she had had too much candy or whatever she'd been eating. But she seemed so sick and kept saying she was cold and that whiskey would help. So I got the whiskey from the kitchen. And—brought it to her."

"Did she drink quickly or sip it?"

"Quickly. I was afraid she'd be really sick. But with all that candy—"

"Where was the candy?"

"The kitchen table had the remains of breakfast—toast, bits of egg, coffee—and an open candy box."

"Candy box?" O'Leary said. "On the kitchen table?"

"Oh, yes. Half empty."

O'Leary waited a moment, then said thoughtfully, "There were some pieces of candy in the refrigerator. Nothing of the kind on the table. You are sure of that, Miss Wales?"

"Oh, yes. That is why I thought that she had taken too much candy and so was feeling a little sick. Oh, yes, there *was* a box on the kitchen table along with the bits of food."

There was a rather long pause. Finally Captain O'Leary said, thoughtfully again, "I looked over the kitchen. It wasn't a very clean and tidy place, but I expect she didn't care. No candy box, however."

"There was one. I'm sure of it."

"Not when I saw that table." He gave a little shrug; probably he was finically neat himself—he looked it.

Lacy nodded. "The whiskey bottle was on a counter. So I took it to her. She drank and talked and then—then just fell over and died. Still talking. I couldn't believe it!"

"Yes, I remember, you told me all that. You went upstairs to get a sheet to put over her and then—"

Then she had sensed rather than seen a kind of blur, moving toward the woods. Don't mention that, Hiram had warned her. She said, "Then the doorbell rang and I went down to answer it. The doctor— You know all the rest of it." She had a vague memory of talking and talking to the police when they arrived; she wasn't sure exactly what she had told O'Leary in her shock and confusion. Now Captain O'Leary looked at her soberly. His quiet New York City cohort coughed, and Jessica took exception to the noise and growled. Raf hushed her with a hand over her mouth.

The coughing policeman didn't like it. "She bite?"

"Not very hard," Raf said. "She's such a little thing."

"She has teeth, though." The policeman edged rather prudently toward the door to the hall.

O'Leary said, "Well, thank you. Thank you. We'll try to find your friend, Mr. Blake."

"Wait a minute," Lacy said rather desperately. "There is someone who may be able to locate the Richard Blake we know. He may know where to find him—that is, the bureau Richard works with."

"Oh?" O'Leary looked and sounded skeptical. "Buddies, are they?"

"Not at all! He is only a close and valued friend and—"

"His name?"

"Burden Smith."

"Address?"

She gave Buddha's address, but suggested that they telephone and ask for an interview before seeing him.

"Dear me," said O'Leary as softly as a snake might mutter to itself (if, Lacy thought wildly, snakes did anything but hiss). He turned toward the door with the envelope in his hand.

Lacy stopped him quickly. "Please, Captain, have they found out what really killed Rose?"

The captain gave her a sober look. "No, not yet. There's got to be an autopsy, you see. Good morning. Thank you again."

As they moved away, their footsteps sounded so heavy that they suggested something fateful.

Raf went to a front window, and said mildly, "That is a smart man, that policeman. O'Leary, did you say? You notice he didn't leave the contents of that envelope—including a marriage certificate." He turned to face Lacy and Inez; the boyishness had left his face.

Inez sank down into the big armchair. "My God," she whispered. "That *can't* have been Richard! He wouldn't have actually married Rose Mendez while he is engaged to you, Lacy!"

And O'Leary couldn't have forgotten the ring. Yet certainly it lay there on the rug. An answer occurred that was not welcome: perhaps he only felt that he was restoring the ring to its original owner. Whatever his reason, aside from sheer forgetfulness, Lacy had to consider the marriage certificate and the snapshot hidden away in her handbag. The certificate was dated about three months ago. Richard had been away for more than his usual absences lately, hadn't he? During the last few months?

Raf said, "I know it is none of my business, but *could* this husband of Rose's actually be your friend Richard Blake?"

"No!" said Lacy too sharply.

Inez said dully, "If he is, I— Oh, I don't know what to do! I suppose there could exist some reason for a marriage like that but—no!"

Raf said, "Reason?"

Inez shook her head and looked at the rug intently. Then she rose, picked up the ring and said, "Lucky the police forgot it, Lacy. *Is* this your ring?"

Lacy nodded.

"You're sure?"

Again Lacy merely nodded. Inez turned and turned the ring.

Raf said, "Well, come clean now, Inez. Explain this Blake you know."

Inez replied flatly. "I told the police. You heard me. He is engaged to marry Lacy. He is with some secret government mission. He can never tell us what he is doing or where he is going. I do not believe it is the same Richard Blake. That is a very, very common kind of name. There must be thousands of Blakes and millions of Richards."

But Lacy wouldn't show Inez the photograph, tucked in her handbag. She wouldn't show it to anybody. Richard had *not* married Rose! He had never, never married her and then murdered her!

Inez said slowly, "That ring may be, well, *like* your engagement ring, Lacy. You said you lost it. How could anybody have got it off your finger!"

"Nobody took it from my finger. I just—lost it," Lacy said again. But of course he could have taken it. She thought back to the night she had lost it. She and Richard had gone to a movie, over on Lexington, nearby. And he had held her hand and—oh, yes, it had been an exciting movie, and when they got back home she had discovered the loss and blamed herself bitterly. Richard had said he'd get her another.

Raf said, "Your O'Leary friend is smart. He knew that if he pretended to forget that ring and leave it here, you couldn't help claiming it."

"No! No—I don't think—" Lacy began, but thought it possible that Raf was right.

"May I see the ring?" he asked.

Inez held it out to him. To Lacy's vague surprise he got out a small instrument of some kind like the one she'd seen Carlos use the day before and fastened it in one eye. Inez said, "Why, Raf! So you carry a loupe around with you! Why?"

Nine

Raf turned the ring in his hand and peered through what Rose called a loupe. "I'd like to see— Yes, it's a good stone. Might even be one of ours, Inez. I can't tell. Looks rather like old Geno's work!"

"Geno?" Lacy asked blankly.

Nobody replied to that.

At last Inez said, "He must have bought it at Cartier's or Tiffany's or any other fine place! How many carats are there?"

"Do you know, miss—Lacy?"

"She doesn't know a jewel carat from an eating carrot," Inez said.

"Yes, I do!" Lacy said. "Richard told me. And he said that the word 'carat' came from some seed, that is, not a seed precisely but—"

Raf nodded. "Sure. A carob bean. All carob beans seem to be the same weight. I believe the word started in the South African diamond mines. Used now all over the world. However, if you must be specific, a carat weighs 3.086 grains. This emerald is not the best but it's good."

Inez stared at him. "Since when have you become an expert, dear?"

"I'm not an expert."

Inez's eyes narrowed. "Are you sure you were not actually in Antwerp, Raf?"

Raf laughed, shrugged and said warily, "Why not? A little close study of lapidary seemed a good idea. Antwerp is still the source of the great diamond cutters in the world—so they say, and so I believe. Nothing wrong with getting some ideas about cutting emeralds. We have a fine lapidary setup right there in Logonda. Under Carlos's control, unfortunately."

Inez said slowly, "They couldn't keep you away from it when you were a boy, Raf. You liked it."

"I loved it," Raf said. "Nothing like the beauty that emerges when a stone is well and truly cut. Sure, I spent days in my childhood watching Geno. Eventually, of course, Carlos decided I'd be better off studying or working in some faraway place. England. But after a while I gave in to my childhood love and went to learn what I could in Antwerp. I'll never be an expert. But I know well-cut stones when I see them. Carlos was smart, getting old Geno to work in Carlos's private lapidary workroom."

"Too private," said Inez shortly but very thoughtfully.

Raf said, "Carlos always had his own way. Keeps everything far too privately for Carlos. All legal, too, I'm afraid, since Carlos makes the laws. As for that ring—yes, it could be one of ours. It could also have come from any fine store. I tell you I'm not that expert. I can't be sure. But after all, how can I help being interested in emeralds? Even the best can be very difficult for cutting. You can easily ruin a fine stone. Diamonds are harder. Topazes come next—"

"Raf." Inez was coldly controlled. "She'll have to know about the emeralds." She turned to Lacy. "You see, that's one of the ways Carlos got to be rich. That land of Carlos's— the entire property he claims and of which Raf and I ought to have an interest—that land— Oh, it's a small country. Carlos is a—"

Raf looked at the ceiling and softly supplied words. "A big wheel."

"Yes. Yes, he has a finger in local politics and in every—"

Again Raf supplied words, dreamily, "Every crooked deal that comes his way. Or he invents a crooked deal. But always just within the law."

Inez took a long breath. "The plain fact is that Carlos discovered—"

"Emeralds," Raf said.

"Yes. You see, Lacy, part of the land that was to have been divided among the three of us is mountainous. We thought it was quite impossible for the production of anything agricultural. All crags, cliffs, valleys too precipitous even for raising cows—"

"Goats," Raf prompted her.

"Anything at all! But Carlos discovered a vein of beryls. Some aquamarines. Various stones. But the emeralds were beauties, most of them. In great quantities—"

"Too great," Raf said gently. "So great that unlimited production—mining, that is, and selling—would depress the market. Once Carlos discovered the emeralds, every land-holder searched his own crags for emeralds and occasionally found them in considerable quantities. Consequently, Carlos felt he had to control the output—that is, the competing output from the other landowners. Not his own. A neat politician, is Carlos, and a man who looks after his own interests. So he manipulated the so-called government—he paid them off or fought it off one way or another."

Inez intervened. "He made enemies, but I suppose, yes, he paid them off."

Raf nodded. "Bribery also as to passing this law," he said flatly. "A limit was set concerning the mining of emeralds. There had proved to be too many veins of beryls, although

85

nothing as big and rich as on the Mendez lands. The legal allowance for the mining of emeralds is three days."

"Yes!" Inez said, softly now. "Three days for emeralds."

"They got the idea from the De Beers diamond mines system in Africa, which limited the mining time and forced strict control over the mining of diamonds, and thus kept up what could have been no market at all if diamonds flowed out over the world without stint. No value. That," said Raf, looking fully at Lacy but with a cold sparkle in his dark eyes, "is merely economics. The more there is of a product, the lower the price. Simple!"

"But," Inez said slowly, "Somehow, some way, emeralds do get out of the country. Not many—but some."

"Smuggled, by Carlos. Secretly," said Raf. "Enough to supply money, money, money for Carlos. Carlos sells through a number of dealers. They sell to jewelers. But Carlos keeps mining going, as well as the lapidary workrooms, all the year round. Carlos has got his hands on the entire Mendez property. Inez should have a third and I should have a third. But what is law in some places doesn't seem to affect Carlos's chums."

There was a long and thoughtful pause. At last Lacy said, "But then how would Richard get the ring? It is mine, I'm sure. But how did it get in Rose's house and why— Oh, Inez, surely Buddha can put the police straight about Richard."

Inez gave her a curious, half-surprised, altogether loving look. Raf strode back to the window, his hands thrust in his pockets. He said over his shoulder, "My dear niece, you are a very, very fine kind of girl."

"You don't mean fine. You mean dumb. But I'm not. I know that Richard is honest and I *know* he was not married to Rose. I don't understand, I couldn't possibly guess how all this came about—not only my ring and the marriage certificate but—" She stopped herself just in time to avoid mentioning the snapshot. "I do know that it had nothing to do with Richard. None of it!" There was another pause and Lacy added, "You called me your niece. I'm not—"

Raf laughed. "Oh, yes, I am. Inez is your stepmother. I am her half brother. I'll grant there are considerable steps and halves but still I'm your uncle by marriage. Too bad," he said over his shoulder, but Lacy saw a laugh in his eyes. "Yes, too bad an uncle can't marry a niece. Just think of what happened after Richard the Third was offered the hand of Edward's daughter. He refused it, properly, but later she married the father of Henry the Eighth." Raf turned back from the window. "You are up on English history, aren't you?"

"Oh, stop it, Raf," Inez said.

Lacy had time to think. "That isn't fair of Carlos to steal from Inez and you!"

"Certainly it was not fair. But I was a minor. Inez—well, women have few property rights in our little country. She trusted Carlos—"

"Not for long," Inez said. "And I could not continue to act as a kind of governess and nursemaid to Carlos's three children. Not that"—her face softened slightly—"they aren't nice children. They are. Too nice for Yolanda. And Carlos. Not that either of them seems overly devoted to their offspring. Oh, Raf, if there had been any other way to get away from the whole situation, I'd have taken it. But I kept thinking of my mother's people and what she had said about America and New England—but then it all worked out magically for me. I met Tom."

Raf was no longer in a laughing and teasing mood. "Obviously it has not occurred to either of you that this engagement to Richard Blake—if he should be your Richard Blake—would give the police a motive for Lacy to murder Rose. Marriage to another woman! Keeping it a secret from you! Going along with your engagement! Oh, yes, quite a motive for you. They'll not forget that you were in the house.

You did give her that unfortunate drink. Jealousy! So, well, there you have it—"

He stopped, for Inez came at him like a tornado. Without the slightest pause she snatched the ring and then slapped him hard across the face.

Raf drew back, then seized Inez's hands. "No more of that, Inez. I'm not a child, you know. It *is* a motive—or will be in the minds of the police and, just possibly, a jury."

Inez was white with anger. "You can't say such a thing about Lacy—"

"She doesn't speak for herself," Raf said. His face was tinged with red where Inez had struck him.

Lacy cried, "But I didn't kill Rose! It was exactly as I told the police. They cannot possibly believe for one instant that—I—killed her."

"I'm sure I hope not," said Raf, anger still in his dark gaze. The doorbell rang, bursting into an explosive moment of silence.

Raf shrugged. "I'll answer it. Neither of you seems capable of moving. Except to give me a very hard slap—" He almost bowed to both of them. There was a dangerous ruby light in his eyes but he sauntered out into the hall and opened the door.

It was Hiram. "I've come to see Lacy."

"Oh, she's here," Raf replied, pleasantly.

Inez seemed to be trying to smooth out the furious look on her face. Lacy sat still, stunned by Raf's quite logical but terrible hypothesis.

Hiram brushed past Raf, took one look around him and said to Raf, "What's been going on here?" He couldn't help seeing the imprint of a hand on Raf's face. All at once Hiram had become very quiet. His whole face stiffened, his body straightened alertly as if he might be called upon to administer a few blows himself. He went on, "Family quarrel or not, I intend to interfere. Who hit you, Mr. Mendez, and why?"

In a second Raf turned into a laughing, teasing boy again. He rubbed his cheek ruefully. "My sister. Didn't like something I said."

Hiram was not to be deflected. "What did you say?"

Raf debated. The boyish look remained, but his eyes had no laughter whatever. "I ventured to suggest that if the Richard Blake to whom, it now develops, Rose was married, is the same Richard Blake to whom my niece, here, has the misfortune to be engaged, why, then"—he gave a very Latin kind of shrug—"the police could begin to question Lacy's story. That is—"

Hiram broke in impatiently. "Lacy didn't go out there and kill Rose. That's a perfectly preposterous notion."

"I hope you are right." Raf was smooth as butter now.

Lacy said quickly, "But Richard Blake *is* the name of the man to whom I was—am—engaged. The police were here. They brought some of Rose's things to me, thinking I was the only person who might be close to her. Among the papers was a marriage certificate: Rose and—and a Richard Blake. So—so Raf thinks that the police will suspect me of—of killing Rose out of jealousy—or something. That can't be, can it, Hiram?"

Hiram was still a straight-edged New Englander, perhaps hardened further by law and New York. His eyes were dark gray searchlights, without any expression but a kind of rigid determination. He was taller than Raf, better built—thanks partially to university rowing. Raf was leaning gracefully on the back of Buddha's armchair. Inez was clasping her hands together and looking as if she'd like another go at her brother.

Hiram said, "You won't need a coat, Lacy. It's very warm. Come out with me. I want to talk to you."

Raf said softly, "You have come to the same conclusion that struck me. So you have some ideas—"

"Yes," Hiram said. "I have. And I'll thank you to keep out of things—"

"Can't," said Raf, smiling sweetly. "Family matters, old fellow—"

Hiram's fists actually tightened.

Inez stirred. "No, Hiram—Mr. Bascom, I mean. Don't—"

"I'm coming," Lacy said swiftly.

But Raf was still angry. "Tell him about your ring. Tell him about Carlos and family emeralds and all that. Might as well tell him where your so-called engagement ring was found."

Inez rose, advancing upon Raf, who had the discretion to slide lower behind Buddha's big chair. Hiram scarcely gave him a glance and said to Lacy, "We'll go to the park. Bring your key."

"Don't forget your ring," said Raf too agreeably.

Ten

Inez still had the ring. All at once the ring meant nothing, nothing romantic, nothing exhilarating or happy; it meant only terror.

"Give me a moment to change my dress—" Lacy said to Hiram.

"You look very nice as you are."

In blue jeans and a limp blue shirt? No. She ran up the stairs. It took, in fact, only three or four minutes to slip into a neatly tailored white linen dress and brush her thick, wavy black hair. A touch of lipstick didn't delay her. At the door she saw her handbag and thought swiftly that she didn't wish to leave the handbag where not Inez but Raf just might wish to explore it. She snatched it up and ran downstairs. Hiram stood at the street door, apparently in deep thought, but smiled when he saw her.

"Didn't take you long," he said approvingly. "Got the key to the park?"

"Oh, I always have that."

It was a beautiful summer day. The trees and vines and shrubbery made dancing flecked greens. The murmur of the city was always there, along with an occasional nearby rush of a taxi or a private car. The rasp of the key to the same park gate they had entered—years ago, it seemed to Lacy—was comforting and familiar, a small part of her known world. Hiram took the key from her hand, almost shoved her into the park and locked the gate after them.

There was, unbelievably, nobody else there. It must be the lunch hour, Lacy thought vaguely.

"Here we are," Hiram said. He was still New Englandish; there was a rocklike determination in his face. He didn't wait to start a conversation. "That little rat, I mean your Raf! He saw it, too. He had more information than I had. I merely thought it possible that the police would wonder if Rose had somehow snared your Richard Blake because—well, the police visited me this morning—"

"In the office?" she said with horror. That sacred lair of the law!

"At my club. This is Saturday," Hiram said. "Never mind that. The police asked me about you. I told them, when they asked, that, yes, you were engaged to be married. I was not acquainted with the man. Then the big cop with the green eyes—"

"Captain O'Leary."

"Yes. He said, didn't I know the guy's name? Wasn't it Richard Blake? Because if so, Rose had been secretly married to a man by the name of Richard Blake."

"Oh, no! No, it could not have been the man I know. No!"

The straight lines of his face seemed to set very hard. "You are sure of that?"

Lacy didn't pause. "Yes," she replied too defiantly, perhaps, for Hiram's dark gray eyes seemed to drive into her thoughts.

Finally, he said, "Well, then, your next step is clear. You must send word to this Blake, tell him what has happened, that he must come home and clear himself."

"I don't know where he is."

"You don't— Why not?"

Miserably she began the explanation about Richard's career.

Hiram appeared to accept it without question. "Fine. Then we'll get in touch with him through the government. He's got to come back, you know."

"Yes. But—oh, Hiram, truly he would never do such a horrible thing! Really! You must believe me!"

He gave her another searching look, which seemed to Lacy as if he were analyzing her defense of Richard. He said, "What did you tell the police?"

"Only that. I knew the name on the marriage license was Richard Blake. But"—she borrowed Inez's phrase—"there are hundreds of Blakes, millions of Richards." Then unexpectedly she had a brain wave of her own. "Somebody could have borrowed that name. That's a possibility—isn't it?"

Hiram drew a figure on the path with the toe of his loafer. "The only fair thing to do—fair to your Richard and yourself—is obviously to find him and give him every chance to defend himself. So—"

There was a long pause. The opposite gate opened with a slight creak and a young woman, a nursemaid apparently, tugged two small children inside, then locked the gate and told her charges in clear, emphatic tones that they must behave themselves, and that they could not bring their dog into the park but she would take it for an airing later on.

"That'll probably be too late," said one of the children, a very cross little boy who scowled ferociously at Hiram.

Hiram caught the scowl, and a flicker of amusement softened his face. A granite face, Lacy thought, but a kind and helpful granite face.

"I can't find Richard," she said.

Hiram's amusement vanished. "You have to. If you love him and intend to marry him, surely you can see that it is your duty to send for him."

"I will—I'll try—but honestly, I don't know where to start."

He thought that over for a moment. Then he said, "Our firm has a few connections in Washington. Someone there might be of assistance. I'll try. But in the meantime, Mr. Smith, your Buddha, might help."

"The police got his address. I suppose the captain is talking to him right now."

Again for a second, all of Hiram's granite hardness became very sober.

After a moment he said dourly, "You mentioned the figure or something you thought you saw going into the woods to the police that day. I didn't stop you. I didn't think fast enough. Don't talk of it again to anybody. Don't emphasize it—"

At this moment a squalling, shrieking uproar arose, which was only amplified by the helpless soprano reproof of the nursemaid. The two children were rolling over and over, yelling; the boy had the little girl by the hair, and apparently the little girl had teeth firmly sunk into the little boy's leg.

Hiram rose. He strode across to the tumultuous group, seized both children by the scruff of their necks and held them. "Now stop that! It's not allowed here. Or anywhere else," he added, grinning at the nursemaid, who was all but weeping.

"Oh, thank you. They—they really are good children until—"

"Until they bite and pinch and fight. Now, you two—" He addressed the children in a very ferocious voice. "If you don't behave you'll never be permitted to enter this park again. Understand me?"

Miraculously the little boy said politely, catching his breath, "Yes, sir."

The little girl looked up and said, "You may kiss me, if you like."

"Well, I—all right." Hiram planted a brief kiss on the

child's cheek and stroked back her tousled hair. "Now promise me, both of you, to behave like the nice children you are."

"Yes, sir." The reply came from both of them. The nursemaid smoothed down her dress and thanked him in a breathless way. Hiram turned and came back to the bench, grinning.

"Little imps! Much like my sister's children. Now then, I'll go to see Mr. Smith myself. I'll make him understand that we need your Richard Blake. He just might be able to help. By the way, that Raf! He deserved to be slapped by Inez."

"He said that I might be a suspect—" Lacy said in a small voice.

"That's a preposterous notion! And what did he mean by family secrets?"

"It's a little—well, complicated," she said. "Emeralds! And my ring—"

"I have time to listen. What did Raf have to say about your ring?"

"My engagement ring."

"The one you lost?"

"Yes. But you see—I—well, that ring was among the things O'Leary brought to me. He brought what he could find of Rose's personal papers and things because I was the only person he could think of who might know something of Rose's people. But then he took away all the papers with him."

"What about this emerald?"

"Well, you see, emeralds seem to be the source of the Mendezes' wealth. That is—it's this way—"

She told it as carefully and clearly as she could. "So you see both Inez and Raf are—"

"After Carlos's scalp. Can't say I blame them. But the ring—are you positive it was your ring that was among Rose's things?"

"I—yes," she said flatly. "But I didn't admit it to the police."

Hiram said slowly, "You are very sure of your Richard."

"Yes! I know him. You don't get engaged to somebody unless you know him."

Hiram seemed to brood for a moment, then he said, rather crossly, that there'd be fewer divorces if people really did know one another very well before they leaped into marriage.

"I'm not leaping."

"No. It looks as if your Richard is the one who's not exactly leaping!"

"That's not fair! He can't help doing what he's ordered to do. You do what you're told, don't you?"

"Yes, I do. But it's no secret, what I do. Although," he said rather ruefully, "Sometimes I feel that I'm not much use to the firm—that is, it doesn't really matter just what chore I undertake."

"Now, that's not true. You know perfectly well—"

He smiled, for the first time that day, down into her eyes. "Good Lacy! Rush to *my* defense, too! But"—he became serious again—"let's get this Richard of yours back home and cleared and then—then, we'll see. Hungry?"

"No. I mean, yes."

"Come on. There's a nice place at the hotel."

As they left the park and crossed the street, they met Raf, guiding Jessica who gamboled at the end of her new leash.

Hiram stopped him. "Mr. Mendez—"

Raf smiled boyishly. "Try Raf."

"Raf, then," Hiram said not very warmly. "I am curious. Where did you really acquire that little—that nice dog?"

Raf's white teeth flashed. "She acquired me. I invented nonsense about a plane just to annoy Carlos. He annoys very easily."

"But the dog—" Lacy was curious, too, although it had nothing to do with her.

"The fact is," Raf said, corraling Jessica who wished to investigate a nice little piece of grass, "I picked her up on the way to Inez's and your house, Lacy. She was trying to get some food out of a garbage can and saw me and ran toward me, and I really couldn't shake her off."

"But she knows her name," Lacy said.

"Certainly." Raf's eyes were laughing again. "I tried all the feminine names I could think of as I walked toward Gramercy Park and your house. The only one that interested her was Jessica. She had no tag, no collar, no means of identification. I suppose I'll have to go around to somebody, some official?" He eyed Lacy, who nodded.

"She'll have to have a license. Her owner may try to find her. At best she could go to an animal shelter—"

But the dog didn't seem to like this idea. She came to Lacy, quite as if she understood, and sat back to paw at Lacy's skirt.

"Oh, dear!" Lacy knew that she was lost.

Raf smiled. "You feel the same way. She's got a home. As long as you and Inez don't throw both of us out."

"There's a law in New York—" Lacy began.

Raf nodded. "I know. Inez told me. I'll be careful. But it's lucky that you and Inez have that lovely piece of back garden. Not," Raf said rather severely, "that you keep much of a garden there. But it is a place where Jessica can run."

Raf saluted both her and Hiram with a graceful wave of his hand and sauntered on along the sidewalk.

"You can't help liking him. A little," she said, watching Jessica bounce happily along, stopping only to investigate some interesting smell.

"All right," Hiram said shortly. "Go ahead and like him. The hotel will give us a good lunch. Also something to drink. Which I can do with."

The hotel dining room did provide them with a fine drink and a good lunch afterward, but they had reached fruit and coffee before Hiram returned to the subject of Rose and her murder.

"What puzzles me—well, a good many things puzzle me—is why the police haven't concentrated on the reason for

Rose's divorce. If Carlos divorced her, and gave her a fine allowance, *why* did he divorce her?"

"His present wife, I suppose. Yolanda. Three children from their affair—"

Hiram lifted a very Yankee eyebrow. "Must have been quite a long affair. Well, then, suppose Yolanda finally made such a fuss Carlos was driven to divorce Rose. And suppose that the romantic spell that so hypnotized him that he married Rose all at once departed. I mean, suppose he just got tired of Rose and wanted Yolanda back (and Yolanda made a great to-do), he still had to have some real reason for divorcing Rose. She had reason to divorce him, but that would put the shoe on the wrong foot. What I would like to know is why."

"Perhaps he offered Rose the money for that?"

Hiram frowned at a fine-looking peach on his plate, which didn't deserve the scowl. "Or perhaps there was another man."

"You mean Rose had another man?" Richard Blake, but not her Richard Blake!

Hiram looked at her as one might look at a backward child. "Seems logical, doesn't it? Surely Rose wouldn't have agreed to a divorce if she hadn't some other plan in her head. It must have come to her as an unpleasant surprise when she learned that her allowance from Carlos would be cut off if Carlos discovered her marriage."

And hadn't Rose said confusedly that the man she had married wouldn't have married her without the money (Carlos's money)? That man might have left her, as Rose obviously feared, but killing was another thing.

"Hiram, as I told you before, couldn't somebody have used Richard's name? Somebody, of course, who must have known or knew of him—perhaps one of the people Rose must have met. Wherever it was, the background of that snapshot looked tropical."

"What snapshot? You never mentioned a snapshot!"

"Oh, dear!" She had not meant to speak of it. "Well, all right." It was still in the handbag she carried. She drew out the by now rather battered photograph. He reached over and took it.

After a long moment he gave it back to her. "That's your Richard, is it?"

"Yes. It must have been some kind of joke. His peculiar writing on it like that. Not even his handwriting. But somebody was there with them, and knew him, and he was on a job, and then—" She concluded triumphantly: "So—when whoever he was married Rose, he just used Richard's name. Why not?"

Hiram sighed. "For one thing, that would be illegal. It would also make the marriage illegal. Rose said she was afraid of her husband, didn't she?"

"It's very hard to be sure just what she meant. Rose did seem afraid that her new husband wouldn't want her if he discovered that she had no more money. I rather think," she said with a twinge of guilt at being critical of a friend, "that Rose must have been spending rather lavishly. So freely that she gave Rich—I mean the new husband—reason to think she was a very rich woman. But that was *not* my Richard!"

"All right. . . . Well, we may as well go to see Mr. Smith. You seem to think he knows everything."

Eleven

As it soon proved, however, Buddha didn't know everything, or if he did, he didn't tell Lacy and Hiram what he did know.

Yes, he said, leaning back in an enormous chair, the police had been there. Captain O'Leary apparently believed he could be of help and that he would do his best to help them. But there was not much he could do. Certainly Lacy had stopped to see him on her way to the country. He showed them the vase she had returned to him and, chuckling a little, explained why she had done so. No one gave it so much as a glance. Captain O'Leary hadn't many questions. Buddha had supposed (this was said with a glance at Hiram) that it was a business errand for Miss Wales. No reason to suspect that Lacy might be getting into such a frightful affair. He wished that he had counseled her to make further inquiries before she blindly followed Mr. Bascom's request.

Hiram didn't fidget at this, but he didn't look happy. Then Buddha launched into his own inquiry. Had Lacy had the faintest idea that someone else was in the house? It would be a help, he added.

"Yes," Lacy said, "But it was only an impression. There wasn't a sound anywhere."

"Oh," said Buddha, with one of his little chuckles.

Lacy cried, "I had only a kind of feeling of someone—listening—or watching. Only that, in the house."

"You didn't look?"

"No."

Hiram said, "Do *you* think there may have been another person in the house, sir?"

Buddha shook his head. "No. It might be a help, however, to Lacy. I don't like the fact that she was all alone in the house."

"Neither do I," Hiram said, so crisply that Buddha's eyes almost opened wide to shoot another glance toward Hiram.

After a second Buddha said, "Of course they asked about the key."

"What key?" Hiram said sharply.

Buddha looked down at his folded hands. "It seems that the back door, a door to the kitchen, was locked. From the outside. No key in the lock. The police suggested that it was used by someone leaving the house and then tossed away somewhere. They are looking for it. And also for"—he shrugged—"a half-empty box of candy. Seems you mentioned that the box was on the kitchen table as well as the remains of breakfast."

"You did mention that to the police, Lacy," Hiram said. "But I don't remember your describing anything else about the kitchen."

"I must have, when I told them how she would go without sweets for a time to lose weight, but then go on a kind of candy binge. It's why I thought she just felt sick from too much candy."

"But you saw nobody," Buddha said. "Too bad. You are sure of that, Lacy?"

Hiram answered again. "Certainly she's sure of it. She had to tell the police. Although I don't think she's entirely sure

101

of anything just now, sir. Look at this snapshot. Is it the Richard Blake you know?"

He rose to give Buddha the crumpled-up photograph. Buddha hastily searched out a pair of gold-rimmed glasses, which he carefully adjusted on his nose; then he looked at the picture for a long time before he nodded. "I'm afraid I do recognize it, Lacy. Yes, I'm afraid that is your Richard."

Hiram took back the snapshot. "We came to ask you if you can tell us where to find him. I mean the Richard Blake Lacy knows."

Buddha thought and shook his head. "I'm not really very well acquainted with him. Of course, I've seen him with Lacy and Inez. I understand he is out of town frequently. Quite often, now that I think of it. In fact, I know very little of his job, whatever it is. Something to do with a government bureau, I believe, and very secret. Not unusual in these times. But, no, I don't know where he is now. I'll try to find him. If Lacy doesn't know—"

"I don't."

"Too bad. He ought to be able to clear himself of any suspicions. I gather from your attitude that the police do suspect him of being involved in the death of this Rose Mendez. As a matter of fact, I gathered that from the general trend of the questions the police asked me. It seems that when they first questioned you, Lacy, you suggested that this Rose was afraid of her new husband—at least *a* husband. Take your choice."

"It couldn't have been Richard. Using his name was some kind of joke," Lacy said definitely. "It had to be somebody who knew him, adopted his name for the marriage certificate and—and for the marriage. He's the one the police ought to find."

"Perhaps they will," Buddha said comfortingly.

"So that is all you know about him?" Hiram asked.

Buddha put his plump fingers together and looked at them. "I'm trying to think back. I do know some of his friends. New York is a small world, in its way. But—no, I knew very little about him until Lacy and Inez announced the engagement. I can't say I know anything of Blake's family, but he was certainly a desirable and pleasant guest and what you might call a man about town. Except, I believe that he wasn't about town very often really. His job, as you know, took him away. I've told you all I know of that. Actually, our acquaintance was pleasant without being at all close." He sighed. "The police kept inquiring about him, Lacy, as if I were your guardian. In loco parentis. They hoped to get more sense out of me than regrettably I could give them. But the police are very smart, you know—especially that O'Leary. Yes, what is it, Spook?"

The small, wizened, but very neat houseman had materialized in the doorway. "It's Captain O'Leary, again, sir. He wishes to speak to you."

"Oh, certainly." With no visible difficulty, Buddha rose out of his chair. "Ought to have a telephone at my elbow here." He walked into the hall, moving as lightly as a ballet dancer for all his weight.

He left a deep silence behind him. Lacy looked at her hands. Hiram looked at the rug. After some time Buddha returned, slid neatly back into his chair and sighed. "Too bad!" He folded his hands together. "The missing candy box has been found. Regrettably, the person who found it was of a frugal turn of mind. Careful about money, not about what he took as a find."

Hiram leaned forward. "What happened?"

"He died. Almost at once."

Hiram got himself together first. "*Who* died?"

"A teacher in that girls' school in Fairview. Seems he was known to be very parsimonious. Couldn't resist anything free for the taking. Once too often. They—the Fairview police—believe he found the candy box somewhere and apparently ate some of it. Dead as a doornail," said Buddha.

"Oh, no!" Lacy cried.

"Too bad!" He said to Hiram, "The police haven't found the origin of the candy. It seems to have been a very popular and highly favored brand. Sold everywhere! The police are now certain of what the few remaining pieces contain. They had a very long name for it. But whatever it is, it's obviously lethal. Induces," said Buddha, "a numbness, a kind of sleepiness which, if combined with alcohol, results in a coma. That, they said, is what caused Rose's death. I'm afraid they are going to question you again, Lacy. They had tried to reach you at home. Inez suggested that you might be here. Naturally, I didn't admit that you were here when that man, O'Leary, told me why he wanted to talk to you further. About the candy, I judge."

"But I don't know anything! The box was simply part of the litter on the kitchen table." A terrible suspicion shot into Lacy's mind. "What's the name of the teacher at that school?"

"I believe it was something like Wandel—Waddell—"

"Oh, no!" It was a wail. "Poor little Tight Wad!"

Both men looked at her as if she'd lost her senses.

Hiram guessed first. "On the faculty of your school? Penurious? His last name was Waddell? So you charming little girls called him—"

"Yes," Lacy admitted, stricken with shame. "Tight Wad. But he did save everything. Even string and scraps of paper, I mean anything big enough for him to write on if he wanted to and—oh, all sorts of things. He put the pennies and nickels he happened on into a piggy bank. Candy must have been a find for him." She said desolately, "Everybody loved him just the same even if we didn't love what he taught."

"O'Leary said Botany," Buddha suggested.

"Yes. But he also taught algebra and geometry and, naturally, we didn't like those subjects. At least, most of us didn't."

"Did Rose Mendez know him?" Hiram asked.

104

"Oh, no! I don't remember where she went to school but it wasn't there. I talked of the school enough so she knew all about it, though."

"It was in her letter," Hiram said slowly, "Why she thought of Fairview as a quiet place in which to hide. Peaceful, quiet—"

"Not so peaceful now," Buddha murmured.

Hiram said, "How about fingerprints on the box? Did he say?"

"Oh, yes. Only other fingerprints were Rose's. There were, I believe he said, some smudges." Buddha sighed. "They interviewed the only merchant in town who sold that kind of candy. Fact is, the policeman said, he was in a state. Said he didn't know and couldn't guess if he had sold it. Fell over in a faint and had to be rushed to the hospital, but it turned out to be nothing serious. You may as well go home, Lacy, and prepare yourself to see the police."

"I don't see why they'd want to question Lacy." Hiram's chin was set stubbornly.

Buddha sighed again. "They have their ways."

There was a long pause during which Lacy could hear only the decorous, seemingly faraway murmur of traffic along Park Avenue.

Hiram said at last, "Well, you did see the half-empty box, Lacy, but that's all. Might as well face them, I guess."

Buddha stirred slightly. "I have a notion that they are pretty busy right now in this little place, Fairview, so perhaps they'll not get to you, Lacy, for some time. Don't get upset about it, and stop crying."

"I'm not crying," Lacy lied, for the tears were starting. Poor little Mr. Tight Wad! They hadn't made life very pleasant for him, those teasing girls. Yet he had always seemed content with his collections of wildflowers—weeds, mostly, she always thought—his carefully painted pictures of various specimens he had found in the woods or fields. The tints were always delicate, very fine and gentle, she thought, grieving for little Mr. Tight Wad, who had, unhappily, come upon a half-full box of candy.

"I'm not crying," she said. "I'm only thinking how cruel girls can be. He was a nice, quiet little man. He didn't deserve—"

"All right, Lacy. Thank you, Mr. Smith—"

Buddha rose lightly and went with them to the elevator. "Now, Lacy," he said, "an investigation like this takes time. Autopsies, facts. Time, yes. Don't get in a state like the man who sells candy!"

"I'll try." But tears came to her eyes just the same. Little Mr. Tight Wad with his bent, thin body and big nose, stooping over, watching for any botanical specimens—or any stray object. "So—so somebody dosed the candy with something—whatever it was," Lacy said. "Who would do that! Surely not—not Carlos. Certainly not Richard! Then *who?*"

Buddha tried to reassure her. "The police will find out. But the thing will have to go to laboratories. Hartford, I should think. You know, all this happened only yesterday. Friday. Today is Saturday. The police do accomplish what they set out to do, as a rule. In the main they are very dependable. But slow sometimes—and this may be very slow. So try to relax. Don't think about it. Here's the elevator, my dear." He nodded at Hiram as they stepped into the elevator, which moved almost stealthily down to the entrance hall.

The doorman recognized them. He had contrived to have Hiram's not very splendid car placed conveniently near the impressive, huge doors.

Hiram turned into the Park Avenue traffic, swerved over to Fifth and went down toward Gramercy Park. "I suppose you want to go home."

"Yes, please! Do you think the police will be there?"

He said steadily, "Not a chance! They are in the middle of two shocking deaths—doing their best on a Saturday, when almost everything is closed. I don't think they'll get a chance to talk directly to you. And anyway—" He stopped for a red light, turned to cross Park Avenue and turned again on Lexington. "It's probably only some inquiry about the candy. Obviously your little Mr. Tight Wad didn't notice any difference in the taste. Neither, presumably, did Rose. Now, brace yourself, Lacy. We are almost home. Your stepmother will want to know why the police phoned you. She'll have to hear the whole story as we know it, which isn't much. It's lucky you didn't sample the remaining candy in that box," he added.

"I wouldn't have! The whole kitchen was so unappetizing. Oh, Hiram, don't make fun of me!"

"I'm not making fun. I'd like to get that look off your face, though. Your stepmother worries about you."

The curtain of the living room moved as they went up the steps. Inez opened the door.

"Lacy—the police—a man—"

"We know," Hiram said promptly. "They phoned your friend Mr. Smith, too. We were there."

Twelve

Jessica dashed down the steps in a flurry of barking and then attacked Hiram's nearer ankle. He picked her up, shook her and said severely, "I have never kicked a dog in my life but there's always a first time. That is, if you really are a dog and not some remarkable, unknown animal."

"She's really a dog," Inez said rather wearily. "Shut up, Jessica. Now come in, Mr. Bascom—I want to hear—"

Raf wanted to hear too, for he came to the door of the living room, greeted Hiram politely and scooped up Jessica. "Friend," Raf said to the dog. "Understand? Friend."

Hiram unexpectedly displayed a knowledge of dogs. "That's a poor word for a command. People keep using it but—"

"What are good words?" Raf asked, his white teeth flashing. " 'Damn you, shut up'?"

"Possibly. But actually, what's best is a word with a definite kind of vowel. Like *bad. No. Stop that.* Oh, all kinds of words like that. But 'friends' they don't seem to care for."

"Like some people," Raf said, gently caressing Jessica, who had settled down but still eyed Hiram with suspicion.

"Now then—" Inez had led them into the living room. She poured drinks for them from a table that stood at one end of the room. "Whiskey for you, Mr. Bascom?"

"Thank you, yes." Hiram sighed and took a chair near Lucy, who had all but collapsed in the comfort of Inez's presence and found herself in Buddha's big chair.

Raf brought her a glass of white wine, at which Hiram looked without much favor. "You have succumbed to an unusual trend, Lacy."

"What's unusual about this wine?"

"Nothing! That's the trouble with it. Everybody seems to be pouring white wine into themselves. Nothing the matter with a fine"—he sniffed at his glass and nodded at Inez—"a fine Bourbon. Mr. Smith said that the Fairview police had phoned here."

Inez said quickly, "They told me that someone else had died, apparently after eating candy from a box on Rose's kitchen table. They want to see Lacy. I guessed you must have gone to Buddha's. The man, the policeman, jumped at it, said thank you and that was all. Now tell me—"

"I expect you already have the basic facts," Hiram began.

"Yes, but what did they tell Buddha?" Inez sat on the bench before the fireplace. Raf rose and turned on some lights. It had been, Lacy suddenly realized, a very long afternoon.

She listened to Hiram as he told of Buddha's report of the police inquiry and of Mr. Waddell. It was too soon, Buddha had said, for the autopsy results and the laboratories to say just what kind of hypnotic had to have been introduced into what Rose took to be only candy, which she could not resist.

There was a long, thoughtful silence. Then Raf sighed. "I never actually knew Rose, but she certainly charmed my brother. For a short time, however. There doesn't seem much anybody can do right now."

Inez stirred. "We'll just have to wait. But they cannot connect Lacy with this latest death—this poor teacher. . . .

Will you have dinner with us, Mr. Bascom? It'll be a pickup meal. I never do much in the way of cooking on Saturday—"

Lacy roused sufficiently to eye Inez with amused speculation. Was Inez preparing for proof of Richard's guilt? Or at least proof of his marriage to Rose? She could almost unconsciously be coming to the conclusion that Hiram Bascom would be a good match for Lacy, in the event that Richard turned out to be an impossibility. There were things that Inez, too, was very forward-looking about.

But Hiram, thanking her, said he had promised to see his parents that weekend at their place in Quogue. So, after some moments of conversation that got nowhere, he left.

He took Lacy's hand before leaving, however. "I have a funny feeling about this whole thing, Lacy. Please be careful and don't go wandering around the city alone after dark. Here's the number of my club in town. I live there. The family number is in Quogue. Call me if anything happens and you need me," he said, and went down the steps.

"Now then," Inez said firmly. "We'll have no more talk of this. Come and help me, Lacy, you too, Raf."

It wasn't a pickup dinner; it never was with Inez. But it was a silent one. Lacy soon realized that all three were listening for the telephone, which refused to ring.

Raf took the dog out while Lacy was putting the dishes in the dishwasher; when she turned it on, its soothing hum was the only sound in the house. Afterward, Inez told her to go to bed.

"Don't worry, Lacy. It'll be all right. You didn't kill Rose, and you certainly didn't poison any candy!"

Later, from her room, Lacy heard Raf return, whistling softly. She turned on her bedside radio, heard all about the weather and turned it off again. Mainly she thought of Rose and of little Mr. Tight Wad. She fell asleep but suddenly awoke, realizing that she had been dreaming a mixed-up, unhappy dream about fields and figures wandering around, and about little Mr. Waddell, mincing along, sniffing out

110

unusual flowers and any pennies and dimes or anything else that someone had lost. She had been crying; there were tears on her face. She wiped them away and decided not to dream again. Whoever had tossed away that candy, which carried quick death with it, had deceived Rose, too.

Sunday was a dull day, cloudy yet warm. Lacy got out her car and took Inez to church as usual. Inez had an affection for St. Ignatius. She was a Catholic and a practicing Catholic. Why she had grown out of the Congregational Church, which must have been her mother's church, Lacy never knew. Once Inez said simply that she liked the Catholic Church, and that was enough for Lacy. Why she preferred St. Ignatius to any nearer church Lacy never knew either, but accompanied Inez and imitated her reverent behavior except when it came to taking communion. That did not seem honest, since she was still Episcopalian. Occasionally, in times of stress or merely because Inez wished it, they had gone to St. Patrick's together and Inez had led her back along the right to the solemn, wonderful calm of the Lady Chapel. This always made Lacy feel cheered and more confident of herself and the world at large.

Inez did not suggest stopping at Buddha's apartment house. Lacy only wanted to get back home and find out from Raf (who had lazily admired Inez for attending church but had not gone himself) if the Fairview police had telephoned again. They hadn't.

Raf left after lunch saying he must collect the rest of his baggage.

Later in the afternoon Hiram telephoned.

"I thought you had gone to Quogue."

"Nope. Too rainy and dull, nothing to see but the ocean and hear my married sister's kids yell and fight. I told you she has two young devils," said Hiram, but fondly. "Any chance of letting me come around just to—just to talk?"

"Oh, yes, do come."

"You sound as if you have a bad case of the blues."

"I—yes, I have. We'll look for you."

"Can't say I care about the 'we' stuff," said Hiram shortly.

"You mean Raf. He's gone out to the airport."

"Airport?" Hiram seemed pleased. "He's leaving?"

"Well, no. He must have left some baggage there. He hadn't known just where he would be staying. He had only a sort of briefcase envelope thing for his razor and pajamas and so forth. Inez has invited him to stay here, so he's coming back."

"I see," Hiram said flatly. "I expect he'll be there for some time."

"I don't know. Do come, Hiram—"

"In fifteen minutes, then."

"Good," said Inez, behind her. "You know, Lacy," she hesitated, but continued, "young Bascom is a—I suppose you'd call it a catch."

"Now, Inez, I know you. You've decided that just in case Richard proves to be the Richard Blake whom Rose really did marry, you're thinking that somebody like Hiram would be a good substitute. You can't fool me, darling."

Inez colored slightly, then laughed. "I'm not! Oh, *why* can't somebody find Richard?"

It was by then obvious that the police had not found him. Once he was found and had come home, everything would be settled. He would explain the photograph and the certificate.

But Hiram's arrival was welcome on that dark day with clouds hovering over the city, over the house, over the park, over everything, like a gray menacing weight.

"So your brother is going to stay on for a while," Hiram commented to Inez as she served him a martini after having graciously inquired as to his preference in the way of a drink. She also produced magically some paté and crisp toast and told Lacy to light the log fire laid in the living room.

"This is great," Hiram leaned back, savoring his martini and looking at the rosy flames. "A dark Sunday in a club in

112

New York is about as dampening to the spirits as anything." He glanced at his empty martini glass rather wistfully, so Inez at once rose and took it from him for a refill.

Hiram said lazily, "My father had a butler—when there were butlers—who was English and very rarely relaxed his dignity. But once when I was home from school and feeling low about my grades, he said, 'If you can't keep your spirits up, Mr. Hiram, put some down.' And brought me a whiskey and soda. Not bad advice. He's gone now."

"Oh, too bad," Inez said instantly, automatically sympathetic to a young and good-looking man.

"Not at all," said Hiram briskly, "He's doing very well. Started a dude ranch out West, making tons of money. I know because I wrote his will for him. He wasn't too sure that I knew how, so he got old Fitterling to check my work." Switching from the idle talk, he said, "I take it you haven't had more news from the police."

"Nothing," Lacy replied.

"Well, it takes a while. Saturday and Sunday are poor times to get anything done. Except for making inquiries, say, of persons who might supply information." He gave Inez a steady look. "I hear that Raf has gone to the airport?"

Inez nodded. Hiram said, "And, of course, Carlos and his wife have probably gone to church or—somewhere. Sunday movie?"

"I really don't know," Inez answered rather sharply. "You can't mean that you think they have been interviewed by the police. Only because Carlos was once married to Rose."

"I haven't the least idea," Hiram said. "It only strikes me that your Captain O'Leary seems to be a man who loses no time or—"

Lacy couldn't help adding, "Or leaves no stone unturned? If that filling-station boy, Hobie, really knows anything of interest, I feel that Captain O'Leary will act upon anything he can tell him."

"Sounds likely," Hiram said. "But as for getting any kind of information from, say, laboratories, where somebody might have to peer into microscopes and such on Saturdays and Sundays—not a chance! Anything good on the TV?"

"If you like hunting in the wilds, there's a set in my husband's study."

They watched hunting in the wilds only briefly—it proved to be a rather tedious description of polar bears—for about dusk Carlos and Yolanda arrived. Raf came at almost the same time.

Raf was carrying a light suitcase, which he took upstairs. Carlos was decorously dressed as if for church. Yolanda was wearing an expensive-looking scarlet dress and jacket and plenty of matching lipstick.

They came in, and Carlos settled himself in Buddha's chair and lighted a cigar. Inez didn't quite shudder but almost; she hated the lingering odor of cigar smoke, which clung even to curtains. Yolanda seated herself with great calm and self-possession, then leaned over, pulled off high-heeled pumps from pudgy feet and sighed as she leaned back.

Inez eyed her dress. And Inez, usually so reasonable and kind, was still subtly but firmly on the warpath. "You spent most of yesterday shopping, did you, Yolanda?"

"Certainly. I've never been in New York before. Such wonderful shops—"

"It's wonderful that you don't care how much money you spend," Carlos said sourly.

"You didn't go out," said Inez nonchalantly, "for a drive anywhere today?" Yolanda opened her mouth and closed it as Carlos gave her a pale blue glance.

"Why should we?"

"A chance to see something of the country—" Inez suggested and Carlos stopped that line of thought.

"We walked a little. Then went to a cinema."

Raf, with Jessica, came in but at Yolanda's remark he gave a very exaggerated sigh. "I'll take a walk. Back soon," he

114

said to Inez. "That is, as soon as I think our family—connections"—he paused before adding too sweetly—"have gone. Good night, Carlos. Good night, Yolanda." Hiram also excused himself courteously and followed Raf out the door.

Raf, Lacy reflected rather enviously, is the kind of person who always manages to escape anything he wishes to escape, and to do it, she had to admit, with a certain gracefulness that took the edge off his rudeness.

Inez said, "Well, Carlos. Anything at all on your mind?"

"Yes. In a way." Carlos sat in as erect a position as he could in Buddha's big chair. Somehow he managed to suggest presiding at some board meeting. "You see, Inez, that boy Raf has been prowling around, hunting out gems here and there." The loupe he carried, Lacy thought. "And also," Carlos continued, "he studied law—rather briefly—in England. Now, we are not subject to British law—"

Inez, looking very severe and New Englandish, sat up even straighter and hauled out, in effect, a verbal tomahawk. "You mean, Carlos, that you are the law in Logonda."

Carlos eyed her, his pale eyes blank, but he did manage a slight smile. "My dear, you know that Logonda is a very small place. Almost, one might say more like a principality than a country." His light blue gaze shifted to Lacy. "If you try to find it on most maps you'll have a hard time. It's that small and really not important. Not important at all to the world at large. Troubles in any part of South America really don't touch us. We—I am simply not a political person. In fact, I know nothing of politics outside our home." He shrugged. "No problems touch us."

"I believe that," Inez said. "Nothing touches you, Carlos, in your own business operation. That is all that matters to you. I talked to my husband about it."

"Oh?" Carlos asked frostily. "And what did this husband of yours say?"

Inez answered bluntly. It takes years and generations, Lacy had often thought, to breed out one's native blood. Inez was always the kind and generous but obviously unforgiving New Englander. "Tom said to pay no attention to any of it. He knew that you are—if I may speak plainly—a crook."

Carlos laughed softly; this was disconcerting to Lacy, but not to Inez. Yolanda surveyed her handsome new pumps: Ferragamo, unless Lacy was wrong.

Inez said, "Go ahead and laugh, Carlos. Tom wondered how you managed to get workmen to dig for emeralds. But I knew."

"What did you know?" Carlos was condescendingly indulgent.

"You threatened them. You made them work for you all the year round instead of the three days that (at your instigation) was required by law. But you, Carlos, managed to smuggle out emeralds."

This time Carlos stirred but kept on smiling thinly. "Oh, Inez, nonsense! Forget all this. What is Raf planning to try? He'll not get far with me, you know. I have the law on my side."

"You mean Logonda law."

Yolanda stopped approving her new pumps and said acidly, "It's good enough for us."

Inez had had enough. She rose. "Good night, Carlos. Yolanda—"

Carlos didn't budge, but Yolanda rose. "My feet are killing me," she said frankly. "Come on, Carlos. If you don't want to come, I'll take your car back to the hotel—"

Carlos rose at that. "You are probably the worst driver who ever got behind a wheel. Not an expensive hired car do you take! That old rattletrap you've shaken the guts out of at home—that's different. Take that when we get home. But not this car—" Without another word he walked majestically to the door. Yolanda paused to shove her feet into the new pumps, shuddered and struggled as she did so and then followed him, saying carelessly over her shoulder, "That Raf—don't trust him for a moment—"

"You don't know anything about him—" Inez was silenced by the street door closing with a bang.

Jessica gave a yelp rather as if prey had escaped her. Inez gave Lacy a look and said, "Carlos is a crook. No getting around it. But he also practically owns the place. Then she added thoughtfully, "I can't see them just strolling around all day."

"Window-shopping?" Lacy suggested with a bit of Inez's own tart humor.

Inez laughed. "I hope so. Good for Carlos's love for money! What's the matter with the dog?"

Jessica was now sitting at Lacy's knee, swishing her huge yellow tail but staring up at Lacy with an anxious appeal that said as clearly as words, Out! This minute! Out!

Lacy understood dog language in spite of being a city child. "All right, Jessica."

"Best take her back to the garden. The fog has come up and, besides, you can't take her into the park. The streets aren't safe at night, especially not in the fog. Take her out the kitchen door and areaway. Want her leash?"

"She'll stay with me. At least she can't possibly get away and I'm sure she has decided that this is her home. Come on, Jess."

Jessica didn't move but continued her imploring stare. Lacy yielded. "All right, Jessica."

The dog leaped and bounded at her side; Lacy led her back to the freshly remodeled kitchen and opened the door, which led down a few steps to what had been an areaway and had always been surrounded by a good strong fence. There were not many flowers, but shrubs were plentiful, though not very carefully clipped, since there had been so little money to spend on controlling madly growing shrubbery. The fog was like a misty curtain. Jessica dashed off into the shadows.

At the end of the narrow but rather long space, called a garden more by courtesy than accuracy, there was a paling gate that opened onto an alley and a row of trash cans. This was concealed by the crowding shrubbery.

Jessica was rustling a little in some dark patch of lilacs, in leaf but past their bloom. The lilacs and the shrubbery made deep dark shadows; there was a faint light coming from a window in the onetime butler's pantry above. It spread a dim path of light across the rather scrubby lawn and the paved path to the back gate.

The sound came slightly nearer. Indeed, it seemed to Lacy that one of the rhododendrons had moved. She felt oddly uneasy, just for an instant, as if someone or something were watching her. That lasted only a second or two, for one of the rhododendrons gave a kind of violent shiver and Jessica shrieked; as Lacy turned, something fell over her face, almost choking her. Jessica yelped again, as if in sharp pain. There was a kind of thud, and for a second Lacy actually seemed to see stars—red and blue and white sparks danced before her eyes and then everything was black.

When she regained consciousness, she realized that Inez was leaning over her and wiping her face with a wet cold towel. Raf held her carefully upright in a kitchen chair. Jessica whined to herself in a corner of the kitchen.

"Who was it?" Raf asked in a voice of fury.

Thirteen

Her head ached. Jessica whined. Raf said, "Shall I take her in to a sofa, Inez? Or upstairs? Shouldn't we call a doctor?"

"*No*—" Lacy managed to say, and with a great effort put her hands to her head. "Out of the rhododendrons. Something—"

"*Who?*" That was Inez, stern as a rockbound New England coast.

"Nothing—I mean, not anybody—I mean—oh, I don't know!" Lacy was as agitated as the dog.

Raf was decisive. "I'll get her upstairs. You call a doctor, Inez. You must have a doctor nearby."

"Yes. Oh yes! Lacy, is it very bad?"

"Hurts, yes. But—" Lacy made herself straighten up by forcing her spine against the rigid back of a kitchen chair. "Who got me out from the garden?"

Inez replied at once. "Raf. He got home. Heard the dog howling. Found you. Brought you inside. Lacy, what happened?"

"I don't know—I fell—"

"Somebody knocked you out," Raf said briefly. "Do you think some brandy would be a good idea, Inez?"

"Oh, I don't know." Inez never wrung her hands but she almost did then. "Let's take her up to her room, Raf. I'll help you. She's heavier than she looks."

"I think I can manage," Raf said, stooping. "Put your arms around my neck, will you, Lacy?" His voice was kind. Lacy made an enormous effort and got one arm up around his neck. He drew her up and was unexpectedly strong but puffed a little all the same as he carried her into the hall and up the stairway. "Go on, Inez, phone."

Raf knew which room was Lacy's. He got her inside the door, staggered a little toward the bed but got her there and then collapsed on the floor. "Inez is right. You're heavier than you look."

Lacy irrationally defended herself. "I'm not too heavy! Just over a hundred pounds—"

"Too much," Raf said and all at once his teeth flashed. "But kindly don't starve yourself on my account. I'm just not in any condition to lug girls upstairs. Now then, what really happened to you?"

She felt wonderful—her own bed, her own soft pillows, her own room with the lights turned on.

"I don't know. It just came out of the dark and Jessica helped. Is she—" Lacy lifted herself on one elbow, tried to ignore the pain that shot across her forehead and said, "Is she all right, Raf?"

The laughter left his eyes. "Whoever hurt you kicked her. But she's fine. Only frightened. I hope that's all that's the matter with you."

"Here you are." Followed by the dog, Inez came into the room with a glass in her hand. "Drink this, Lacy. It's only brandy."

But her memory of Rose and the drink she had given her was too recent and terrifying. "No," she cried and nearly sobbed. "No! I'm all right! Just—just knocked out—"

"Did you get a doctor, Inez?" Raf asked.

"Only his answering service. All I could do was to leave my name and number and say it was urgent," Inez said despairingly. "Shall I try the emergency ward at the nearest hospital?"

"No!" Lacy sat up, clasped her head, groaning as pain lashed through her temples, and said, "Hi—"

Raf was puzzled. It took Inez only a second to understand. "But Lacy, dear, Hiram Bascom can't do anything. You need a doctor. The emergency—"

"*No!*" Lacy said. It came out as a shout, which Jessica didn't like; she wailed shrilly and tried to climb onto Lacy's bed. Raf scooped her up and began to feel the small, furry body for broken bones. He's kind to animals, Lacy thought; this was a plus. But she wanted Hiram Bascom and she knew clearly why she wanted him.

"Inez, his number! It's on a piece of paper in my handbag. He's staying at his club. Please," she said defiantly as Inez seemed to feel uncertain. "I want to talk to him."

"All right."

Inez must have remembered that the handbag was downstairs in the hall, for she went out and Raf said slowly, "I don't think Jessica is seriously hurt. Scared still. Tender in spots. I'd like to see whoever it was kicked her. She's got a very sore spot just—just here—" He poked lightly at the little dog's back. She whined but wagged her tail.

Raf looked over the little bright-eyed head and said, "You mean that you want to tell Bascom all about this thing tonight. Naturally. A lawyer. Your friend. Your very good friend, I should say. I wonder that you got yourself engaged to this Richard Blake."

Lacy mumbled something, but a few words did emerge. "Friend—my boss—"

Raf brooded for a moment. "Why would anybody take such a swing at you?"

She didn't reply. She knew one possible reason. A shadow,

but really a nothing; only a blurred movement near Rose's house. Hiram had warned her not to talk about it.

Raf went on, "I know there is a gate at the back of the garden. If anybody wants to call it that. I shouldn't have said that because I know you and Inez have had a rough time—thanks to Carlos's piracy of the family funds and your father's death. Certainly you have had no money for extras. To me, it's a garden—that's enough. But there is a gate at the back. I saw it the times I took Jessica out. It has only a latch, anybody could open it. I do hear that New York has become a rather dangerous place, in some vicinities and in some ways. But I didn't have the faintest notion that that's true of this special neighborhood."

She had to defend her home and the surroundings, which she loved. "It hasn't been true here! Even though there have been occasional purse snatchings and attempts at break-ins—that kind of thing."

Inez came in. Lacy cried, "Did you reach Hiram?"

"Yes. He's coming. First, though, he practically ripped the skin off my ear for letting you go out alone. But it was just in the garden! Do you feel better?"

"Oh, yes." Lacy felt her head for the sore spots as gently as Raf had searched little Jessica for bruises.

The doorbell rang in a repeated and imperious way. Inez ran down the stairs. It was the doctor; he had received her message. He didn't explain more than that, but sharply asked where the patient was.

Inez had to follow him up the stairs again. It was lucky, Lacy thought, that Inez had kept her breath and her figure, but then Inez was by no means an old lady.

The doctor was youngish, fattish, very authoritative. He went over Lacy with quick and able hands, took her temperature, felt her head gently but thoroughly for contusions, nodded and asked, as if surprised, "Didn't you call the police?"

Inez cried, "No! We never thought of it."

"Should have," said the doctor and shoved his stethoscope back into the black bag he carried. "Take two of these. If you have any continued pain, let me know. Here's a card where you can find me as a rule. Just leave your number." He glanced around him with a look of grave disapproval. "We have had some muggings in this area, but very few. However, it's never prudent to go out alone at night." With which he took his slightly pompous but brisk and able presence down the stairs again. This time Inez stopped at the head of the stairs until the street door closed. Then she came back into the room.

"He seems to think you are not much hurt, Lacy. At least—oh, he'd have known it if you have even a slight concussion. Take the pills—"

But the doorbell rang again in sharp vigorous peals. "That's Hi," Lacy said.

Raf said, "Sit still, Inez. I'll go! All this running around—"

"I'm not that old," Inez snapped, quite her usual self again now that her worry over Lacy had been quieted.

They could hear the men's voices floating upward. Hiram's was the stronger and sounded furious. He burst into the room and glared at Inez. "Why did you let her go out in the garden? Lacy, I told you to stay at home and be careful! But no, out you go, inviting trouble. . . . How's your head? Mr. Mendez here tells me you did have the sense to get a doctor. I saw his car drive away."

"I'm fine," Lacy began, and moved her head but found it wasn't quite so fine.

Hiram's quick eyes saw that. "Keep still. What did the doctor say exactly?"

Inez replied, "That it didn't seem to be a concussion. He left her a couple of pills to take just to quiet her down, I expect. And he said to call the police—" She clapped one hand over her mouth. "I never thought of calling the police!"

Hiram was now really angry and didn't attempt to conceal it. "Why not?" He all but yelled, "I'll call them and get somebody here—too late probably. But—"

"There's a phone in my room at the front of the house," Inez said rather weakly.

Hiram had disappeared in leaps. They could hear him. The address, what happened, when it had happened. No robbery. A mugging.

He came back, wiping his forehead with the back of one hand. "Well, you did call a doctor," he said to Inez forgivingly and sat down at the foot of Lacy's bed. "Now tell me everything."

There was not much to tell, but what there was obviously was too much.

Inez tried to pacify Hiram a little. "This is a very safe neighborhood. We've never had a mugging."

Lacy said, "There was that break-in at a club. Somebody got away with all the wraps from the cloakroom."

"Oh, that. That was years ago. And that well-known collector who lived in the neighborhood—Hiram, you might remember, it was a famous name, a very famous man but I can't think of his name—he had a whole houseful of the most beautiful furniture, paintings, treasures of all kinds. He never had a break-in—"

"Probably had alarms, too," Hiram said dryly. "Well, I really think you're lucky. I mean you," he said to Lacy. "Didn't I tell you not to go out alone in the city? To stay with someone all the time—"

"But it was only out the back door—"

"Dangerous!" Hiram said and nobody denied that. But Hiram, Lacy knew, had a different view of the matter than either Inez or Raf. Raf leaned forward and picked up one of the pills the doctor had left. "If you are not going to take these, Lacy, may I give one to Jessica? She's still shaking, poor little scrap."

"Better break only a little off the pill," Inez said. "She's very small."

Raf made no objection. Jessica did. After spitting out indignantly several times the portion of a pill Raf gave her, she left Raf's knee and crawled under Lacy's bed. She whimpered a little before falling into a deep sleep.

The police arrived and Raf again went down to let them in. There were two of them—from a prowl car, they said—and they came up to Lacy's room to ask questions. Very polite questions, but after they had both heard what happened—a girl out at night in the garden—one of them looked at the other and said, "Vacant place back of the house" as if hypothesizing, but in fact this was more exact than he knew, for it was indeed neglected and empty but for the scrappy shrubbery and dancing shadows. There was a knowing glance exchanged between the two policemen and a moment of complete silence. New York's finest, Lacy told herself, and they certainly lived up to the name: tall, well-muscled, bright-eyed, very observant as well as kind and polite.

Finally the one who did most of the talking for the two gave a nod to the other and thanked everybody in the room. "Now, we'll take a look at the garden. We'll take a prowl through the whole neighborhood. There's not much trouble around here, you know. Very quiet neighborhood." He addressed Inez rightly, as the one in charge. "It might be a good idea, ma'am, to put some kind of latch on that back gate. I mean a real latch, a lock."

"Yes. I will." Inez had got back a touch of color in her face.

Rather to Lacy's surprise, Hiram had listened without uttering a word. He now accompanied the police when they left, and then came back. He turned to Inez and said, "Please, Mrs. Wales—I know this is an intrusion but—"

Inez had recovered her usual quick perception now that things were calmer. "You wish to stay here overnight?"

"If it's not any trouble for you. Actually, I doubt that anyone is going to try to enter your house tonight. It was probably only some vagrant, hoping to get Lacy's handbag or something—"

"He didn't take anything. I didn't have anything for him to take," Lacy said.

"Well, he might have been only frightened. About to break in and you caught him in the act." Hiram was being a little too glib.

Inez said, "There's another room. Small, but it will do. I'll make up the bed—"

Raf knelt down to drag Jessica out from under Lacy's bed. "Come on, now. Stop your trembling. I'm not going to hurt you."

Hiram watched as Raf pulled out the dog, who whimpered and shivered. "Sure *you* didn't kick her?" he said in an absent way.

Raf's handsome face turned perfectly white. "I'm sure. What I'm not sure about is why you barge in here, my sister's home, asking all these questions, sending for police—"

"Why didn't you send for them yourself?"

"Because it never occurred to me. All we wanted to do was get Lacy into the house and get a doctor and—" Raf stroked Jessica gently. She stopped whimpering. "I should have thought of it. But I don't know New York, you see. I didn't realize—"

"You realize now. Thank you, Mrs. Wales," Hiram said as Inez returned.

"It's rather small," she said tonelessly.

Raf, with an impish light in his dark eyes, strode over to Lacy and kissed her. His kiss fell on her cheek and was brief, but Hiram's fist clenched. Raf either saw or felt Hiram's reaction, for he laughed softly, said "Good night and sleep well," and departed, Jessica leaning over his shoulder, her beady bright eyes still looking worried. Inez followed him.

126

"So," Hiram said grumpily to Lacy. "Can't you even wait until your Richard Blake is found and returns? Do you have to form a new attachment?"

"Oh, don't!" Lacy's laugh was rather shaky. "Not Raf!"

"You could have fooled me." He reached over and very softly closed the door. "Lacy, you know you are in danger. You did believe that you saw some kind of movement near Rose's house. You did tell that to the police—there was no reason then not to. At least no reason you'd have thought of that afternoon. You were in a state of shock. You just babbled out everything you saw or didn't see."

"I didn't really see a person. Or anything!"

"But if it *was* someone, he doesn't know that. Not for sure." Hiram sat down on the chair Raf had been using. "Your Raf is certainly attentive. Found you. Carried you in!"

"Hiram, Raf is not my anything!"

"He is your stepmother's brother."

"I don't want to talk about him! Hiram, do you really mean that perhaps somebody was hiding around the back, waiting, just hoping that I might come out—"

"That could have happened. In the morning I'll ask the doorman of the hotel if there were any cars sort of lurking on Lex last night or in the streets around the park. Not that I think we or the police can trace anybody now. Good night." As Inez opened the door and nodded he said, "This is very good of you, Mrs. Wales."

"I borrowed some pajamas from Raf," Inez said. "He seems to have brought a small supply of clothes."

"Making a long stay here?" Hiram asked in a polite way, but didn't wait for an answer, told Lacy to sleep and disappeared. Inez came in. "Let's get your clothes off. Here's a nightgown. Want a shower? No, you'd better not try that. Might get dizzy."

Dear Inez, Lacy reflected—always sensible, always helpful, always protective of her. As Lacy slid down between her own sheets at last, Inez said, "You didn't take the pill the doctor left."

"Neither would Jessica," Lacy replied, and suddenly Inez flashed a smile at her, said good night but to call her if she wanted her and departed, closing the door after her.

It seemed strange to feel herself floating away into sleep. That must be a reaction to the fright, the terror and the pain. But also she knew it was because of Hiram's presence in the house. How could she make anyone believe that in fact she had only seen—or imagined—a kind of blur, nothing else, vanishing before she got her distance lenses in her eyes?

Then she thought of little Mr. Waddell and the candy he had found and of Jessica's angry soprano yelps when she had been kicked, and then told herself that Hiram was so near that he could hear her if she called—but that wasn't going to happen. No murderous hand could come out of nowhere and attack her.

Her sleepy, vastly tired, mixed thoughts became hazy and finally vanished until quite suddenly she awoke to see that she had left the bedside light on all night. Daylight, rather gray and threatening rain, came in at the windows around the shades, which Inez must have drawn. Inez herself brought in a tray with coffee and orange juice. "Feeling better?"

Lacy sat up. "Yes, yes, certainly. Good heavens!" She saw her bedside table and its little clock. "I've got to get to work—"

"Not today," Inez said flatly and put down the tray on the table, shoving the clock out of sight.

"But I want to keep my job—"

"Forget that for today. Mr. Bascom said you were not to go to work today, he'd see to things. He left about an hour ago. I suppose he didn't feel that a sweater and— Honestly, Lacy, he had jumped into blue jeans. Well, you saw him. But the very proper young lawyer scooting around at night to come to the aid of a maiden in distress in a sweater and blue jeans!" Even in her tense state Inez found herself laughing a little. "Now get this into you and come down. There will be some breakfast waiting. Hurry up."

Raf lounged in as Lacy, much refreshed after showering and dressing, was eating what Inez's New England forebears considered a correct breakfast—bacon and eggs and toast and more coffee. Raf smiled.

"I see you're able to take nourishment. Come on, Jessica."

Jessica had quite recovered and she bounced in to eye Lacy's plate hopefully.

"Oh, she's been fed," Raf said, interpreting Lacy's expression accurately. "I suppose Inez told you that you are to go to Fairview today."

Fourteen

"What!"

"They wanted it to be this morning, at first. But my sister told them you were not able to go up there this morning. Somehow they settled for the afternoon. It seems your friend Mr. Bascom talked to Inez and he is prepared to take you to Fairview. He'll be along, I expect, quite soon now." Raf sighed but with no expression of sorrow on his mobile face. "Oh, by the way, did Inez tell you? Your Richard has been found."

Lacy gasped. *"Where? When is he coming?"*

"That is uncertain." Raf was smiling a little. "That is, he was not exactly found, but they know where he was at the time of Rose's murder. Where he is now—"

"Surely he'll come here at once."

"One hopes so. It was your Mr. Smith who discovered where he had been at the time of Rose's murder. He remembered some acquaintance he and Richard—your Richard—both appear to have had. So Mr. Smith got in touch with the friend—his name is John Lyon, if you want to know. After that Smith phoned the Fairview police. It seems"—Raf was still smiling but his bright eyes were watchful—"your Richard was delayed in Washington, so he spent the time there playing poker with friends, including the one whom Smith knew slightly but well enough to inquire if he knew anything of Richard—well, in any event, there are three perfectly sound alibis for your Richard."

"But Richard couldn't need an alibi!"

"Oh, yes, he could! However, it seems, by the word of three good men and true, to quote Smith, that Richard is in the clear. O'Leary sent a man by a Sunday-night plane as soon as your Buddha informed them, and this man—a detective in good standing, I'm sure—questioned the three other poker players and there is no doubt of it, your beloved Richard was nowhere near Fairview at the time of the murder. I thought you'd be pleased."

"Oh, I am! But then I knew Richard could have had nothing to do with Rose—"

Raf had a sudden wicked gleam in his eyes. "Did he ever admit to their marriage? That's what you want to know, isn't it?"

"I do know!"

Inez came in from the kitchen. She gave Lacy a shrewd glance. "I see you've heard about Richard. That's all we know, but it does prove his complete innocence of any accusations."

Raf nodded. "We hope so, indeed."

Inez shoved aside a plate of toast and sat down near Lacy. "I suppose Raf has told you everything."

"I'm not sure—" Lacy felt rather as if a very swift elevator was starting downward and sinking her with it.

Inez's kind but often severe expression was like a mask. "Did you tell her, Raf?"

"No," Raf said. "I did not tell her that the police have discovered nothing to indicate that Richard has any connection with any government bureau." With an air of tolerance he added, "Of course, I understand that many of these things are of necessity secret. But this is very secret! Isn't it, Inez?"

Inez replied defiantly, "We've known that for—oh, ever since we met and *liked* Richard. Not even the Fairview police would be likely to be told just what he does or where he is."

Raf lifted a slender black eyebrow. "You could always address the secretary of defense, I should think. Or even the president, couldn't you? I understand that in America anyone who wants to get in touch with your president is at liberty to do so."

Inez took that up indignantly. "You don't understand, Raf. Any letters or phone calls or—anything like that, have to go through various offices—"

"Oh, I understand." He looked off at the far distance and said dreamily, "The British have an excellent phrase for that. The Official Secrets Act. Of course, you Americans—well, I'm an American, too, even if South American—you citizens of the United States, do not openly use such a very descriptive and I might say at times convenient phrase, but there must be something—"

"Oh, shut up, Raf!" Inez rapped it out sharply. Jessica growled, a tiny but definite growl. Raf leaned down to pat the dog.

Lacy forced herself to rise to the occasion. "Richard had nothing to do with Rose's death, and certainly he didn't marry her. He has a perfectly fine government post. It's not his fault that it's top secret."

Inez put her hand on Lacy's arm. "You have been asked to go to Fairview. Did Raf tell you that Hiram Bascom will take you there?"

Raf said pleasantly, "Surely. He said it was only his duty."

"That's right," Inez said hotly. "He got Lacy into this— this—"

132

Raf supplied the words. "Shocking affair of murder."

"That's exactly what I mean. But I don't see why the police—or at least that Captain O'Leary—couldn't have come here to talk to you, Lacy. And, further, I cannot see what on earth you could tell them that you haven't already told them."

"I've told them everything I know. Everything—" And too much, perhaps, Lacy thought. There was the stunning blow in the garden the previous night that could easily have killed her, that just may have been meant to kill her. Always supposing the attack was not that of a common or streetwise mugger who happened to find a gate that could be opened and who waited in the shadows—or more likely darted into the shadows when she appeared at the back door. But Hiram didn't really believe in the mugger notion.

Raf said blandly, "Are you keeping something back, Lacy? I mean that business last night really does suggest that somebody wants to silence you. Or—might need to silence you." His eyes were sparking; Lacy tried to keep her face a blank. After a second he went on. "The Fairview police wish to question you more minutely, that is all."

He picked up a silver spoon and turned it so he could examine the marking on the back. "I see you managed to keep some fine silver, Inez. Now, if only Mr. Bascom— Very chummy, I'm sure, Inez—"

"Raf, I have slapped you many times when you were a child. I slapped you—"

"Oh, yes! But you'll not do it again," Raf said agreeably. "I'll not let you." He put down the spoon.

Inez said, "Lacy, you have to go to Connecticut, I suppose. Perhaps the police we called last night have reported the attack to the Fairview police. They do work together, don't they?"

Lacy didn't know. Raf said rather hastily, "I'm not up on criminal law here. Or anyplace else, as a matter of fact, Inez.

133

But it does seem to me a little unusual that two policemen, out in a prowl car would report Lacy's accident to the Fairview police."

It didn't seem likely to Lacy either. Inez shifted the toast dish and said very softly, "Were you in Fairview yesterday, Raf?"

Raf looked at her for a moment, then laughed. "I told you what I was doing. But never mind. Your new man—I mean admirer—is to be here at two o'clock, Lacy."

Inez looked at her watch. "All right with you, Lacy?"

"It will have to be."

Inez went on thoughtfully. "Of course, the tragic death of that teacher, Waddell, may require more information from you. Yes, that must be it. I don't believe that the men from the prowl car last night, no matter what their report, ever connected what happened to you with Rose's or Mr. Waddell's—" She didn't want to say murder, so she stopped there.

"And they do know that your Richard has a perfect alibi." Raf whistled to Jessica who shot out from under the table, tail wagging, toward Raf who picked her up. "Time to go out."

"And time for you, Lacy to get into a suit or something," Inez said. "But are you sure you feel able—"

"Oh, yes. There's a kind of sore spot on my head. But no concussion, if that's on your mind, Inez."

"The way we found you—Raf and I—I was actually afraid for a moment— Well, go on then. But not that white linen you wore yesterday. It's very wrinkled. I put out the blue cotton skirt and jacket and a clean white blouse."

Lacy rose and on an impulse stooped over to kiss Inez. She was so loving and feminine that it was always a surprise to be reminded of her resolute view as to self-control, to say nothing of her stern conscience. Inez gave a brief kind of sound, which she wouldn't permit to emerge as a full-fledged sob and said only, "Do be careful, Lacy. Remember they'll make notes of every single thing you say."

"They've already done that. Except of course for last night."

"Lacy, do you have the faintest idea of the identity of that—that man last night?"

"No. There was only a kind of rustle and movement of shadows and then—" Lacy tried a grin but felt it was not successful. "Then I saw the finest collection of stars outside a planetarium."

And, she thought, I'll not say another word about that blur I saw yet didn't really see near Rose's house.

Hiram arrived before she had finished dressing as decorously as Inez wished. When Lacy came downstairs they were standing in the hall conversing in very low voices. Hiram looked up and smiled. "So you really are all right. Good girl."

"But you'll not let them tire her too much," Inez said.

"Not me. If I have to shoot my way out of the police station. Always supposing they give me a gun to shoot with. Come on, Lacy."

"See you," Lacy said to Inez and went down the stairs with Hiram to his rather battered but safe car.

Safe? That was a word that up to then had meant something like dodging traffic or locking street doors of the house or even gargling if Lacy felt a cold coming on. She got into the car and Hiram said, "No ideas about that business last night?"

"Only that I had a crack over the head and someone did it."

"Have they told you about locating Richard? That is, not actually locating him, but proving that he had an alibi for the time of Rose's murder?"

"Yes. But then I knew he couldn't have killed her. And I know, too, that he didn't marry her. He—" She stopped.

Finally, she said, "I am perfectly sure of that. And I am perfectly sure that as soon as he knows of—"

"Of that marriage certificate?" Hiram got his car in gear. "Or that snapshot you found?"

"Certainly. He'll explain. And he'll come home as soon as he possibly can. There just may be more important things he must do than to run for home to—to—"

"Clear his name?"

She nodded, and sat in silence while Hiram drove and frowned at all other cars as if they were encroaching upon his right to the street.

This time they didn't pass the filling station with the eagerly inquisitive boy, Hobie. "This is a different road," she said.

Hiram nodded. "Not so very different. It goes in the same direction—that is, this one leads past some tennis courts and swimming pools. But anybody could have taken this way. You'll see—" He slowed up a little to point out two perfectly kept tennis courts and a long, clear swimming pool. "See? Someone could have shot through those streets, come out here, having, say, parked a car somewhere along this road. Hobie's filling station and Winding Lane do have more than one access. By the way, did Carlos and his wife actually go to see the police yesterday—by invitation, I mean? Or your friend Raf?"

"I don't know. Inez tried to question Raf, but he only smiled."

"My guess is that O'Leary— Well, we'll soon know. Perhaps. Now, where, I wonder, is the police station?"

She was still a little ruffled by his manner of referring to Richard. She said, "You ought to know. I take it someone gave you directions."

"The police. Sure—ah, this way, I think."

The police station had once been a small, red brick schoolhouse. They had cherished it in Fairview, and some taxpayers had insisted that it be given historical landmark status,

136

but the obvious need of the police had outweighed that argument. The place itself was mysteriously redolent of generations of schoolchildren, apples and scuffed shoes. However, the police had probably endowed it with more authority than any teacher had ever done.

O'Leary himself greeted them. "Come in. Please be seated. How are you feeling, Miss Wales, after your unfortunate experience last night?"

"All right." Lacy couldn't help the slight edge in her voice. "I didn't have a concussion. I can't understand why it was reported to you."

Hiram looked at the ceiling very innocently. Lacy cried, "Hiram, you did that!"

O'Leary said softly but firmly, "That was his clear duty, Miss Wales. Why would anyone try to kill you? What haven't you told me—us?"

"I tried to tell you everything at the time."

"Ah, yes. Well, now—you knew this teacher, Waddell?"

"Yes."

"Like him?" O'Leary said unexpectedly.

"Why, yes. All of us liked him, though we made fun of him a little. Schoolgirl fun."

"Schoolgirl," O'Leary said flatly. "I understand you called him Mr. Tight Wad."

"Yes, we did. It was very wrong, very cruel. In fact we all liked him."

"We have talked to a member of the teaching staff who sometimes—this year, for instance—remains at the school for the summer holidays. The dietitian or cook. She was as informative as she could be."

"He—he picked up things, you know," Lacy said feebly. "He would wander around hunting for some kind of flower or anything that interested him for botany classes."

"Also any stray dimes or pennies, or some candy, tragically in this case, already filled with a very dangerous drug?"

137

Hiram picked that up. "So you have the laboratory reports?"

"Yes. In a crisis we get results very quickly. There was some—enough—remaining in the candy. You can look at the report."

He handed Hiram a very official-looking paper. Hiram took it and read it carefully. His lips pursed in a soundless whistle. Finally he said to O'Leary, "All these Latin words— I did have a short course in chemistry in school, but it was obviously too short."

"The lab boys explained to me." O'Leary grinned briefly. "It means a form of sodium used as a hypnotic. It can be a very strong hypnotic, usually in a white crystalline form—I am quoting them again. The fact is, it does provide very heavy sedation, so it is almost never used. The lab boys aren't sure just where it was procured. That information will take time to run down. But the point is, it can be reduced to a liquid and thus introduced into the candy by the use of a hypodermic syringe. You understand, I'm sure, that any hypnotic can be dangerous. The sad fact is that this heavy sedation, if combined with alcohol in any form, induces a completely comatose state. Or in many cases death. Whoever put that drug into a well-known brand of candy did it purposely. So the whiskey Miss Wales gave her—"

"But I *didn't* know! I thought she only needed some kind of stimulant. I told you—"

"Are you quite sure you told us everything you saw—or even guessed? Sometimes a guess can be revealing."

The snapshot! So Hiram had not told him of that. But O'Leary had the marriage certificate! "Captain O'Leary, Rose was never married to Richard Blake. At least, not the Richard Blake I know. He is away, yes. Mr. Smith phoned to me—that is, my stepmother talked to him—and he said that the Richard Blake I am going to marry has a firm alibi for the time of Rose's murder."

O'Leary was nodding rather impatiently. "Yes, yes. All

the same, Miss Wales, even you—and indeed I admire your loyalty—must admit that his disappearance has raised some questions."

"But only they—the bureau—know where he is."

"Of course, Miss Wales—perhaps your stepmother or someone else has told you—the police so far cannot find that Mr. Blake has any connection at all with any government bureau."

"Yes! Inez—my stepmother—told me that this morning. I don't know what your inquiries have been—"

O'Leary's eyes twinkled. "You mean, my police may not have approached the right government bureau in the right spirit. I assure you, everything we could possibly do has been done. I can see that you don't believe that."

Fifteen

"Why, I—yes, I believe you. I just cannot believe that Richard could or would want to carry on such a deception."

O'Leary sighed. "We are trying to find him, of course, and question him about this Acapulco marriage certificate. But it is true he was in Washington at the time Rose Mendez—or Rose Blake—was killed. Mr. Smith was kind enough to let us know that he—Richard Blake, the Richard Blake you know—was playing poker that afternoon and evening—a rather prolonged session, we were told. We sent a man down to Washington on Sunday to talk to one of his friends, John Lyon, who, we were informed on good authority, is a respected member of the bar. Seems he didn't know your Blake well. They had just met casually before. John Lyon and some friends were making up a table for poker. He saw your Blake sitting in a hotel lobby and asked him to join them. Said he had always liked Blake—that is, the few times he had met him. He had a notion that he was pretty well-heeled but didn't know more than that. He, too, had an impression that Blake was a government employee. But you see," he added rather apologetically, "the husband—"

"Is the first suspect," Hiram said, finishing the sentence. "But this Richard—"

Captain O'Leary nodded. "Yes. We'll find him."

Lacy pulled herself together defiantly. "Have you talked to Rose's first husband? I think he was there at her house that morning."

"Not *her* house," O'Leary said, half apologetically. "A rental. We talked to the real estate agent. The house had been empty for some time. It is on an estate and not an easy house to sell. Your friend Rose rented it about a month ago."

"Have you talked to her first husband, Carlos Mendez?" she repeated. "And his wife? The filling station boy—"

O'Leary nodded. "Certainly. Young Hobie is very informative and, I might add, a bright and observant boy. He came of his own volition to see me—very praiseworthy. He described the visitors to Mrs. Rose Mendez that afternoon. This young Rafael Mendez with a—dog. We talked to him yesterday."

"Oh!" So that explained Raf's long absence.

"Also yesterday we talked to Carlos Mendez and his present wife. They both said that they had tried to see Rose, but the door was locked and nobody answered it. So they went away. A simple story certainly. Nothing to disprove it. Agrees with Hobie's statement that they came back very quickly."

"Oh," said Lacy again. Carlos and Yolanda, too. Hiram and Inez had both thought such questioning likely.

O'Leary went on. "We talked to Hobie's father—a most respectable citizen. He owns two filling stations. He takes the night trick at the station on the other side of Fairview. Permits Hobie to take the station on the road you took. Oh, yes, Miss Wales, we even tried our only bank. Banker stopped by after church to see us. Nothing doing there. Rose Mendez had no bank account. And I am sorry to say that according to the real estate agent she had not paid her bill for the rent to him as she had promised. Please be patient with us. There has been very little time. We have had no reply whatever, so far, from the police in Acapulco." He sighed. "As a matter of fact, your friend Rose was a bit of a mystery woman. That is, she came here, rented that house, moved in immediately. Husband never turned up as far as anyone knows—I talked to somebody at the drama school. They seem to keep records for a long time, probably in the hope that one of their students would get a stage job somewhere. So someone there knew and recorded your job in Mr. Bascom's law firm. That was how she tried to enlist your help in getting a lawyer. Although I don't see just what a lawyer could do. There is the divorce agreement, of course, but all that is clear. She succeeded in arousing your interest—or pity, I expect—Mr. Bascom. Certainly she got Miss Wales out here, and admitted that she was in terror of her husband. The problem is which husband. The first or the present husband." O'Leary said gravely, "Which did you believe she was afraid of, Miss Wales?"

"I told you, didn't I? She mentioned Carlos by name. She said he had—a bad temper, pride, something like that. She was confused—"

"As well she might have been," said O'Leary in a parenthetical way.

"—and so was I. I'm really not perfectly sure of anything I said or did except—that whiskey I gave her. She said she was cold. I told you that afternoon."

"Yes, you did. You've been as helpful as possible. Now then, about this candy box— It has certainly struck both of you that only somebody who knew Rose Mendez quite well would know of her problem about eating as much candy as she could and then, so to speak, going on the wagon for a time. Who are the people you can remember, Miss Wales, who might know about that?"

"Why—why, everybody at the school! It was a sort of joke. She was so lovely when she wasn't tucking away candy, but—no, I can't think of anybody special—"

"Her husband?"

"I—yes. Perhaps. I don't know," Lacy said rather desperately. "Please, Captain, I hadn't seen or talked to Rose since her marriage until—"

"Yes, yes. I understand. Any particular, say, attractive man at that drama school?"

Lacy gave free rein to her indignation. "You should see them. All intending to be stars sometime. Barely paying for their room and board. No, Rose would never have looked at any of them! Not—well—" She stopped herself.

"Not with the glittering prospect of money that came with Mr. Mendez," Captain O'Leary said. "Never mind explaining. Now, this candy—"

"How about fingerprints?" Hiram asked. "I know I'm speaking out of turn but—"

O'Leary took no offense. "Not at all, Mr. Bascom. Quite correct. Mrs. Mendez's fingerprints were on the box. Also Mr. Waddell's. Nothing else but smudges. Now, there is another reason I requested you to come up here, Miss Wales. Did you have any idea that anyone else was in the house when you went into the kitchen—or at any time?"

"No. Well—no. I did have a kind of feeling of something or other. Nothing I could identify."

"Try to remember!" said O'Leary.

"I can't! It was only that the house was so dreary and depressing and I kept thinking somebody might be there. But I didn't see anybody or actually hear anything."

"Did you try the back door? There's a small entry there."

"No. I never thought of it. Why?"

"Because the back door was locked," said Captain O'Leary, looking out the window absently but, Lacy was sure, noting at the same time any reaction from her. He added, "Locked from the outside, and the key was gone. The key was found this norning. Out in the woods. Not far, as nearly as we can tell, from the spot where Mr. Waddell picked up the candy. That afternoon when we arrived and questioned you, you did say that you saw something near the house." He withdrew his gaze apparently from some faraway space, and looked directly at Lacy. "You say you can't describe that—thing?"

"No! I just *thought* there was a movement! It was, really, Captain, just a small moving blur, if that. Possibly a deer. But really nothing identifiable. I think just a shadow. I told you I have to put in my contact lenses to see anything more than ten or fifteen feet away, so I got out my lenses and by that time whatever I thought I had seen there really was just nothing."

"You are not wearing those contact lenses now."

Lacy reached for her pocket and remembered the skirt she was wearing was new: Inez simply had not yet added neat little pockets. But Lacy had always carried a pair of rimmed glasses in her handbag. She slid them over her ears. Instantly Hiram's face, the desk, the captain became pale blurs. "These are for distance. I have contact lenses. But these, too."

Hiram said as if he were speaking only to Lacy, "I must say I like them better than those contact lenses. More—more—oh, something. I think I must have the usual inexperienced person's idea that contact lenses are very difficult to wear."

"Not at all difficult," Lacy began, but the captain stirred in an authoritative way. "We are not discussing the comparative ease of any aids to vision," he said, and looked rather hard at Hiram. "Are you by any chance Miss Wales's counsel?"

"You mean," Hiram said quickly, "if she should by any mad chance need counsel?"

"I mean, are you acting as her lawyer?"

"Certainly," Hiram said decisively.

"I see. Yes. This attack upon you, last night, Miss Wales—the police you summoned, and very wisely I might say, report that they found no signs of any intruder. But then I gather by the time the attack—"

"The mugging," said Hiram.

The captain shot a chilly glance at him. "Thank you, Mr. Bascom. I am aware that you promptly reported the circumstances to me. Also the chief of police in your precinct, Miss Wales, thought it proper to report to me. Very thoughtful of him. After our conference it seemed to him advisable to communicate anything unusual to me."

"The old boys' network," Hiram said not quite under his breath, which drew another hard glance from Captain O'Leary.

"You might have a bad time sometime, Mr. Bascom, if there were no such friendly links between police forces. However, we'll let that pass for the moment. Now again, this teacher—Mr. Waddell, Miss Wales. Can you tell me anything of his family? Anyone who ought to be notified of this tragic accident? The dietitian at the school knew nothing about any relatives."

"Neither do I. Surely some of the school faculty can tell you."

"The few we questioned didn't know, and the rest are all taking vacations in some out-of-the-way spots. You kids must make it hard for them."

Lacy thought back and said honestly, "I rather think we did. I suppose the present classes are no easier to cope with than we were."

"Harder, I should imagine." The captain sighed and looked down at a report—at several sheets, in fact—spread out on his desk. "Well now, Miss Wales, I have to ask you to go over all the events that occurred before and during your visit to Mrs. Rose Mendez's house. I want to check a few items. If you please."

Again. She looked at Hiram, who looked at the floor. Nothing else to do, his attitude seemed to say. So she began.

Captain O'Leary had a pen in his hand but made no further notes on the papers or notebook before him. They contained, Lacy supposed, everything she had blurted out during the shocked, almost hysterical time after the police had arrived. Nothing new at all. When she finished her recitation, O'Leary said wearily, "You still insist that this blur you thought you saw, you really didn't see."

"No—I mean, yes. I didn't see anyone."

"Any ideas about who knocked you out last night?"

"No."

"How many people have you told of this vanishing blur you saw near the house?"

"Not many. Hiram told me not to speak of it."

This time O'Leary favored Hiram with a definitely approving look. "Smart of you, counselor."

"Only sensible, Captain."

Captain O'Leary shrugged. "All the same, someone did attack Miss Wales last night. The city police were unable to discover the presence at any time of any suspicious car—or even bicycle, for that matter—lingering around the neighborhood. Muggings are not unusual in a big city. We all know that. But this one—" He shook his head. "Why did you call the doctor first, rather than the police?"

"Why, I—my mother—I mean stepmother—did that—"

Hiram broke in. "She was hurt. Nobody knew how seriously hurt. Raf—that is, Raf Mendez, her stepmother's younger brother—found her and brought her into the house."

O'Leary just looked at him in such a patient way that Hiram stopped, almost blushed and said, "Sorry. Forgot. You know all about him. You have questioned Raf and Carlos and Carlos's wife, too. Sorry."

"Oh, that's all right," O'Leary said cheerfully. "You are not in my business." He looked rather as if he felt grateful for that, and Hiram's ears reddened.

O'Leary went on. "However," he said rather gloomily, "we have not succeeded in finding just how Rose Mendez received her allowances. Mr. Carlos Mendez was willing to

146

say it was by check, which Mrs. Rose deposited wherever she happened to be. We naturally inquired who sent her the check. Carlos Mendez himself—or who?" Here O'Leary shook his head. "There is where he stonewalled us altogether. Wouldn't say who, beyond saying the intermediary was a longtime friend of his from Logonda and would not like being questioned by the police. I insisted. I even impressed upon him the importance of how he discovered Mrs. Rose's residence, but he refused to answer. Couldn't get a single word out of him about his proxy—"

"Wait," Lacy cried. "Rose called him a spy—she was very confused, so I wasn't sure I understood her. But I think that's what she said."

"A spy? Well," O'Leary said, considering the word. "That seems possible. I think we'll have to bring a little pressure—" He fell silent and began tapping the desk with his pen. Finally Lacy said, "What about services for Rose? I mean, if she has no blood relatives you can find—"

O'Leary looked at her thoughtfully. "Oh, young Raf Mendez has tried to see to that. His brother seemed the likeliest person to feel a kind of responsibility. However, when I broached the subject, his wife—" O'Leary looked a little embarrassed. "To tell you the truth, I was thankful there was no weapon handy. Young Raf said somebody had to make the arrangements, so it was decided to wait for a little. Have to, anyway." He twiddled the pen. "We'll see. But there's a good side to that young fellow."

Oh, yes, there was a good side to Raf—a very kind side; all the same he could and did lie, happily, and as it suited him. This time, however, Lacy was inclined to give him full credit for a humane and touching offer.

It was remarkable that while Raf, Carlos and Yolanda had spent so much time during that long, dreary day just past, actually being interrogated by the police, nobody had mentioned the visit to Fairview. But it was certainly an unpleasant experience, and none of them wanted to talk of it.

147

Raf had returned, he said, from the airport carrying only a very small suitcase.

It had been a rather long pause after O'Leary's last comment. Hiram asked, "Is that all, Captain? We have a drive back to New York."

"I think we're finished here for the time being," O'Leary said, and suddenly and frankly added, "That hypnotic had to be procured somewhere. I'll have to ask you to keep what I've told you about it to yourselves. I don't intend it to be of use to any other persons who just might wish to induce such heavy sedation that a little alcohol would put away any person someone wished to dispose of." O'Leary unexpectedly revealed a small chapter of his own past. "My father warned me about that kind of situation. He was a country doctor. He told me that an easy way to get rid of anybody was to use insulin—a very heavy dose. He said that an autopsy would not reveal anything. Somebody had asked him about it, and before he realized what he was doing he had given out the information. When he realized what he had done, he kept a strict watch upon the person who had received such information. However—" Captain O'Leary gave a rather wistful little sigh, which suggested an eager dog cheated of his bone. "Actually there were no unexplained deaths among any of that person's friends and relatives. Even a quite rich grandfather lived happily and for many, many years beyond anybody's expectations. So you see that luckily the knowledge my father had imparted did no harm. Of course"—he returned to the present—"we have now developed more exact methods of ascertaining any use of a hypnotic." He gave a little laugh. "I really don't think either of you are about to set out on a course of mayhem. If it relieves your mind, Miss Wales, I cannot see why you would wish to murder Rose Mendez unless—well, I have to admit, unless she had married your—er—sweetheart and you were so jealous that—"

"She had no opportunity," Hiram said sharply. "And no means, no purpose—"

148

There was a soft and respectful knock at the door. O'Leary said, "All right, Sergeant."

A policeman in blue uniform, looking rather puzzled, said, "A Mrs. Maria Llamas wishes to see you. Spelled with two *ll*s."

O'Leary's face suddenly brightened. "Show her in—thank you—"

The policeman stepped aside and a slender woman, about forty and very chic and composed, came in. She glanced past Lacy and Hiram as if they were not there at all, and said to O'Leary, "Mr. Carlos Mendez sent me."

"Ah," said O'Leary, clearly pleased. "I hoped that he would. A chair—"

She sat down near him and folded gloved hands over a very elegant handbag. "He said I was to tell you the whole story. As—" she added very positively, "I know it."

"Well, yes, please continue, Mrs.—"

"I am Maria Geno Llamas."

Geno—why, that was the name Raf had mentioned, saying something about old Geno's work; the emerald, of course. Lacy leaned forward. Maria Geno Llamas did not deign to glance at her.

"I'll put it as clearly as I can," she said calmly. "My father works for Mr. Mendez. So does my husband. Mr. Mendez made an extraordinary yet quite comprehensible request of me. He asked me to act as his intermediary—in a way. That is, I was to send a certain sum of money once a month to his young half brother, Rafael."

"Ah," said O'Leary. The bit of money Raf had said was barely enough to live on?

"And also—I cannot say that this was quite to my taste— but I and my father and my husband—"

"I understand. You were to send money also to Mrs. Rose Mendez." O'Leary took up the pen again.

"That is quite all right," said Maria Geno Llamas, referring obviously to the pen. "He wished you to make a record of the chore and for me to explain it to you. In short, after his divorce he asked me to follow Rose Mendez and inform him of her activities. You see"—she studied her hands for a moment—"the money to go to his former wife was a very large sum." She spoke steadily and clearly, her English not even touched by a Latin accent. "The amount came close to a hundred thousand a year—in your money. So, in order to protect his own interests, Mr. Mendez employed me to keep in touch with his ex-wife. He was quite sure that she intended to marry again and therefore he had a clause in their divorce agreement that his generous allowance was to be cut off if or when she did remarry."

O'Leary did lift his eyebrows a little at that. "So you followed Mrs. Rose—"

"Certainly. Indeed, I made friends with her. That was easier than it may sound. She did not remember me from Logonda. I doubt if she had ever seen me. At this time she was very lonely and spending a great deal of money. But then—she did marry. As Mr. Mendez expected her to do. It was cheaper, you see, much cheaper in the long run to employ me than to keep on paying such a very large sum to his former wife." She added simply, "It was quite easy to become her friend. I had been taught English. My father and my husband owe a great deal to Mr. Mendez. I can't say I really liked the task he gave me, but there was nothing else I could do. But then after I told Mr. Mendez of her marriage, Rose did escape my constant vigilance. While we did make friends in a way, I couldn't watch her at all times. She simply disappeared one day. I was told by the owner of the house which she had rented that she had gone to New York. Mr. Mendez wanted me to find out where she was, so"—she shrugged—"I came to New York. I wrote a short note to her, at the rented house in Acapulco in the hope that it would be forwarded to her. It was. I had given her the address of the small apartment I had sublet in New York. She came to see me. It was—" Her voice wav-

150

ered just slightly. "I did feel sorry for Rose. So I lent her a little money but had to let Mr. Mendez know where she was. He said he would arrive by plane as soon as he could and asked for her present address. I gave him that and then phoned young Raf Mendez."

O'Leary interrupted. "Why did you do that?"

She looked a little surprised. "Why, because Carlos, his brother, was coming. I hoped they would have some kind of reconciliation. You see"—a faint color came into her cheeks—"Raf was a nice boy. Inventive perhaps—not quite accurate about, say, truth telling. But only a boy, sent away from home and—of course, I liked him. That is," she said, looking rather like Inez, "I liked him but could never be sure when he was telling the truth about anything. The point is, I'm afraid they arrived here the same day—"

"Mrs. Llamas, did anyone at all, just anyone else, ask you for Rose's address?"

She looked a little, but only a little, startled. "Why, yes. He gave his name but I didn't make a note of it—something like Williams or Jones—oh, I understand a very common name here. He said that somebody in Acapulco had given him my New York number, but he knew so much about Rose and the Mendez family that I believed she had deputized him to talk to me. Yet all he asked for was her address."

"I see." O'Leary fidgeted slightly with a pen. "So you gave it to him. Naturally. Did you happen to tell him that Mr. Mendez—that is, Carlos—and also this young Raf were on their way here?"

She blinked. It was the only time she had seemed the least uncomfortable. "Why, I—yes. Yes, I did mention it, as I recall."

"I see. Are you sure this voice over the phone was a man's? Describe it as best you can."

"Why, I—I thought it was a man, but now that you ask me—" She seemed to cast back in her memory and shook her head. "I cannot say positively. It could have been either. I only told whoever it was that both Carlos Mendez and Raf were expected to arrive Friday."

Unexpectedly O'Leary gave a sudden thrust backward to his chair so that it sprang away from the desk, and he looked as if he might give an exultant leap into the air. However, he calmed down sufficiently to pursue his inquiry.

"But you never saw the man Rose had recently married."

"Oh, no. In fact, I only remember her air of—oh, I can't describe it—but sort of"—she colored a little again—"being secretly happy. After I learned of her marriage I understood."

"But you're sure you never saw the new husband? Didn't know his name either, I expect."

"No! Certainly not! When Rose came to see me—I believe I told you she had—"

"Yes. Quite enough." O'Leary fiddled again, sighed and said calmly now, "I thank you for coming forward. Also Mr. Mendez for advising you to see me. He's a very smart man. I'll tell you something, I can believe in a single coincidence—police work takes one coincidence almost for granted, it happens so frequently. But it was hard for me to accept that so many people interested in Mrs. Rose would arrive at the same time of the murder. . . . Thank you, Mrs. Llamas."

With great dignity she said, "If you wish to question me further, here is my address. Not that I can tell you anything more." She slid a neatly lettered piece of notepaper from her handbag; and put it on O'Leary's desk, closed her handbag with a decisive snap, bowed with great composure and left.

"Dear me," O'Leary said after a moment. "Dear me! Well, much cheaper than paying out all that money for years and years."

"So this woman acted as his agent," Hiram said.

And spy, Lacy thought. A reluctant spy but a spy all the same.

"You heard her. Mr. Mendez admitted there was someone. But he wouldn't tell me who. I take it he had second thoughts."

There was a long pause. Finally Hiram said, "But she never knew who the man in Rose's life was? I mean the next one she married?"

There was another knock on the door, this one hard and angry. Without a pause the door was flung back and Richard Blake strode in. "What the hell is going on?" he demanded.

Sixteen

"Richard!" Lacy sprang from her chair.

He gave her a nod. He did glance around, as if surprised. "Is this—is this actually a police station?"

O'Leary interpreted both the question and the air of surprise. "Why, yes. You see we're old-fashioned around here. None of the new equipment but only—"

"Only your own ideas!" Richard said sharply. "I see. What are all your ideas? Why have you got my fiancée here, questioning her? And who are you?" He glowered at Hiram.

Hiram took it very quietly. "Hiram Bascom. A friend."

"Richard, you don't understand," Lacy began.

Richard cut it off. "I understand too much. I heard from John Lyon that Mr. Smith was trying to reach me and a man from the Fairview police was asking all kinds of questions about me in connection with some woman's murder. So I came. . . ."

"How were you able to get away?" Hiram said mildly.

Richard whirled around as if ready for a fight. Even his usual very discreet, dark gray suit, spotless white shirt and neatly knotted tie seemed to join him in expostulation. "I hadn't left. I was to leave this morning. But when I reported this—problem, the bureau gave me what in some government jobs is called compassionate leave."

There was a marked silence. He gave a swift glance around and, being Richard, alert and sensitive, guessed. "Oh, I see. You've been inquiring about my post, have you? Well, my guess is that you found out nothing, Mr.—or whatever your rank is."

"Captain O'Leary," said Hiram.

"Captain O'Leary. Well, if you inquired about my bona fides, so to speak, you can't have been informed."

"Why not?" O'Leary said almost lazily.

"Because of orders given to me," said Richard shortly. "I am only to do or die. However, to make this clear, I must explain my presence here. I don't know exactly what a compassionate leave is called in my branch of the service but it operates in the same way. Naturally they don't want anyone connected with the bureau to be called for questioning in a murder case. I did not kill anybody! Let's get that straight. I know that you have already checked my alibi for the time of some poor woman's murder. Doesn't it satisfy you?"

"Not entirely," said O'Leary very, very quietly. "Since you have come, do you mind just signing your name here?"

He pushed a paper toward Richard, which, as far as Lacy could see, was perfectly blank.

"Sign?" Richard cried. "Sign what? Do you intend to write something above my signature, a confession, say?"

"No," O'Leary said, again very quietly. "See, I'll scratch out the empty space you leave. I'll do it now so there's just enough room for your signature."

Hiram made a restrained but interested kind of move. "Here is a pen."

Richard took two quick steps toward the desk, leaned over, his fine tailoring scarcely showing a wrinkle as he took the pen from O'Leary, didn't even glance at the lines O'Leary had scrawled down the paper, but signed with a flourish and an extremely steady right hand. "Satisfied?" he asked O'Leary.

"I think so. Now, do sit down, Mr. Blake. Let's get things a little straighter. How did you get here so quickly?"

Richard was still white with anger. He sat down, however, in one of the uncomfortable stiff chairs and automatically pulled up the legs of his trousers so as not to disturb their knifelike creases. "Easy. The moment I got away from my chief at the bureau I made for the airport, got a plane to La Guardia, phoned your mother, Lacy, found out you were here, rented a car and here I am. Let's have an end to this nonsense. I never heard of this Mendez woman who died. I know nobody by the name of Mendez, except, of course, your mother, Lacy."

"Inez's name wasn't really Mendez," Lacy heard herself say defensively. "She was born Susan Timpkins. A plain New Englandish name. But when her widowed mother married Carlos's father—"

"Yes, yes," Richard said. "I remember, she told me something of that. Now, what else do you want to know?" he asked O'Leary.

O'Leary looked down at the paper Richard had signed. "I want to know everything about Rose Mendez's death," he said.

"Well, I can't tell you." Richard was obviously still angry. Hiram, Lacy happened to see, was very quietly leaving the room, behind Richard's back.

"Surely you are troubled about her murder," O'Leary said.

"About your questioning Miss Wales? Yes. No sense to that—"

"But you do know that she was in the house when Rose Mendez died." Richard gave a quick nod. "And you do know that she gave Mrs. Mendez a drink of whiskey just before her death."

"What's wrong with that? I'm sure Lacy thought there was no harm in it."

"I'm telling you that it contributed to her fatal collapse. Also, since we have a certificate of marriage in the names of Rose Mendez and Richard Blake, naturally we have to question you."

"I am Richard Blake. But certainly not the same one."

"Can you suggest anyone who might be likely to use your name? Remember, that is a legal document."

"I suppose I am permitted to see it."

"Of course." O'Leary went to a rather antiquated safe in the corner, pushed aside a last year's calendar hanging on the handle and opened the safe. He drew out the marriage certificate and handed it to Richard, who gave it one disdainful look and shook his head.

"That's not my signature."

"But it is your name," O'Leary said.

"Oh, I can see that. And I can't say that I have any friend who would forge my name. I don't know any other Richard Blake either. There undoubtedly are others—clearly there must be at least one, but I don't know him."

Hiram slid quietly back into the room. Lacy saw Captain O'Leary's eyelids flicker once in his direction but he said nothing to Hiram, who moved quietly into a chair again.

"Now then—" Richard settled his perfect tie. "Do you permit me—us—to leave?" he asked in his formal way. In all probability he had cultivated that studiedly polite voice, which made explicit his confidence in his own authority and assurance that he was backed by the government.

O'Leary half smiled. "Oh, sure," he replied pleasantly. "Any time. Now, if you don't mind letting me see your passport—"

"My— Sorry, I can't do that without asking permission from my chief."

"But you have it with you?"

"No, sir. No use searching me, if that's in your mind."

"Oh, come, Mr. Blake! We don't use such strong-arm methods. Unless, of course," Captain O'Leary added thoughtfully, "it is necessary."

Richard eyed him for a moment. Then he said, "I'm certain you would do anything that is properly within your power, Captain. Very wise. Now then, you have my address. It's a small apartment in New York. Merely a pied-à-terre. My card—" He pulled out a handsome leather billfold with gold corners, drew out a spotless card—engraved, Lacy felt sure—and put it down on the desk. He turned to Lacy. "You'll come with me, Lacy. My car is waiting—"

Hiram had risen too. He had an arm under Lacy's elbow. "Oh, dear me! I'm afraid I acted too hastily."

Richard flashed his eyes at him. "What do you mean?"

"Why, I—" Somehow Hiram managed to convey a kind of boyish apology. "I'm afraid I sent away your car, Mr. Blake."

Richard's face turned white again. "You sent away *my* car!"

"I shouldn't have. But I thought of it—a hired car and driver, standing out there, waiting for who knew how long. I do know something of what the government pays its servants, and I really thought I was doing you a favor. You might not have thought of the cost of keeping an expensively rented car and driver waiting for— Well, naturally I didn't know how long. But my car is here. Do ride with us."

It was not in the nature of the Richard whom Lacy knew to explode. He came near it then. For Hiram pulled out a bunch of keys from a pocket and tossed them toward Richard, saying, "These were in the car—"

Richard caught the ring of keys quite adroitly with his left hand, glanced at the keys and said sharply, "These are not mine. In any event I assure you I do not leave keys around in a hired car—or anywhere."

Hiram took them as Richard tossed them back, looked at

them and said, "Oh, I *am* sorry. These belong to me. Now, how—what did I bring from the hired car— Oh well, it doesn't matter," He opened the door, turned to nod at O'Leary, who had a half-smile on his face, and ushered Lacy out.

Richard followed.

"Good day," said O'Leary cheerfully to their departing backs.

"Mine is not much of a car," Hiram said. "Nothing like the grand car you hired, Mr. Blake. However, it works, and we can all three sit in the front."

"No, thank you," Richard said, still angry. He all but shoved Lacy into the backseat and got in beside her. Hiram clapped a hand on one of his pockets, muttered something and ran back into the police station. Richard said nothing. In a moment Hiram returned.

"Sorry. Forgot— Now we'll be off." He took the driver's seat. Somehow he adjusted the mirror so he could see not any traffic behind him but Lacy's face. He gave her a pleasant little nod. "I think we'll take the road past that filling station. I must need gas."

Still Richard said nothing, but Lacy knew he was fuming. However, he adjusted his perfectly creased trousers, touched his perfectly knotted tie, smoothed back his perfectly neat black hair and said, "Mr. Bascom, I understood from Lacy's stepmother that you permitted Lacy to see this Mendez woman. What a foolish thing to do—"

The car shot ahead as Hiram stepped hard on the accelerator. "Yes. I wish I hadn't."

"I should think you would indeed regret doing anything so unprofessional. As I understand it, you claim to be a lawyer."

"I am a lawyer," Hiram said. "But you are right, it was a very foolish thing to do and I regret it. But try to stop Lacy? I couldn't!"

"Then it is certainly your duty to get her out of this."

There was a pause. Finally Hiram said, "I'm trying to do just that. Oh—" They had come to the filling station and Hobie appeared as the car came to a stop. "Will you just take a look at that right rear tire, Mr. Blake?"

"Do it yourself," said Richard. "It's your car."

"Sure. If I had the right gadget here—but it won't take a minute." He rolled down and leaned out the window. "Hi, Hobie! May have a soft tire. Take a look, will you?"

"Sure," Hobie was very cheerful. His face grew keen with interest. "Say, did you just come from the police?"

"Yup," said Hiram, at which Richard gave a sigh of exasperation. "And," Hiram added, "Mr. Blake here wants you to tell him about that tire."

"Mr. Blake does nothing of the kind," said Richard, but nevertheless he slid out of the car gracefully and disappeared from Lacy's view. Hiram neatly altered the mirror, the barest trifle, so he could watch Richard and Hobie.

Richard came back and slid into the seat again, closing the door hard. "Tire is fine."

"Good. Thank you."

"What is it, Hobie?"

Hobie's keenly freckled but serious face appeared at the window beside Hiram. "Well, Mr. Bascom. So you've been seeing the police."

"Sure," Hiram said good-naturedly. Hobie's bright, eager eyes shot to Lacy. "Hello," he said cheerfully.

"Hello," Lacy replied.

"I thought," Hobie said, "that gentleman—" He nodded at Richard, who did not look particularly gentlemanly, and certainly not polite, but Hobie could not be discouraged. "I thought he might have turned out to be the young guy who went to see Mrs. Mendez that day. Day she was murdered. But he's not the one. I told you, miss. That one had some funny kind of animal with him. Wasn't a cat. Think it was maybe a dog. At least, I never saw a cat wag his tail. Funny kind of—"

"Right," said Hiram. "Fine, Hobie. See you!" He shoved his foot hard down on the pedal.

There was clearly nothing the matter with the car. Hiram concentrated on traffic. Richard did not speak.

There had to be a serious talk with Richard, Lacy thought; it had to occur as soon as they could be alone. The marriage certificate, yes; that must have been done by someone who simply faked Richard's name.

But there was the snapshot; there was the ring. There was the police statement that Richard was not associated with any government agency. Suddenly it occurred to her that Hiram had sent Richard's car away on purpose, to prevent or postpone her own mandatory talk with Richard.

It would have to be a very private talk between them. She glanced at Richard and his handsome profile was unrevealing; he was merely silent—probably, she thought, it was the kind of diplomatic silence that had become a habit.

He wouldn't even have said a loving word, not with Hiram's ears ahead, practically sticking out, she thought, with what ought to have been anger but was instead amusement. There was certainly nothing at all in Richard's manner to remind her of the suddenly ardent expression of his affection when he had gone away. True, there had been no audience to that scene of passion, which almost called for applause and a curtain call, but now, she thought, there also was no audience—with Hiram sitting in front.

She chided herself: the present situation was too serious for any embraces or indeed anything else to remind her that she was still his wife-to-be. She couldn't expect that of him, not under the circumstances.

It seemed a very long and certainly a very silent ride.

Richard made no comment at all on the murder of Rose Mendez. Hiram whistled a little, softly, as they maneuvered along Lexington Avenue and around the corner toward Gramercy Park.

"Expect you'll want to talk to your fiancée," Hiram said

as he stopped at the Waleses' house. He turned off the engine of his car and, without an invitation, came up the steps beside Lacy. Richard was still coldly angry. Lacy thought he was probably angry at being questioned as to his identity, his government post, and at being obliged to dig up alibis for himself. Also probably at Hiram's high-handed way of getting rid of the luxurious car that Richard must have intended to invite Lacy to share with him.

Raf met them at the door, smiling, showing his fine white teeth. "Back so soon? They didn't shove you into jail? That's great. Oh—" He seemed to perceive Richard only then. His curved black eyebrows rose. His teeth gleamed whiter. "You must be Mr. Blake. Come in."

Inez appeared beside him. "Lacy, dear! Well, we'll all have tea. That is, unless— Why, *Richard!* I can't tell you how thankful we are to see you! So much has been happening. May I introduce my brother."

Jessica bounced out, sniffed at Richard's highly polished oxfords and growled.

Richard, taken by surprise, kicked her.

Seventeen

This Jessica did not approve of.

Raf took an angry step toward Richard and Inez cried, "No, no, don't!" Lacy clutched at Richard's arm. "You mustn't—"

Jessica could help herself, however. She gave one high soprano yelp, got her teeth into Richard's ankle and held on.

Lacy swooped down, and tried to gather Jessica up—no easy task, as it happened, for the dog refused to give up her grip on Richard's ankle although Richard tried hard to shake her off. Raf came to Lacy's aid, Jessica held on, Inez cried, "Let her go, Richard—let her go—" This was obviously the wrong thing to say. Richard's usually immobile face was flushed with anger. "Let her go!" he cried. "Get off me, you—whatever you are—"

Things were a little confused until Hiram and Raf both took action. Lacy contrived to get her fingers into Jessica's mouth, which baffled the dog because she really could not bite a friend. Raf and Hiram between them detached her from Lacy. Richard shook out his trousers, got himself together and said stiffly, "Any iodine in the house?"

Inez and Lacy both assured him that there was iodine, but Richard rolled down a neat sock, surveyed a row of red dots and said, "I'll have to get a shot now." He looked up at Inez. "I mean against hydrophobia. That dog of yours is dangerous. Ought to be put away."

Lacy snatched at Jessica again and got her away from Raf and Hiram, neither of whom objected, for Raf was rolling up his coat sleeve with a dangerous look in his eye and Hiram was already squaring off, also prepared to do battle. Inez's voice was sharp. "Now stop that! On the doorstep, too! What will people think! Come on, all of you. *Now!*"

Inez seldom spoke like that; but when she did, she was obeyed. Once in the hall she turned to Richard. "That dog does not have hydrophobia. However, if you want to be vaccinated, that's up to you. But just now—"

Carlos appeared in the doorway. "Well, well—" he began as Inez said hurriedly, "This is my stepbrother, Richard. Carlos Mendez. Richard Blake."

Richard looked at once sober and dignified yet still ruffled, for there were two angry red spots on his usually rather pale face. He gave Carlos a strange, perfectly blank glance, which Carlos returned. Richard bowed slightly. Carlos did not even nod. Jessica showed her wounded feelings by giving another growl in Richard's direction. Raf reached over to smooth down her yellow fur.

Hiram said to Carlos, "Good afternoon." Carlos muttered something and in a moment they were all in the living room, even Yolanda, who was seated swinging one foot and half smiling. It struck Lacy that she had enjoyed the drama, if it could be called that, on the steps, which she and Carlos must have been able to hear. But Yolanda nodded in a friendly way and spoke to Richard. "Why, it must be Mr. Blake! I'm Lacy's—Lacy's aunt, I guess. By marriage—"

Richard gave her a chilly glance but bowed.

The meeting was not precisely propitious and the center of a chill came from Carlos's glacial formality and his blank, cold blue eyes. For some reason, he looked at Richard as if he were eyeing a remarkably offensive bug. Raf's dark face was no more friendly. On the other hand, Yolanda was frankly interested and almost beamed at Richard, who did not return the flash of her dark eyes.

Inez said in a low but commanding voice, "Perhaps we should all have drinks."

Sooth the savage beast, Lacy thought wildly, and sat down. Richard politely but coldly waited for Carlos to seat himself, as he did, and in Buddha's chair. Buddha was the only one missing in the little coterie, and Lacy wondered how it happened that Inez had not sent for him. She didn't wonder long, for the doorbell rang; Jessica barked. Hiram was near the hall door, so with a shall-I-answer glance at Inez, he went to let in—of course—Buddha.

He came into the living room jovially, gave a graceful bow mainly directed at Carlos and Yolanda, and smiled. Then he glided softly over to Richard and stuck out his hand. "Richard! Glad to see you, young fellow. Had a hard time running you down. Hope you cleared yourself with the police."

Richard's face was still stony. "I think so, sir. I assure you I did not kill this—this Rose Mendez. Oh"—he turned in formal courtesy toward Carlos—"I understand that she was your wife. I beg your pardon—"

"His former wife." Yolanda's flashing eyes now flashed nothing inviting. She didn't snarl but the effect was the same.

Carlos was completely self-possessed. "My ex-wife, yes. It seems that lately she contracted another marriage." He turned to Richard. "Do you mean to say that you persuaded the police to believe you are not her husband?"

"Yes!" Richard's response was like the snap of a steel spring.

Carlos said with, at least, frigid approval, "Good. They always say the husband is the first to be suspected. But then—who did marry Rose? Our family name, you know. Mendez. Like to keep it—"

165

Raf broke in with one smiling and sarcastic word. "Clean?" Carlos did not appear to hear that.

"Certainly I didn't marry or kill her," Richard said with force.

Buddha selected his chair, barely foiling Jessica, who was making for the luxury of the big chair. She stopped and curled her lip. All her femininity had been outraged—first by a kick, then by being pried from what she considered logically to be an enemy and now ousted entirely from the chair she had taken a liking to. Carlos looked at her with distaste; Yolanda again tucked up her feet, instep bulging above sparkling new pumps. Hiram said, "She's upset, Mr. Smith, pay her no attention. May I help you, Mrs. Wales?" Inez nodded, and Hiram followed her to the kitchen. Raf smiled and strolled after Hiram.

There was a moment or two of strained and frosty silence. Then the tinkle of glasses came from the hall. Inez came in and went to the table. Raf followed and deposited a tray of glasses and ice. Hiram obligingly carried the bottles.

But if Inez had fully intended to turn the occasion into a cozy if not entirely friendly sharing of drinks, she was mistaken. Buddha accepted whiskey and demanded soda, which Raf had not brought and strolled back to the kitchen to secure. Carlos helped himself to a rather large drink of vodka with nothing in it but ice. Yolanda sighed, refused, and then relented hungrily, taking vodka too, without ice, which interested Lacy, who did not quite believe her eyes. But when she glanced at Hiram, she saw he was only amused; she could tell by the glint of humor in his eyes. He turned then to mixing drinks. He glanced at her, "Martini for you, Lacy?"

Her favorite, he had remembered. She had asked for it before dinner in his club. He brought a glass to her, and again with a twinkle of humor, quoting her said, "But you said only one."

She took the glass, set it absently on the table beside her

and watched the others. She must take Richard aside and if possible get answers to some questions.

Carlos frowned at Yolanda, who tucked in her feet and drank from her glass.

Somehow, at that point, Richard was leaving. He had to go to his apartment, he told Inez politely, because there might be a message for him. Lacy heard this and said distinctly, "I have something to say to you first, Richard."

"Oh, I can't talk now." Richard looked at his ankle. "I really must tend to this bite—"

"Yes, yes," Inez said as always and usually successfully when she tried to bridge any kind of awkward social gap. "Yes, of course, but you'll want a little talk with Lacy. After all—" Her hint was easily translated: she's to be your wife, you know.

Carlos put down his glass. "Well, then, if there is no further news about whatever those police are doing—"

"I know of none," Hiram said.

Carlos gave Yolanda a glance. She had begun to push her feet into the handsome new pumps when Carlos crossed over to her quietly and as quietly put a hand on her shoulder. To Lacy's vague surprise, Yolanda became motionless at once. Carlos said, "Oh, we mustn't leave sister Inez so soon. We've seen very little of her—"

Inez didn't say the less the better but looked it. Buddha sat in his chair sipping his drink; Yolanda drank the remaining drops of her own drink. Carlos said nothing, but Lacy was sure that the pressure of his hand on Yolanda's shoulder did not lessen and Buddha said, "Well, my dear Richard, I'm certainly pleased you managed to clear yourself with the police. I never expected to be able to track you down. But—"

"But you did," Richard said. "Now I'll be going—"

"No, Richard, not now," Lacy said in a voice of command that was new even to her own ears. "I'd like to talk to you."

Richard lifted an eyebrow. She thought that Hiram, who

stood at one side, gave a kind of encouraging if slight wink in her direction. Inez said quickly, "Oh, certainly you wish to talk to her, Richard! We've been so deeply concerned! There's your father's study, Lacy."

"Yes." Lacy put her martini on a table and stretched a hand out to Richard, who didn't seem to see it; he was eyeing the fine dark spots on the sock Jessica had sunk her teeth into. "Let it bleed," Lacy said in that new voice. "If it does, it will cleanse itself. Come along, Richard—" She looked for her handbag and saw that it lay on the same table where she had put down her martini. She needed that handbag for its special contents. She took it and started for the hall. She saw that Buddha was smiling. "Right. Yes, you two will wish to have some private moments—" He stopped and gave one of his little chuckles. Hiram looked at nothing but whistled softly to himself.

Inez said, "This way, Richard." She stopped as Lacy drew her a little near and whispered, "The ring—"

Inez was never slow to grasp anything in the way of a hint. She walked ahead of them, entered Tom Wales's study, went to a small safe set in the chimney of a tiny fireplace, twirled the dial to open it and drew out the ring. Richard was eyeing the study and looked a little puzzled. He had never been in the room before.

Inez kept it as Tom Wales had left it; it was not a shrine but a place where she and Lacy often retired to think hard thoughts when their finances reached a very low ebb. It always seemed to give Inez courage. Tom Wales had been her husband, her bulwark, her everything, except for Lacy who was Tom's daughter. Lacy didn't think Richard saw Inez transfer the emerald ring to Lacy's hand. Then Inez murmured something and went out, closing the door carefully.

"Interesting!" Richard said, "but small. I should think your father would have had a larger study—library—whatever he called it. Something more luxurious."

"You've never been here," Lacy said. She didn't add the fact that her father had liked its simplicity. It was a slit of a room really, a space that had originally been part of the small dining room, narrow but long. The fireplace was never used since Tom died. Two leather chairs were drawn up near it; a table was still laden with magazines. She knew they were dated the year her father had died. Dear Inez; she couldn't bring herself to change anything in the room that spoke so eloquently of Tom. Tears came to Lacy's eyes. "Rather out of date," Richard said, dropping a couple of the magazines he had picked up. "Bookcases, a dictating machine—that's outdated too—"

Lacy braced herself. "Richard, *did* you marry Rose?"

He jerked toward her. "What a question! Certainly not. You heard me—"

"Then what is this?" Lacy was to be a little surprised later, thinking of the interview, by her own icy calm. At the moment she felt nothing as she yanked the snapshot out of her handbag and gave it to Richard.

He took it; he looked at it; he frowned; he seemed to try to think back into some forgotten incident, and then he smiled. "Oh, that's a joke!"

"But you said you didn't know Rose."

"I didn't. Not at all! That is, in a way, maybe. It must have been at one of those parties—oh, tennis, I believe, or something. Could have been in—possibly Aruba."

"Not in Acapulco?" Lacy suddenly heard a kind of echo of her father's sometimes peremptory voice and didn't care; indeed she felt a kind of pride that she could take that tone. Take the bull by the horns! Not that Richard was lowering his head and charging at her, but she left that fragment of a notion unfinished, for Richard answered, "Acapulco! Good heavens! I don't think that's possible. Yet I do travel a lot, as you know. I may have met her in any of those places where the ultra rich seem to gather and invent games that amuse them."

"And you may have been in Acapulco. Why?"

Richard shrugged his finely tailored shoulders. "I go where I'm told to go and do what I'm told to do to the best of my ability. Things go on, even among the very rich sometimes. Odd things, but the bureau must have some definite idea of precisely what some people are doing. You do understand, I'm sure. You—" He looked at the snapshot. "Not a bad picture, is it? But somebody certainly had a poor idea of a joke. Utter nonsense. Probably meant nothing. Not even my writing!"

Lacy thought it a poor joke, too; not believable—yet it might be true. Richard's government chores were ordered by somebody, possibly to get himself invited here and there to observe. Oh, yes, observe—that could be a way to discover anything contrary to the national interest. However, she said steadily, "The same kind of joke somebody played on the marriage certificate?"

Richard gave her a long look and did not reply.

"I mean it. You say it's a joke. Who would use your name on a marriage license and write on a photograph of someone who is certainly you. You can't deny it."

"I'm not trying to deny it. Lacy, you don't realize—you don't know the kind of things I have to put up with on my job."

"What was your job in Aruba? Or Acapulco?"

"I'm not sure if it was either. There are many trifles the bureau wishes me to check. Nothing that concerns you."

"I think you are lying," Lacy said firmly.

"Lying?" He was not at all angry. His eyebrows lifted and he gave a cool little laugh. "Oh, come, now, Lacy. Don't make a fool of yourself. Why should I lie about—"

"You can't lie about this!" She opened her hand. He stared at the ring.

"Well?" she said as his silence lengthened.

"May I look at it more closely?"

"Certainly. But give it back to me. You did give it to me once, you know."

He took it from her. He turned the ring this way and that. He moved to a lamp on the magazine table, switched on the light and held the emerald closely below it. Finally he looked up. "It does look like your ring—your engagement ring, darling. Where did you find it?"

"I didn't find it. The police found it among Rose's papers and other personal property. They showed it to me. Also the marriage certificate with your name and Rose's. This is my ring. The one you gave to me."

"But how did this Rose Mendez get hold of it?"

"Oh, Richard! I lost it—that is, I thought I lost it. But you took it and gave it to Rose, and that snapshot was on her dressing table, and—"

Richard was shaking his head. "You aren't making all this up, are you, Lacy?"

"Certainly not." The stubborn wall of loyalty she had imposed upon herself all at once vanished as if it had never been. I've just been a fool, she thought sadly yet angrily. The deceptions that she had taken for truth and defended with loyalty (and believed, too, she reminded herself swiftly) had simply crumbled away. She said in a voice she had never heard herself use, "Richard, tell me the truth!"

"I have told you the truth, I've told the police the truth, too. See here, what have you been doing all the times I've been out of town since we became engaged. This young fellow Bascom, how does it happen that he has become such a good—such a very good—friend? I think you owe me an explanation."

"I don't owe you anything." Lacy was drawing on a well of defiance in times of stress that may have been native to her, endowed by her father, but only rarely put to use; it might also have arisen in part from Inez's own determined courage. In any event Richard looked at her as if he were a stranger.

171

Thought I was a pushover, she reflected; and I have certainly acted like one!

"You can't mean that you don't believe me!"

"I don't believe you. That ring, that marriage certificate—"

"I suppose you can't get that silly marriage certificate out of your head."

Lacy had never felt such a wave of fury as she did then. She paused for a few seconds in order to be sure her voice was steady. "I can't get any of it out of my head."

Richard said sharply, "Do you really think I murdered her?" He laughed. "Well, there's proof I didn't. Alibis galore."

That was true. And she had defended him all along constantly, loyally and very foolishly. Yet there were certain arguments that were mandatory, too. "I know you didn't murder her," she said steadily, "but I can't believe you about that snapshot—"

He interrupted. "You would believe me if you had to circulate among some of the partygoing people I've had to associate with. All sorts of people. Part of my job—"

A new Lacy had certainly emerged or had been there all along without her knowledge. "What was your investigation in Aruba? Or in Acapulco."

"I don't remember—even if I could remember or asked for my records in the bureau, I couldn't tell you. But that silly snapshot could have happened easily. There were water sports, tennis, golf and—it seems—joke playing as well."

"How about my ring?"

"I don't think that can be your ring."

"It is."

"Then how did the police find it at this Mendez woman's house as you said?"

"I told you, Richard. There is one way. You gave it to her. So now you can have it back."

She didn't fling the ring at him but he dodged a little as if she might throw it.

"Listen, Richard! I mean it! That is my ring."

"Oh, no. . . . I'm no connoisseur of jewels. I can't identify one from the other, but—"

"Raf can!" Lacy said.

Richard's eyes opened. "Who is—oh, that young man Inez said was her brother?"

"Yes." She opened the door of the study and called him. "Raf! If you please!"

There was a slight commotion in the living room. Then Raf walked in leisurely, white teeth shining. "You called me, Lacy?"

"Yes. Will you look at this ring?"

She took it from Richard and put it in Raf's palm.

He looked puzzled. "But I did look at it, Lacy. It's an emerald."

"Richard thinks it is not the ring he gave me."

"Well," Raf said lightly, "he should know. All I can say is that is the ring the police found at Rose's house."

Richard said nothing. Raf looked more closely at the ring; again he got out the loupe and fixed it in one eye. After a moment he looked up. "Yes, Lacy, as I told you, I can't tell where it came from—the stone I mean. But the lapidary work does look like old Geno's." Old Geno, whose daughter had been Carlos's rather reluctant but constant emissary and spy, Lacy thought swiftly.

Raf went on, "I can't say positively, but my opinion is that it was Geno's work." He turned to Richard almost lazily. "How did you come to buy it?"

"I didn't," Richard was angry again. "I know nothing about jewels. I gave Lacy an emerald, yes. It was like that one, yes. But I know nothing of stones—only their price," he interpolated. "Lapidary—what does that mean?"

"You have a dictionary," Raf said, smiling with all his white teeth.

173

"Not with me," Richard said, smiling now, also showing his own teeth too much.

Raf shrugged. "Look it up sometime. Carlos would certainly be able to speak with more authority, but may I ask just where you purchased this particular ring?"

"That is not the ring I gave Lacy!"

"Well, where did you purchase the ring you are sure you gave Lacy?"

Richard said smoothly, "I don't like to admit this, Lacy, but the government is not noted for generosity to its employees. I have to admit I saw it in a pawnbroker's window. Over in the Forties somewhere. I liked it. I bought it. And gave it to you and you liked it and lost it and—"

"Then," Raf said softly, "it turned up in Rose's house."

Richard thought for scarcely a second. "And so apparently did you."

Eighteen

Raf was taken aback. His teeth still showed wolfishly in a smile but rather as if the wolf had been cheated of a coveted prey.

"How do you know that?"

"There is a filling station along the road. I stopped there today on the way to see the police in that little place—Fairview. The filling station boy said a good-looking young man had passed the day of this murder. There wasn't much time but the boy thought something like a cat was with him." Richard looked a little smug. "A yellow cat, but it was wagging his tail, so he decided the creature must be a dog. Now will you stand aside so I can get to a doctor? Your little yellow pet has given me a nasty bite. Puncture wounds are dangerous," Richard added, leaned over to Lacy so quickly she couldn't move, kissed her swiftly, bowed to Raf and went smoothly out into the hall. Inez met him. He said something to her about going to a doctor. The street door closed hard.

Raf was no longer smiling. Lacy had to speak. "Raf, the police told me you were there yesterday."

"Certainly. They had me out there for questioning. Also, I might add, Carlos and Yolanda."

She was momentarily diverted. "It was good of you to offer to see to Rose's services."

Raf shrugged. "Somebody had to. Unless the police unearth some blood relative. Or somebody who is familiar with the terms of her will or—oh, it doesn't matter, Lacy. She is still, in a way, this family's responsibility. Not that Carlos will see it that way."

"No. No—but, Raf, tell me why *did* you go to see Rose that day?"

Raf tossed the ring up and down in his palm. The emerald was a single lovely piece of deep green.

"I knew that she had married Carlos—after a rather swift courtship. I knew that he ought to have married Yolanda. Occasionally his agent did send me some money—enough to live on. His conscience or more likely a sense of guilt made him do that. Through a . . . friend from Logonda who now lives in New York."

"Maria Geno Llamas," Lacy interrupted him. His curved eyebrows lifted. She said, "She went to see O'Leary. Today. She told him all she knew. That you and Carlos were expected the same day; that she had talked freely to you both in the hope of a reconciliation between you—"

Raf showed his teeth but not in a smile.

Lacy continued. "Well, she said that and she meant it, I'm sure. She passed on to Rose her allowance from Carlos and reported everything she found out about her. She told Carlos—and you—that Rose had remarried."

"Maria is a nice woman," Raf said unexpectedly. "I always liked her. I thought it was a pity that Carlos had roped her in to keep an eye on Rose. Yes, she did tell me where to find Rose. I had to find out just what kind of deal Carlos had given her and why. Oh, I'm not a nice guy, Lacy. But I really did want to make sure that Carlos was not taking—call it revenge. Since Rose had married again, I couldn't help wondering what Carlos was doing about it. I knew of the allowance he had given Rose. I even knew that there was a catch to it. He'd cut it off if she remarried."

Lacy interrupted. "How did you know that?"

"By asking, of course. Indeed I'm afraid Maria Geno was impressed by my brotherly affection for Rose." This time the white teeth shone. "At any rate, she gave me her address. So I hired a car. Jessica was with me, yes. I stopped at a hamburger joint and fed Jessica. Then on the way I stopped at the filling station to get more exact directions. As you know, I found Rose at home. She peered out the door and wouldn't let me in at first, until I said I had a message from Carlos. I stayed perhaps ten minutes and left her in—well, I can't say in good health but certainly alive. But she did seem a little peculiar."

"What do you mean, 'peculiar'?"

"Oh, a little vague. Didn't seem to associate me with Carlos. She asked me for his message. I couldn't tell another lie." The dancing light was back in his eyes. "I told her only that I had to talk to Carlos again now that I'd seen her for myself. She didn't seem in any kind of condition to answer questions so I left. That's all. She was alive then. You found her alive."

Lacy sat down in one of the big leather chairs. "You said she seemed peculiar. Didn't she seem at all natural? Herself?"

"I couldn't possibly tell you that. I never knew her, remember. But she did seem rather cloudy and vague. A little on the sleepy side, I suppose—unless she was drunker than I thought. Yet—" He frowned, puzzled. "She didn't seem drunk exactly either."

"Raf, how was she dressed? Tell me everything."

"Nothing much to tell. How was she dressed? Seemed to me she was wearing some kind of dressing gown, loose anyway. Hair wasn't neat. Fact is, she seemed a little on the sloppy side. I can't think of anything else. Except I did wonder why Carlos had such a passion for her that he'd actually married her instead of Yolanda, with her three kids."

Lacy said slowly, "Then she *was* already eating some of that candy. Did you tell the police all of this, Raf?"

He wriggled a little and grinned like a naughty schoolboy.

"You were with O'Leary this afternoon. You ought to know. Or didn't this fine cop tell you?"

"Yes. And Carlos and his wife met with him, too, on Sunday. But you were probably the last person to see Rose alive."

"Except you," Raf reminded her too gently. "You'd better put that ring away. Isn't that a safe by the fireplace there? Unless, of course, you intend to wear it."

She didn't debate. The ring, beautiful as it was, had taken on an ugly aura of malice. Richard could have bought it from a window at some pawnbrokers. It might even be a quite different ring; she had always believed she had lost her own. But who can accurately distinguish one ring from another, the same size and kind of jewel?

Raf guessed her thoughts. "Carlos can tell, he'll know in an instant."

"He never saw the ring Richard gave me."

Raf's dark face took on a look of skepticism. However, he said only, "I think he'd know something of it. But if you don't want to ask him, put the bauble away. There's that safe, gaping open carelessly, it seems to me. Stick the thing in there and close the door. Give yourself all the time you want to think things over."

It seemed sensible. She shoved the ring into the safe, closed the door and twirled the dial. Raf, she knew, was watching over her shoulder. Intently watching? She was beginning to believe that nothing much missed Raf's dark eyes.

"Good," he said. "Now that is secure for the moment. I'm going back to my drink. I'd advise you to do the same, niece."

She was by now too shattered and bewildered to take exception to his mocking "niece." She went with him into the hall, where Inez met them, her eyes troubled. "You know Richard left," Lacy said in Inez's ear as Raf continued on into the living room, "I'll tell you later. No time now—"

Hiram was in the doorway. Raf made a courteous gesture and passed him.

Hiram came to Lacy. "Things all right?"

Inez answered. "She looks white as— Are you really feeling well, Lacy? No pains where you were hurt?"

"Hurt? Oh, my head." She had actually almost forgotten that ugly mugging in the back garden. She felt for a bruised spot, winced as she found it but said "No."

"Why did Richard—Mr. Blake—streak out of here like a scalded cat?" Hiram asked.

"He went to get a shot or something for his ankle," Lacy replied.

"He was going to his apartment, he told me when he left," Inez said. "But he intended to see a doctor first."

She linked an arm through Lacy's as they went back to the living room.

Raf said over his shoulder, "Come on, Lacy. Here's your drink, where you left it."

The living room still seemed crowded. Carlos sat with dignity on a straight chair; Yolanda was bent over nursing one foot. Buddha sat in comfort having made peace with Jessica, contented now, on his lap.

Hiram put his hand on Lacy's arm and said very softly, "Did Blake satisfy all your—that is, the questions?"

"I—yes—no!"

"Better make up your mind and be sure, hadn't you?"

"Come on," Raf said. "You need a drink, Lacy." He put

the glass she had left on a table in her hand. "Don't drink too fast. You'll choke yourself."

Buddha sighed, "Excellent liquor, Inez. You have never lost your taste for good things."

"Tom's taste," Inez said and gave Yolanda an icy stare, as cold as the granite of her native state. "Why don't you all go home?" she said politely but firmly.

Yolanda's eyes flashed; Carlos again put a hand on her shoulder. "We are just leaving." Probably he was reluctant about thanking Inez, Lacy thought absently, but he did say, "Thank you very much for your kind hospitality. Come, Yolanda."

Yolanda finally got her feet shoved into the glossy new pumps. She and her husband started for the hall, and Buddha began to rise.

Hiram said, "Is your car here, Mr. Smith, or may I drop you off somewhere?"

Buddha gave one of his wheezy chuckles. "My car is somewhere outside. Good night, Lacy. Things will work out. I gather you had a very satisfactory talk with your young man. Blake, I mean." His eyes gave Hiram a single glance.

Hiram replied not for Lacy but to Buddha's glance. "Quite satisfactory, I believe." There was a certain gratification in his eyes. "He's gone to a doctor and then—" He looked at Inez. "Didn't he say something about his apartment?"

"Yes. He has a small apartment. Somewhere in the East Seventies, I think."

Buddha nodded, smiling, as if Inez should know. Raf smiled, too, but not so agreeably.

Hiram said, "I'll go with you if I may, Mr. Smith." But first he leaned over the sofa, under which Jessica had taken refuge from the unkind world, called to her, and as she stuck out her funny, small face with its perked ears and bright eyes he leaned down, patted her gently and said, "Good dog."

She wagged her tail vigorously. Hiram rose with a dancing look in his eyes, which was not like the occasional look of mischief in Raf's eyes but which still indicated a very personal satisfaction.

He then said a proper good night to all and departed in the wake of a light-footed Buddha.

The street door closed. Lacy took up her drink and was pleasantly surprised to see that it was a martini. "Why, Raf! I didn't say martini, did I? Oh—oh yes, Hiram gave it to me."

"Mr. Bascom said you like martinis. He mixed it carefully. Don't you want it?"

"Yes. It really is my favorite, although"—she tasted it— "not quite so heavy on the gin—"

"Darling niece," Raf said, "that is vodka. You can't taste it. Now then, Inez, a confession was forced out of me today."

"Nobody forced it," Lacy mumbled over the drink, which was indeed refreshing.

"Same as that," Raf said, good-naturedly. "The fact is I saw Rose the day she died. Yesterday morning, the police sent for me. So I went to Fairview."

Inez's lips set firmly. She gave him one of her piercing looks. "Tell me—"

"Sure. But, first, I did lie to you about Jessica. I picked her up at the airport. She was lost or hungry or something, so I just took her with me, hired a car and went up to see Rose. That was after I had done some telephoning and actually had gone to see the emissary Carlos had entrusted with sending Rose her allowance—and also to watch her. Even to follow her."

"Go on," Inez said.

Lacy listened as he told what was a rather well-constructed account of the events. Certainly it agreed with the story he had given O'Leary. Inez listened, her clear eyes steady.

Hiram's departure had left Lacy with a ridiculous feeling of being snubbed. She took another swallow, which was so large that tears came to her eyes. A strong martini!

181

After Inez had listened to Raf's tale, she questioned him; Raf's replies corresponded precisely to what he had told O'Leary and later to Lacy. So he must be telling the truth; surely he couldn't repeat a whopping lie with such fidelity to detail. But then, Lacy reflected, Raf *could* remember what he had said. Raf was as slippery as an eel when he chose to be.

But Raf had found her in the garden after she'd been attacked and had carried her into the house. In short, Raf had rescued her. It wasn't fair to permit suspicions of him to surge into her mind.

Or—it struck her like a blow—was it?

Finding her like that didn't prove that Raf hadn't been the person who crept up and knocked her out.

From what she knew of Raf it would be like him to assume the role of rescuer instantly if Inez came out of the kitchen door and called her, or saw Raf—oh, what an ugly idea that was!

But all the same, Raf could have dealt the whack that might have killed her. And he *had* gone to see Rose, and just could have left something for Rose to take or drink, something lethal, even in the few moments he admitted to having been in her house.

Raf was Inez's brother, but he was also Carlos's brother. Blood tells, she thought rather vaguely. She had had too much to drink. She put her glass down, aiming for the table beside her but missed. The glass fell to the floor. Jessica uttered a growl of disapproval. It was very odd but the room itself was slipping away.

Then it did slip away. She was sure that she felt Inez's hand and heard Raf's voice, but that was all.

After a time, how long she did not know or care, she became aware of wet, cold towels over her face and at her wrists. Then a voice she knew, but could not just then identify, said, "Hold her arm for me, Mrs. Wales—that's right." She felt the prick of a needle in her arm.

182

"I think she'll do now," the voice said. Why, she thought dimly, that sounds like the doctor we called—Inez called, no, Raf called, anyway, the doctor who came Sunday night. What's he doing here?

She opened her eyes with a tremendous effort. It was the same doctor, fattish, youngish, holding a stethoscope and looking down at her, this time with a perceptible question. "I think you'll do now," he said to her, "but, tell me, Miss Wales, what are you trying to do to yourself? Mugged on Sunday. Doped tonight—" He looked across at Inez. "What's this girl up to? Doesn't seem likely that two *accidents*"—his voice underlined the word "accidents"—"could happen to the same person in such a short time."

"No," Inez said and nothing else.

Raf said, "I didn't put anything in that martini, Lacy. Had no chance to."

"What was it, Doctor?" Inez said tensely.

"I don't know. Can't be sure. But it seems to me as if a very strong hypnotic got into this girl somehow. If she got it by way of a martini—or any food or drink—I think I must report it to the police. Unless, of course, Mrs. Wales, you know that she is in the habit of taking any kind of hypnotic."

"This isn't your idea of a joke, is it, Raf?" Inez said.

Raf shook his head. "No, Inez! I wonder—"

There was a long pause while Lacy tried and did not quite succeed in gathering her wits together. Then Raf said thoughtfully, "Bascom mixed it. Before she went to have her talk with lover boy. She did leave it on the table beside the chair she had been sitting in. Then—" He stopped.

There was another silence. At last the doctor put his fingers on Lacy's wrist again, seemed satisfied but said, "Well, I—really am not sure what to do. How about it, Mrs. Wales? Shouldn't I report this to the police?"

Raf intervened. "There was only family here, Doctor. Family and—"

"And Hiram Bascom," said Inez, "and her fiancé, Richard Blake. But they all left. Then Lacy sipped her drink."

The doctor sighed and slid the stethoscope into his black bag. "Somebody gave her enough of something or other to kill a horse. Good thing I could come. Good night. But if— Well, good night."

Nineteen

Lacy could hear the doctor and Inez having a low-voiced colloquy as they walked down the hall. Had Raf carried her upstairs again? Probably.

Raf said, "I expect that maybe we will have to report this to the police."

"*Oh, no!*" Lacy cried.

"Why not?" Raf's eyes were shining. "After all, do you *know* who gave that stuff to you? It was done expertly. Must have been slipped into your drink while you were talking to lover boy. Now, Carlos—" He paused but shook his head. "No. I don't think—but who can be sure of anything Carlos might do. Or Yolanda, for that matter. But I can't see why *anybody* would give such a drug to you. Lacy, tell me the truth. *Do* you know anything—anything at all, no matter how small or slight in your view—that would make you a—well, target? No getting around the fact that somebody in your own home—"

Lacy had to rouse herself. "And you were here. Your brother and his wife were here. Buddha was here."

"And your Hiram Bascom. Don't forget him. He's taken

185

a very strong interest in this business of Rose's murder. I wonder why."

"Because—why, because he feels my presence there was because of him. I mean, he allowed me to go to see her—"

"Yes, so I've been told." Raf scuffed one foot absently against a leg of the chaise longue, frowning. "I can't see why he was such a fool as to let you go out there to Rose's. Unless of course, he has some ax to grind that we know nothing about."

Lacy was feeling better—not much better but certainly more like herself. She lifted herself on one elbow and saw with a shudder that somebody had forced her to empty her stomach into a little bowl. There were towels around too. Raf said quickly, "Here, I'll take all that away. The doctor took a sample—I'm sure in the event he decides the police must be notified. He'll let us know tomorrow as soon as he gets around to it just what it was that you took." He went into the bathroom adjoining, came back with more towels and, as carefully as a laboratory assistant, cleared up every drop. He carried the towels and basin into the bathroom.

"There, that's better." He returned. "Are you sure you did not eat or drink anything on your way home from the police in Fairview?"

"Positive! Nothing! Until I started to drink that martini."

Raf stared brightly into space and said very, very smoothly, "Your friend Bascom mixed it, remember. I handed it to you when you had finished your talk with lover boy and came back into the living room. Bascom— I wonder just why Rose asked for his help."

"Raf! She never heard of him! She found out where I worked—"

"The Wales name is in the phone book."

"Yes, but Rose must have believed that my boss would have some influence over me when she sent me that note asking for help. Hiram told me it was all right to see her if

I insisted. He thought she needed help. But then he told me not to go. And now I wish I hadn't!"

He swerved neatly. "How did your talk with lover boy come out?"

"Don't keep calling him lover boy!"

"Well, then your loving little conference?"

She simply could not continue her stubborn defense of Richard. Still, he did have a foolproof alibi for the day of Rose's murder, so she could not accuse him of that. She shut her eyes and did not reply.

Jessica barked shrilly downstairs. Lacy didn't hear the street door close, but Raf said, "I think the doctor has gone. I wonder if Inez convinced him that there is no need to report this to the police. Although I wouldn't be sure. He seemed a follow-all-rules kind of guy. Well, that alibi of Blake's, you know, if the police are right, is simply no alibi at all."

"But it is!"

"Use your head for a moment. And don't think the police haven't thought of this, for I feel sure they have. Also your other—friend, Mr. Bascom. By the way, you're not doing badly, niece. Two young men, both very attractive, I'm sure, to women. Practically fighting over you. It's not every girl, even as good-looking as you are, who gets so much attention."

"Oh, Raf, don't tease me! I feel awful!"

Raf leaned over and adjusted her pillows. "Better? But, Lacy, that alibi—surely you can see that whatever killed Rose could have been put in the candy at any time."

"No—that is, yes. Rose would never have resisted a box of candy! That is true."

"Then whoever did give her the candy must have known that."

"Yes. We talked about that. Captain O'Leary and Hiram. But we could settle on nobody in particular."

"Well, indeed I hope it was not your—I mustn't say lover

187

boy, must I?—your dear friend Blake. But he could have done it; almost anybody could have done it. At almost any time. It was only a matter of waiting until Rose sampled the candy, and then continued eating it. Right?"

Lacy took a long breath. "I don't know!"

"Do use some sense and admit that the whiskey or candy could have been loaded at any time."

This was true. It hadn't occurred to Lacy, but certainly it must have occurred to the police. Yet it was not reliable evidence; supposition could not take the place of fact.

"But, tonight, I must have had some of that whatever it is! Probably the same thing. I just felt peculiar and things vanished—" Her voice seemed to fade, too.

"I want you to understand, Lacy, that I was the one who caught you. I got the idea of what had happened. I phoned for the doctor. Then we waited, Inez and I, until he came. Luckily he had just arrived home from something or other. So he was able to come at once. Alarmed, I'm sure. After the mugging. I carried you up here to your bedroom as soon as the doctor told me to. But I did not put anything in that drink. Please believe me! Or if you don't want to believe me, I can't help it. Here's Inez."

Inez came in with Jessica trailing behind. Neatly dressed as always, with never a hair out of place, Inez somehow managed to look disheveled now. She glanced at Raf and quickly away again.

"I phoned for Hiram, Lacy. I couldn't reach him so I asked him to call back. I hope you don't mind."

Raf gave Lacy a wicked look. "Oh, she doesn't mind. How about the other guy—this Richard Blake you all are so devoted to."

"I don't have his number. You have it, Lacy."

Fired by the gleam in Raf's eyes, Lacy motioned toward her small desk across the room. "In the address book."

Inez found the little red book, leafed through it and took it with her out to the telephone in her room.

Raf grinned like a malicious cat. "Now you'll have both your pets rallying around. But I was here first. And yet," Raf said more slowly and soberly, "you don't trust me. I saved you twice. I really did—"

"Unless it was you who—" Lacy stopped herself but Raf finished the thought angrily. "Unless I did it myself? First mugged you! Then dropped a strong drug into your drink in such a neat way that nobody saw me do it. And, oh, yes, I had gone to see Rose the day she died. Let me tell you, if I meant to get rid of you for any reason, I wouldn't make such a botch of it."

Inez came back. "He's not there. Probably at his doctor's."

At once Raf was good-natured, but at the same time, in an odd way, wickedly suggestive. "May take that doctor a long time to sterilize the bites or cauterize them. It would take some time to heat up a red-hot poker."

Inez replied sensibly, without a flicker of any kind of emotion in her face, "They don't do it with red-hot pokers now, Raf. They use some kind of sterilizing agent."

Raf shrugged. "Science makes strides. Well, in any event it couldn't take very long to give a rabies injection."

"Maybe you should have one, too. You act a little peculiar sometimes," Lacy could not help murmuring.

Raf heard it. "Now, now, niece. That was not at all nice! I am far from having hydrophobia. No symptoms at all!"

Inez said quietly, "Oh, Raf, nobody likes being attacked by your—" But her voice softened. "By your funny little dog."

Jessica heard whatever special inflection was in Inez's tone; she poked her head and bright eyes out from under the bed.

"All right, Jessica," Raf was now truly in a good humor; there was no edge to his voice at all. "Come out if you like. How about a walk?"

Jessica understood the word "walk"; she crept out, wagging her tail at the world in general, went over to Lacy, put her tiny forepaws on the bed so she could give Lacy's hand a lick and then ran to Raf, who laughed like a schoolboy, caught her under his arm and went out, chuckling at her delighted wriggles.

Inez said soberly, "He really is a good boy, Lacy." She paused and frowned. "At least, he always was my baby brother and— Oh, Lacy, who could have given you a drug here in your house, our home, among our own people—no, I can't say Carlos and Yolanda are really my people. But I wasn't watching them. I blame myself. I felt that I must get some kind of food for them all, so I went to the kitchen. I was there most of the time you were with Richard. Lacy, why should anybody try *twice*," she said with horror, "to— injure you?"

She wouldn't say the word "murder." There was no need to.

Lacy was beginning to feel as if she might live. She boosted herself further upright. "Believe me, Inez, if I had the faintest idea, I'd tell you. I'd tell the police. I'd tell everybody."

"Of course." Inez sat down and clasped her fine hands together. "Well, then, what Raf said about that stuff Rose got and—if it proves to be the same drug, that you got tonight— Oh, honestly, Lacy, I cannot think that either Carlos or Yolanda would have any grudge against you, at least not such a terrible— Why, there must be a need, a driving and frightened need for someone to—well, to put you out of the way. Can't you think of anything, anybody you threaten or any evidence you have that threatens somebody?"

"By somebody you have to mean the people who were in the living room while I talked with Richard."

"I don't know. I guess so. But not necessarily, there could be some way, I suppose—" She frowned. "Yes. I suppose there could be some way to introduce that drug, whatever it is, into your drink. It just stood there, I think. I'm not sure.

What did Richard have to say? You didn't tell me. He didn't actually marry Rose, did he?"

"He says no. He says the photograph was some kind of joke. He explained that. In a way. The marriage certificate too. Same way. A joke. I think he was lying!"

"What! Richard?"

"Yes."

Lacy repeated the conversation with Richard as nearly as she could remember it.

Inez took it in, listening hard. "But you did not believe him."

"It sounded possible. His job. No! I could not really believe him."

"But what about your ring?"

"I showed the ring to him. He said he didn't know. He said that he had bought my emerald at a pawnshop. It was in the window or something."

"But then how did it get to Rose?"

"He didn't feel it could be the same one."

"But you were not satisfied?"

"No."

Inez said after a moment, "What did you do with the ring? Give it back to him?"

"No. I put it in the safe."

"You closed the door of the safe?"

"Oh, yes, and twirled the dial."

"Was Richard watching you when you did that?"

"I don't know!"

"Raf brought this up to me. Now, Raf was always a good boy, but he does make up things. Always did whenever it suited him as a child. He is my brother. I loved him, do love him. But he has some little quirks. He so hates Carlos, for instance, that he'd say anything, make up any sort of tale just to exasperate Carlos. You've heard him—"

"Stringing out that preposterous story of how he happened

upon Jessica? Oh, yes, he admitted that. I told you. And about Rose, too, he admitted everything but nothing incriminating. He saw her and came away. Jessica was with him. He told the police—"

When Lacy had finished an account of her interview with Captain O'Leary in Fairview, Inez thought for a long time, then sighed. "You see, deep down Raf is dependable. That was very kind about Rose. Carlos wouldn't have offered it. Raf wouldn't harm anybody"—Inez's lovely face seemed to harden—"except Carlos. And I just might help him! Oh no!" She realized what she had said and retracted it quickly. "I wouldn't kill even Carlos."

Raf stuck his head in the doorway. "Still gossiping? Wouldn't it be a good idea to let my nice niece get some sleep?"

Inez pulled herself up from her chair. "Yes. Lacy, if you need anything—"

"Oh, she'll be fine. After I took Jessica out, I saw to it that the doors are all locked. And besides"—Raf gave his cat grin again—"I'm here. Go to sleep, Lacy. Come on, Inez."

"Yes, Raf. If Hiram phones I'll take the call in my room and tell him you are better and sleeping, right, Lacy?"

"Yes." But she didn't really like it after Inez had followed Raf out into the hall and closed the door. After a long time, Lacy got up, and noticed for the first time that Inez had put her in her best nightgown. For a doctor to see!

She still felt just a little fuzzy, not dizzy, nothing like that but not quite as full of energy as was natural to her. She got to the window overlooking the park, opened it and stood there, taking in deep breaths of air—thinking, in spite of herself, of a little scene at the gate to the park, directly opposite the hotel. Obviously, it hadn't meant anything to Hiram; he had been barely friendly and polite when he left with Buddha.

There must have been some lingering traces of the hypnotic with which her martini had been laced, for she was thankful when she reached her bed again. But then she couldn't sleep.

Some facts that were questions, too, arrayed themselves forbiddingly in her mind.

Who had doped the drink that had really put her into a sleep, which she knew could have been a permanent one?

Well, who? Carlos, Yolanda, Buddha, Hiram all were in the living room. Raf had been there, too, during her talk with Richard. Inez had been actually in the kitchen. It was simply not possible, but it had happened.

No reason for it unless, of course, one of them had also mugged her so fiercely in the back garden.

Raf had rescued her both times. All the same, he could have struck her the first time, been interrupted by Inez and turned his attack into a rescue. Same thing with that martini. She would never, never drink a cocktail again; in fact, she doubted if she would ever taste anything again that other people had not tasted first. It was such a devastating, terrifying thing to be threatened with death in one's own home with one's closest friends and family.

Now, get yourself together, she said, low but aloud.

Yet her thoughts persisted, taking their own stubborn course. It did seem remarkable that neither Richard nor Hiram could be found. Probably there were perfectly sensible reasons. Actually Richard was the only person in the house who'd had no chance to doctor that drink. Her thoughts inexorably whirled around this name or that until the whole finally vanished.

She awoke when Inez came in, wrapped in her tailored blue dressing gown, carrying a cup of coffee. "All right? I can see you are better. You don't look so—so—" Inez put the cup down on the bedside table.

"Like something the cat dragged in," Lacy finished, eyeing the coffee with satisfaction. "Or Jessica."

"Raf is out with her now." Inez smiled. "You do feel better?"

"Yes." The coffee was already restoring Lacy to something like herself. "Has Hiram phoned?"

Inez shook her head. "No."

Lacy was caught by a shade of evasion in Inez's voice. "You tried to find him again this morning."

"Well, I—yes, I did. It's ten o'clock. So I phoned the Bascom office. Hiram wasn't there. Girl at the switchboard said somebody had called in to say he wouldn't be in the office today."

Lacy took more coffee. "That's not like Hiram just to phone and say he'll not be in the office. I think—Yes! May I use your phone, Inez?"

Inez was uncertain. "Sure you feel like it?"

"Oh, yes." Lacy shoved her feet into the elegant red slippers that Inez had given her, along with the red dressing gown, two Christmases ago. She finished the coffee quickly and pattered into Inez's big room. The room was very neat in pleasantly muted colors of gray and yellow: a big four-poster bed, shining woods, pastel rugs, a telephone and clock on a table near the bed. She dialed the Bascom office.

She recognized the voice of the girl who answered. "Annie, it's me. I mean—"

"Oh, I know your voice, Miss Wales. If you want to speak to Mr. Hiram he's not here—he *was* in the hospital."

Twenty

"He—*what?*" She ignored the obvious fact that, in an arcane way, the girls at the switchboard were informed of everything. There were only two of them, and as a rule they never repeated anything. "Did you say *hospital?*"

"Oh, yes, Miss Wales. He was mugged last night—that is, not mugged really but knocked down by a car. He is out of the hospital now."

"Is he all right? *Annie, what happened?*"

"I—overheard—" Annie cagily did not say just how she had overheard, and Lacy, knowing that Annie could not admit having listened to a call she wasn't supposed to hear, did not question her. But Annie said quickly, "I just happened to overhear. He phoned his father. Said he was knocked down by a hit-and-run driver and wound up in the hospital—"

Lacy broke in. "*Is he badly hurt?*"

"It didn't sound like it, but that I didn't happen to hear exactly," Annie said regretfully. "Mr. Fitterling came out of his office just then, so I had to—well, you know—"

"*Where is he?*"

Annie perked up. "I gather he'd had enough of the hospital and insisted on coming home. That's his club, you know—" In a different and very formal voice, Annie said, "Thank you, I'll remind him. . . . Yes, Mr. Fitterling." She had to cut Lacy's connection and undertake whatever chore old Fitterling demanded.

At least Hiram was out of the hospital, and at his club. Her address book lay on the table, where Inez had put it after using it the previous night. As she snatched it up, the telephone rang. Lacy answered. "Yes— Oh! Hiram! Are you all right?"

"Sure. I see you heard about it. Just got knocked around a little. People rushed to aid me. I was offered glasses of water, brandy, a wheelchair! Bellboys from the hotel rallied. The desk clerk had the good sense to bundle me into a taxi, after the doorman whistled one up, and gave the driver the name of a hospital. It's really all right, Lacy."

"It is *not* all right. Who hit you?"

"I don't know. Just a very fast-moving car—"

"Where were you hit?"

Hiram sighed and gave a small yelp of pain, obviously the result of a careless movement. "Sorry. A rib or two. Can't do anything about them. They don't even strap you up nowadays! You just have to wait until they heal by themselves."

"Where were you?"

"Well, fact is, I was coming back to your place. Just as I was crossing Lexington, a car swooped at me going very fast, knocked me over as I jumped out of the way, then went on, as fast as it could go. I couldn't even get the license number. I was so thankful to get out of it more or less intact that I never thought of it. The hospital emergency ward staff patched me up. Now I'm back at the club." Hiram said with admirable nonchalance, "How are you?"

"I—*oh, Hiram!*"

There was a faint chuckle at the other end. "Dear Lacy!

You don't like that hit-and-run car. Me neither," he added. "But the ribs will heal. I was really very lucky."

"But *why*—oh, Hiram, why would anybody—"

"How should I know? Somebody in a hurry. Big car—that's all I noticed. But hereafter I'll look both ways and step carefully."

"He might have killed you!"

"Didn't," said Hiram and squawked a little again. "Sorry, can't laugh. But I'll tell you this! Whoever said if you want to live dangerously, just cross a New York street slowly was right. I was on my way back to your place, as I said. Wanted to talk things over a little," he said rather evasively.

She thought hurriedly that this was not the time to tell him of her own near murder. Murder? No, no, her common sense said that couldn't be true.

"I'm coming to see you. May I—"

"Oh, sure." Hiram's voice quickened. "I mean, yes, do come. Right away."

"See you then."

She put down the telephone. Inez in the doorway said, "I couldn't help hearing part of that. Was he really knocked down by a speeding car?"

"Yes. Inez, I've got to see him—"

"Better put on a dress first," Inez said crisply.

"Oh! Yes." She gave Inez an impulsive hug.

The doorbell rang. Inez said, "I'd better answer that. I don't know where Raf is." She went down the stairs. Lacy heard her. "Why—why, Raf—I mean my brother—is not here." There was a loud squeal of joy, the sound of a frantic leaping and scramble, and Lacy ran to the head of the stairs to see what was happening.

The street door was wide open. Beyond Inez, Lacy could see the yellow, wagging body of little Jessica.

Lacy could also see the girl who stood on the doorstep. She was rather tall, slim, blond and, somehow, looked British.

The girl resembled Inez a bit in her calm and friendly yet dignified way. Jessica wriggled and tried to lick the girl's hand.

"That's enough—I'm Jessie," the girl said. "I have to see Raf." She waited a moment and said, "I see that he didn't tell you. I'm his wife. I've been staying at that hotel over there. Very nice, indeed. But they wouldn't take a dog after Jessica forgot herself and bit the doorman, so Raf said he'd see to her. He said he was sure you'd take him and little Jessica in. And—you did."

"Come in, my dear," Inez said without choking.

Raf's wife! Lacy longed to go downstairs and hear more. But what about Hiram? She ran back to her room.

It didn't take long to dash into the shower, toss on her blue cotton dress, run a comb through her hair, snatch her handbag and make sure she had change for a taxi. She took a second or two to apply some lipstick and a drop of the perfume Inez had given her, extravagantly, for her birthday. Then she ran downstairs. Jessica was wagging her tail so hard that it was a blur of yellow. The girl, Raf's wife, was seated upright, looking pleasant but also self-possessed.

Inez said, "Come in, Lacy. This is Raf's wife, Jessie. Been staying at the Gramercy Park Hotel all this time. You could have come here, you know, Jessie."

"How do you do?" the girl said to Lacy, and then replied to Inez, "Raf thought it better not to. There was something he wished to do first. So he didn't tell you of our marriage?"

Inez simply shook her head.

The real Jessica? Or rather, as she had said, Jessie. How very odd to name a pet so close to one's wife's name! Yet how very like Raf! And how very, very like him to tell such a preposterous yet convincing lie about picking up the dog. Obviously he had merely deposited wife, baggage and some money at the Gramercy Park Hotel, walked across to Inez and invited himself (and Jessica) to stay. Or at least he had known that Inez would invite him.

The girl, Jessie, said directly, "I'm sorry to surprise you. But, of course, that's like Raf when he has something on his mind. He can't seem to think of anything else. That is"—there was a flash in her blue-gray eyes—"he has what one might call a single-track mind. But I have been a little bored, sitting over there." She nodded her neatly coiffed head toward the hotel. "Of course, my window overlooks your house, so I could see a little of the comings and goings here. I was interested—" There was the faintest, smallest something—not a sob in her voice—that gave her face a rather desolate look.

Inez leaned over. "Certainly you were bored. Lonely—"

The girl sat up straighter. "Raf came to see me often. They permitted him to bring Jessica up to my room but wouldn't let her stay. But I'd like to shop or go to some cinemas or do other things, so this morning I decided I'd had enough of sitting there alone until Raf could do whatever he had in his mind to do. I'm afraid he'll not like my coming here but—"

Again Inez spoke kindly. "Of course you came here! You should have made Raf bring you here in the first place."

"Oh, no." The girl was permitting no pity, but Lacy was sure she didn't mind Inez's sympathy and kindness. "It's been all right, you know. Besides, so much seemed to be happening over here."

And how right you are! Lacy thought but didn't say.

Inez nodded. The girl said, "I couldn't help seeing police cars—at least, I thought they were police cars—"

"They were." That was Inez.

"But surely nothing is wrong."

Inez straightened up, eyed the girl and said calmly, "A great deal has been happening. Raf should be back again—there's the phone, Lacy."

"Yes. Certainly." Lacy ran to the telephone in the hall.

It was Hiram. "I was so pleased by your promise to come that I forgot. I'm living in a men's club, you know. No women allowed above the dining room floor. Anyway I'm

199

coming over there. But not to the house. I remember you have a key to that park of yours."

"Oh, yes, I do. But Hiram, are you sure—"

"Certainly. I want to talk to you. I'll be there in, say, twenty minutes, as soon as I can—" There was a smothered but pained "Whoops!"

"Try not to move," Lacy cried. "I mean—"

"Oh, I know what you mean. It won't hurt long. So they say. Wait for me in the park, will you? I've got to see you."

"Yes! Oh, yes!"

He hung up with a click. She put down her own phone slowly. Had there been something very urgent in Hiram's voice?

It was possible. Anything was possible. Even Raf's wife, showing up like that, unknown to any of the family and having been, all that time, so near. All that time? It hadn't been the year or two it seemed. Rose had died Friday; this was only Monday. The police had actually worked fast and hard, never stopping even for Sunday.

Lacy returned to the living room. The two women there looked so alike that they might have been blood relatives. There was a certain likeness in their straight backs, their calm, intelligent and attractive faces, their steady blue-gray eyes, and in the impression they gave of knowing just what they were, and where they were. It was as if each unconsciously carried years of inherited dignity. How she knew that Raf's wife, Jessie, was just what she appeared to be—a well-bred, well-brought-up girl—Lacy couldn't have said but she knew it.

Inez's eyes questioned.

"Hiram," Lacy replied and glanced at her watch.

"Oh, you're to meet him." Inez nodded.

Raf came in suddenly, bounding up the front steps and into the hall. Jessica gave an excited yelp, jumped down from Jessie's lap and ran to him as he paused in the doorway.

All three women looked at him: Inez steadily, Jessie steadily; Lacy wasn't sure how she looked, but she knew Raf had some more glib explaining to do.

But Raf paused only a second or two. He came over to his wife, lifted her up, gave her a very enthusiastic squeeze and a kiss, and said, "How nice! You've met my wife, Inez. My sister—" he said to Jessie. "And—" There was a dancing light in his dark eyes but all the same he was slightly disconcerted. "And my nice niece. Lacy Wales."

"We've met," his wife said.

But Inez herself had a word or two to say and did so. "Really, Raf! You ought to have told me. You ought to have brought her here."

Raf held Jessie close to him, but there was still a dancing but not exactly pleasant gleam in his dark eyes. "You've been comfortable there, in the hotel, haven't you, darling?"

"Not entirely," Jessie replied as calmly as Inez. "That is, the hotel service, everything is very good, but"—she paused, then let the words come out coldly—"I could also see some odd things that went on here. Police cars. I thought a doctor's car once. I was afraid a doctor had come to see you, Raf, but then—"

"You said you had to go out to the airport to get your baggage!" Lacy reminded him, accusingly, "and you didn't even admit your visit to Fairview!"

Raf shrugged. "I had to invent a few things, sure. You don't mind, Jessie, do you?"

Inez's chin was very firm. So, as a matter of fact, was Jessie's. Only little Jessica seemed full of joie de vivre, leaped on Jessie's lap and nestled her tiny head into her shoulder.

Raf went on lightly. "I knew you would understand when I told you later—"

"When?" asked his wife.

"I told you. There were a few things I really had to do—"

"Raf," his wife said. "You are not to do what I am afraid you intend to try—"

"Now, now, darling—"

"You have some plan. And I think that tall, thin man who's with a very well-dressed woman—He is the brother Raf doesn't like, isn't he?" She turned to Inez, who nodded.

"There! Raf, you cannot—I mean it—I will not *let* you try any wild, fancy means of hurting him."

"Now, Jessie. I wouldn't hurt anybody! You know that!"

"I don't know it," Jessie said steadily. "Not if you can hurt your own brother—"

"But, Jessie—"

Inez said automatically, "Half brother." She rose. She stood very still, and the likeness between her attitude and Jessie's was, to Lacy, pleasing. Neither intended to permit Raf's tricks. If, of course, either of them could stop him. Inez said, "Now, Raf, you've gone too far. Your wife, and you never even told me! You invented stories about how you happened—*happened*," she said, her eyes steely, "upon that little dog. You didn't tell me that you intended to see Rose. You said not a word of that until you had to."

Raf gave her a quick hug.

"Of course I didn't mention it. Wouldn't ever have if it hadn't been for the mouthy filling station boy. Why should I admit to having been around then—" He stopped with a glance at Jessie.

Lacy saw the glance. "You see, Jessie," she said, "I mean, Mrs.—"

"Jessie will do." The girl's face warmed.

"Well, then, Jessie, Raf's sister-in-law was murdered. The afternoon he had visited her. Rose—"

"Now, really, Lacy—" Raf began, but his young wife put a firm hand on his wrist. "I want to know what happened," she said and meant it.

Inez sighed. "You've let yourself in for trouble, Raf. Coffee anybody?"

Lacy looked at her watch. "I've got to go. Tell her everything, Inez. Make Raf come out with a few facts. Such as what he's planning to do that makes him try to hide from his wife."

"Go on, Lacy. I'll see to—to things." Lacy knew that she meant to tell Raf's wife every single little detail she knew of the problems of the past few days.

Only last Friday, Lacy thought, as she left them together. And O'Leary had done so much, but he still did not know who killed Rose. Yet this kind of investigation must take time. Years, sometimes!

It was again a clear and beautiful day. When she reached the gate opposite the hotel, Hiram was already there, one arm in a large black silk scarf, which gave him a rather piratical air, but otherwise he looked merely like a well-dressed young lawyer, possibly meeting a client. "This sling," he said hurriedly, "is only to remind me not to use this arm."

"Oh, Hiram—" she began. "Raf has a wife! And last night I was—I'm all right now but—"

"Give me the key first." He winced as he stretched out a hand from the sling.

"You'd better do the heavy work yourself, Lacy. Hurts me to move. Not much," he added swiftly. "Only a twinge or two."

She opened the big gate quickly and they entered the quiet park. She went through the little formality of relocking the gate and looked around. There couldn't have been a better place for talking alone. Just then there were no children, no people sitting in the sun, leisurely reading newspapers, nobody.

Hiram said, "Lunchtime. Good. Nobody else here. Lacy, I think—I'm not sure, but I think I have got onto something. I can't really tell you yet. Indeed, I'm not perfectly sure I'm right. It's perhaps just a straw in the wind but— What happened to you last night? You said you were all right now."

"Where were you when the car hit you?"

He waved at the gate. "Right over there. Across the street. I had just got out of a taxi, intending to walk directly to your place instead of going around the park. As I got out and my taxi went on, a big car came zooming out of nowhere, and I jumped for the entrance of the hotel, missed the curb—the car gave me a toss and got away. I didn't even see the number or the kind of car or anything. One doesn't," he said ruefully, "when one has been knocked out of the way like that. However, as I told you, the boys at the hotel and the desk clerk and a few other people rallied around and before I knew it had shot me off to the hospital. They patched me up and let me go back to the club. Dosed full of painkillers. But there's something else—"

"Yes. Whoever did that meant to get rid of you. Why?"

"May think I know too much. But I don't! Now, Lacy, what happened to you last night? You said you are all right but—go on, tell me. You might as well, for I won't give up until you do."

"After you had gone, I took the martini you had mixed for me—oh, Hiram—"

"Wasn't it good?" Hiram said too tensely. "Don't tell me somebody tried to—"

"Yes. I went out like a light. Inez and Raf got a doctor. He said I had got some very strong hypnotic in the martini. He made me—" She paused; not an attractive thing to say. "That doctor made me throw up and—"

"Sure. He had to make you get rid of whatever you had taken. I did mix that martini, but I certainly didn't put any drug in it!" He was very white and had a cold look about his gray eyes.

"I know you didn't! But it had to have been done while I was talking to Richard in my father's study. Inez had gone into the kitchen; she always has this New England notion that people must have food or—"

Hiram didn't smile. "Care," he said. "Sure. She's great,

but that leaves Raf and Buddha and that brother Carlos and his wife and me to dose your drink. After I mixed it, I saw you set it down on a table when you went into the study to talk to Richard. I don't remember anybody approaching your glass before that. So—no, I don't see how it could have been Richard."

"It couldn't have been Richard. Right afterwards he left to see a doctor."

Twenty-one

"Seen him since?"

"No."

Hiram gave her a long searching look. But he said only, "You really are all right, aren't you?"

"Yes. I don't like to think of it. But, Hiram, somebody who was there had to have doped that drink."

"Not many people there," Hiram said in a faraway voice. His bandaged arm moved uneasily.

"That hurts," Lacy said.

"Not much. Whoever dosed you nearly to death might be the same person who tried to run me down in a car and nearly succeeded. Did succeed but not, I am glad to say entirely. A warning?"

"No. It was meant to kill! Somebody is trying to get rid of me, and you, too. Because I've told you everything I know!"

He waited a moment. "Oh, I don't know—"

"You said you had something to tell me."

"I didn't mean that I was sure about it, I only suspect it. But no proof."

"What do you suspect? Who then?"

He thought for a long moment. A church bell somewhere tolled twelve slowly. She had often heard the bell during the evening hours, never at night; she worked very hard and, as a rule, slept too soundly.

Hiram said, "For one thing, there may be something that we both know that has scared Rose's murderer. Granted?"

"I didn't kill Rose. You didn't. But Raf was there. Oh, I forgot, Raf's wife has been here! In New York. All along."

"Raf's wife!" Hiram gave her a half-flashing smile. "Raf was certainly paying ardent attention to you."

"She *is* his wife. I'm perfectly sure. She'd never bother to tell a lie. She's like Inez—" she finished inadequately.

Hiram, however, seemed to understand. "I think I know. Inez is a pretty fine, strong woman. Good-looking too—"

"So is this girl. She's been staying at the Gramercy Park Hotel."

"Do you mean to say, Raf parked her right over there and made her stay there until this morning? When did he let her out?"

"She let herself out. She got bored and tired of watching our place. Oh, Hiram, she saw the police cars and the doctor and—anyway she came looking for Raf—"

"Hadn't he seen her since he left her there?"

"Oh, yes. He made walking Jessica the excuse. He saw her frequently, I'm sure, making up excuses to Inez and me. Any excuse. Raf may know the truth but he's very wily about not telling it, if it suits him."

"What's he going to do with her now?"

"Inez will see to that. She'll stay with us, of course."

"How did Raf take this unexpected development?"

"Raf! He never gets upset about anything. He always has a fine and circumstantial story to tell. And then tells it," Lacy said venomously, thinking of Raf's many deceptions. "But the girl, his wife, seems to think that he has some peculiar goal, something he is determined to do. Do you think he could have been planning to—"

Hiram could follow her train of thought, too. "To involve Carlos in Rose's murder? It's possible. Raf is a rather intricate character."

"He's a liar! He told different stories even about how he got hold of that little dog. Kept saying he picked her up because she looked hungry."

"She's a nice little dog," Hiram said and added, "By the way, how is your Richard and his dog bite?"

"I don't know."

"You don't know? Why, Lacy! Your loved one—"

"I haven't talked to him this morning." She was evasive. Hiram sensed that. "Did you try?"

"No!"

"I really wonder just where he is, by now."

"At his apartment, I suppose."

He considered that for a moment before he said, "Don't get all upset about that man. It does seem to me that he is quite capable of caring for himself. I'd say he has a good strong sense of self-preservation." Again there was a silence. Lacy could not accuse Richard. Yet she wanted to tell Hiram of her revealing talk with Richard.

Hiram sensed something significant in her silence. At last he said, "Do you think that this project of Raf's, whatever it is, concerns Carlos?"

She thought for only a second. "He hates Carlos. But Inez hates him, too. I think he brought all that family hate upon himself."

"Raf can't do much legally. That is, I don't think so. From what little I know, I gather that Carlos *is* the law in Logonda. Not titular ruler certainly, but the power behind the powers. Isn't he?"

"Inez and Raf say so."

"Lacy, now don't yell at me, but tell me. Do you think it possible that Raf went to see Rose, that he gave her an

208

inviting box of candy, and then left because he knew from this Maria Somebody that Carlos proposed to visit Rose that day and he hoped the police would fasten on Carlos as the murderer?"

"No!" It was a shocking notion. But murder was shocking, too. And Raf! "I don't know . . ." She felt a horrid little chill crawl up her back. She said, trying to resist it, "Raf did save me after that mugging. He did help Inez with me last night. He was really very kind."

"I don't doubt that. But he is also a very wily young man. Charming, too. It does seem to me he is quite capable of performing any kind of action he decides upon, perhaps not right but justified in his view. Carlos has treated both Raf and Inez very badly, hasn't he?"

"Oh, yes! Took the whole family estate—"

"I know. Buddha told me. How he knew—"

"Inez, probably. Remember Buddha was my father's friend. He knew about Inez's background. He probably knew what my father thought of Carlos and his rapacious greed."

"Yes." Hiram poked at a bit of grass edging the path.

"What's the matter?"

"By the way, Lacy, you do look much better with just those spectacles on your little nose. Easier, too, aren't they, than all that sliding and rinsing and certainly easier to grab when you need them than those contact lenses. I only wish you had grabbed the spectacles when you saw somebody leaving Rose's house."

"I didn't see *anybody!*" she said hotly.

Hiram's face was a blur—he was so near her; but all the same she knew every feature of it, as if she could see him clearly.

"Could it have been Carlos you saw disappearing into the woods? Or just possibly Raf hurrying off with the candy box before the police came?"

"I tell you I saw nothing! I only thought for a moment that it might have been a person."

Hiram said slowly, "If it *was* Raf, he'd have had to get back in his car with the dog in time for Hobie to have seen him leave. Of course, there are other ways—one other at least—to reach Rose's house. You're sure whatever you saw moving was not Carlos?"

"I'll not even talk about it. There was nothing on two legs!"

"From what I've seen of Carlos he might be more at ease on four legs. Also his wife—what's her name? Yolanda?"

Unexpectedly Lacy heard her own little giggle. "She's a cat, yes. But not really from the animal kingdom."

"How do you know?" Hiram said skeptically. "Looks tigerish to me."

Lacy considered that for a moment with a small and mean satisfaction, but the bell across the park and several streets gave a single toll. "Hiram, what did you have in mind to tell me? You said you had the hint of something—"

"I thought I did," he said glumly. "Now I'm not so sure. That is, I wasn't sure at all before either, but I think that the police really should take a keen interest in your Richard's affairs."

"But they have! I mean they do! I think—"

"Yes. It's been a very short time. Investigation like that—government jobs, passports, all that. Richard has been away from New York for quite long periods, hasn't he?"

"Yes. Inez and I always knew that."

"But his alibi concerns only that day Rose was killed, doesn't it?"

"I—yes."

Hiram said wearily, "I wouldn't blame him for anything he didn't do. But I do blame you, I guess. You've been such a stubborn fool."

"Hiram—"

"You didn't even know that your boyfriend is left-handed."

"What difference does that make?"

"Of course, some left-handed people really are ambidextrous. Born to use the left hand, taught to use the right, ending with a fair degree of accuracy with either hand. Oh, yes, your Richard! Lacy, how did you happen to know so much about emeralds? Beryls and all that!"

"Why, Richard told me about them."

"I thought so. But I don't see—" He kicked a little at the grass below and said, "You must have had letters from him. Loving epistles, constantly."

"Not constantly, no. He was traveling so much, and it wasn't a good idea because of the postmarks on his letters and—"

"You *are* a fool! Why did I ever take a second look at you! Listen." He took a long breath. "Remember at the police station when I tossed that bunch of keys at him?"

"Well, yes. And he caught them."

"Sure. With his left hand. And I made an excuse to go back to the captain and that desk where he had, still, Richard's signature on a paper. I got a look at it. Good firm signature—"

"And easily done. I saw him—"

"But the signature on that snapshot could have been made by his left hand. Think now, his letters, those passionate cries of love!" said Hiram acidly. "Surely you remember the handwriting on those letters."

"Well—they were usually postcards, typed," Lacy said coldly.

"I'll bet. That boy doesn't like taking chances. Oh, Lacy, you've been so very damn foolish. Why I bother with such an idiot, I don't know. But I'm stopping all this. That man, your Richard Blake, is a fake, and if you'd only think a moment—"

"I have thought. But I can't throw him to the wolves when I know he has an alibi." She rose.

"Just a minute!" He caught her arm and swung her around to face him. "I've done whatever I can. From now on—no!

I've had it with you, my dear. None are so blind as those who will not see. In short, you are just not worth anybody's trouble—" He broke off. "I see Raf. And Jessica. Coming hell for leather."

It was Raf, striding along. Jessica had to gallop on her short little legs, her huge tail floating like a banner behind her. Her pink tongue lolled out. Raf stopped at the gate.

He didn't see them at once. He peered through the iron grillwork of the gate but could not see them, sitting as they were just in the shadow of some thick shrubbery; he grasped the gate and shook it violently. "Lacy! Jessie says you went into the park. You've got to come home. Hurry!"

She hurried around the shrubs. "Stop shaking the gate! You'll have somebody after you—"

"Come home. Hell's to pay."

Hiram sauntered out to stand beside her. In spite of his explosion he seemed as usual, friendly, though perhaps now a little distant and cold.

"What's wrong, Raf?" Hiram asked.

"Everything. Police from Fairview. Also a precinct officer. Carlos. Yolanda. And nobody can find Richard. Inez told the police about the stuff in the martini last night. Come on, Lacy. They want to question you. My wife doesn't like this business at all. She's a very nice lady. Now hurry up." He shook the gate again.

Hiram firmly took the key from Lacy's hand. "All right, all right! We're coming."

Raf gave him a wicked glance. "I didn't ask for you. What did you do to your arm?"

"Ribs. Somebody else did it," Hiram said with justifiable emphasis. He turned the key, swung the door wide, and Jessica, seeing green grass, scampered inside.

"Oh, stop her! Dogs are not permitted here!" Lacy said.

Hiram caught at her with one hand and missed. Lacy ran after Jessica and scooped her up in her arms; the dog did not growl but settled down crossly, not a tail wag out of her. Hiram, his face enigmatic, went with them back to the house.

They were all there. Carlos, white-faced, in an icy fury, Yolanda sulky but eyeing O'Leary with interest. O'Leary was really a very handsome man, Lacy thought with surprise. His New York City escort made himself inconspicuous.

O'Leary as always was very polite. A gleam in Yolanda's eyes approved this. Carlos grew if anything a shade paler. Hobie stood in a corner, not at all awed by the company he was in but very curious. He said, "That's the dog. Hi, dog!"

Jessica did not respond. Hobie said, "And that's the man, Captain. The thin, tall, Spanish-looking guy. I'm *not* mistaken."

Carlos bristled. O'Leary nodded. "I've talked to him, Hobie."

Yolanda became very firm and almost threatening, "I was with Carlos. I swore to you that Carlos only came to see Rose. I sat in the car. He didn't stay at all. I told you. Nobody answered the bell."

"Yes, ma'am, yes," O'Leary said politely but added in an official voice, "We have the record."

Yolanda sat back, but not in a relaxed way. Carlos touched his neat beard and watched. Jessie stood quietly beside Raf, underlining her status as wife and a solid position.

Inez said in an aside, "Your hair is all anyhow, Lacy."

Inez seemed entirely calm, but then she never showed any deep emotion. Lacy put her hands to her hair and tried to smooth it down. O'Leary turned politely to Inez. "May we all just sit down for a moment?"

"Why, yes. Certainly. Drinks anyone?"

O'Leary replied. "Not for us, I'm afraid, Mrs. Wales."

Hiram said, "On duty, huh?"

O'Leary replied, "Yes, Mr. Bascom. Do you happen to know where we can find this Richard Blake, the man who came to see us yesterday?"

"Haven't the slightest notion," Hiram said mildly.

O'Leary looked hard at the sling holding his arm. "Accident?"

"Somebody in a car ran me down. A big car. That's all I know, if you're interested."

"I am interested. I understand that Miss Wales took something or other in a drink. We can guess what, but it will have to be identified by the New York lab boys."

Hiram's eyes got the steely look in them that Lacy now recognized as meaning trouble. "I must ask for some protection for Miss Wales."

O'Leary nodded. "Do you feel that there is some connection between the murder of"—he looked at Carlos whose pale cheekbones seemed higher and his pale eyes set more deeply—"your former wife, Mr. Mendez, and Miss Wales? If so, I must know what it is."

"None," Carlos said angrily but added, "—that I know of. Why?"

O'Leary replied, "Somebody may believe that Miss Wales might be able to identify something she saw entering the woods near the house. If, that is, she saw a person and not a shadow. Also I have to ask if you have any ideas that might account for a mugging. Miss Wales was hurt, and there actually was an attempt upon her life last night. If you can help us in any way, to suggest a reason for these attacks, please do so."

At this Hiram moved one arm; the sling itself advertised his escape from possibly fatal injury. O'Leary ignored it. So did Carlos, who, stately as a judge, replied, "Miss Wales admits that she did not see any person. As I understand it, she simply felt that there was a kind of blur, moving, perhaps. By the time she got her spectacles on—that is, her lenses—there was nothing to be seen. I am afraid Miss Wales may have drawn too much upon her imagination. I don't think she saw even a shadow!"

It was like a statement of fact. Hiram didn't like it; he drew

214

up the unbandaged arm as if to take a good whack at Carlos then and there.

"All right, all right," O'Leary said peaceably. "Now just let Miss Wales tell me about that business last night. You really were drugged were you, Miss Wales?"

"Yes." Lacy locked her hands together.

"I can tell you about it," Raf said.

"Thank you—Miss Wales herself, please."

Jessie moved nearer Raf; her simple little blue and white summer jacket and skirt were a charming contrast to Yolanda's rose-pink, full-skirted summer dress, which looked as if she might be going to a fancy lawn party somewhere. Yolanda's hands were covered with emeralds, possibly to conciliate Carlos.

"We are waiting, Miss Wales," O'Leary said.

Twenty-two

Hiram gave her an encouraging nod, so she started. As she went on, everybody in the room listened. O'Leary, as if by sleight of hand, suddenly was holding a notebook.

The man near the window spoke deferentially yet firmly, "Captain, by the way, you know—the Miranda warning—"

"Oh, certainly. I'm not trying to incriminate anybody."

"Aren't you?" Hiram said. "I'm a lawyer, you know."

"I realize that. All right, then—anything any of you may say will be written out, signed by you and may be used in evidence against you. Good enough, Mr. Lawyer?"

Hiram narrowed his eyes. "I think it is sufficient. I can't honestly say I've ever heard it recited word for word anywhere. But it seems right to me."

Carlos lifted his eyebrows haughtily; Yolanda's dark gaze no longer dwelt upon O'Leary with flirtatious interest but was sharply focused on him, rather as a cat might watch a mousehole.

The animal kingdom again. Lacy waited.

The whole room had stiffened as if a cord had tightened about everybody there.

"Go on, please, Miss Wales," O'Leary said. "You had gone to this other room to talk to Mr. Blake. What then?"

Did she have to tell it all?

Hiram noted her hesitation. He broke in, "All of it, Lacy. Every word you can remember. The photograph. Everything."

"*What* photograph?" O'Leary demanded.

"Oh, I had—have—"

"Where is it?"

"In my handbag."

"May I see it, please?"

Nobody spoke while she took her handbag, drew out the snapshot, rather battered by now, and gave it to O'Leary. After a long moment he slid the snapshot into a folder of some kind of plastic material. "If you please, I'll keep this for the present, Miss Wales. How did he explain it?"

"A joke. He told me that the marriage certificate was a joke, too." She went briefly into Richard's explanation. She was aware of the disbelief in the room with which she herself had to agree. She could accuse Richard of lying. But not of murder.

She ended her account. There was a short silence. Then Inez said in a troubled way, "Tell him about the emerald ring, Lacy. In the safe—"

O'Leary lifted his eyebrows. "I brought you a ring. Left it here."

Inez said quickly. "You guessed it had something to do with us."

"Thought it possible. Thought I'd let you think things over—that's all. Where is the ring now?"

"In the safe," Lacy told him. "In my father's study."

"May we have another look at it?"

Carlos became simply an iceberg, and Yolanda covertly slid off one pump.

Lacy said, "Certainly," went into the study and brought

217

the ring back. As far as she could see, nobody had moved, probably nobody had said a word.

O'Leary thanked her and took the ring. Then he spoke to Carlos, "Have you ever seen this ring before, Mr. Mendez?"

Carlos gave it a glance, frowned and replied, "Perhaps. I'm not sure." Raf's ears were practically sticking out; there was again the shine in his dark eyes. Jessie held his arm tightly.

"Will you look closely?" O'Leary put the ring into Carlos's hand, which Carlos had put out reluctantly. He held it close to his eyes and shook his head. Raf started forward. "Here, Carlos, take this—" He had got his jeweler's loupe out of a pocket. He put it in Carlos's other hand. "Your eyesight is getting poor, Carlos. I could see at once. It is old Geno's work, isn't it?"

Carlos had to shove the loupe in one eye and gaze at the ring. Finally he said, "No jewelmark on it."

There was a silence. Inez said clearly, speaking apparently to Lacy and Hiram, "You see, every good jeweler has a little secret mark he puts on his jewels."

"There's none here," Carlos said flatly.

"But it does look like old Geno's work," Raf insisted.

Carlos pursed his lips and shot a glance of something like hatred toward Raf. "You hung about the lapidary when you were a kid. Wouldn't surprise me if you smuggled away some stones of your own and kept them, too—"

Jessie stepped forward with dignity yet ready for combat. "You must not say such things of my husband!"

The spirited attack surprised Carlos. "Why, you—you—" He turned to Raf. "Where in your travels did you pick up this woman?"

Raf's fist shot out. Somehow Hiram was there first and deflected the blow. Yolanda sprang up squealing. Carlos stood very tall and furious. Raf was so angry that his eyes not only held ruby gleams but were like fire. "I could kill you,

Carlos. I could kill you for a lot of things. You've gotten away with robbery, larceny—"

But at that Carlos, to Lacy's amazement, summoned up a kind of smile. "Not in Logonda, my boy."

Inez said, "We must calm down a little, really. If you two—you, Carlos, and you, Raf—really must fight, don't do it in my house. My husband always told me to leave you alone, Carlos. He told me that all your stealing of Raf's and my property was really small potatoes and that I must forget it. So I did."

"Do you know where Blake is now, Miss Wales?" O'Leary broke in. His rather pleasant we-are-all-friends-here tone was entirely gone.

"No! No, I don't. He left to see the doctor—"

"Mrs. Wales told me. Mr. Raf Mendez told me about the little dog's taking a bite out of him and that he went off to consult his physician. But that shouldn't take all night and most of the day. Where is he?"

Lacy sat back. "I have no idea."

Carlos turned the emerald ring back and forth with his long fingers. He readjusted the loupe and examined the stone over and over again. Lacy knew he was putting on a show of careful examination; so, contrarily, she decided that Raf was right and the cutting was the work of Geno, as Raf had called him, in the lapidary rooms Carlos maintained.

She said unexpectedly, "Mr. Mendez, if that ring came from your place, how did it turn up here in New York?"

Carlos lifted his eyebrows. "I'll explain. I sell only to dealers." He turned to O'Leary. "Dealers sell the stones to jewelers to be set and later sold. I never see the jewelers themselves. Indeed, I see only a few dealers."

O'Leary said softly, over his notebook, "How many? Their names—"

Raf gave a wolfish grin. Carlos adjusted his dark tie and then loosened it. But it was indeed a very warm day. Carlos

219

was slender, and his summer-weight suit looked very proper, not like Hiram in jeans and a cotton shirt with a black sling on one arm. Carlos coughed a little. "Why, really—I don't remember exactly—"

"Oh, but surely, sir, your books would show the information." O'Leary was polite.

"Oh, certainly. I don't carry business notes in my head!"

"But you must trust your memory to some extent."

Raf intervened, "You see, Captain O'Leary, Carlos *is* the law in our home. He pretends not to be interested in politics, and that is true in that he doesn't care about anything outside his own little bailiwick. But he does care about that. He keeps the lapidary going. He mines emeralds, and then he smuggles them out."

"Raf!" Carlos was white now. "How dare you accuse me of a—a criminal enterprise! Smuggling emeralds! The very idea! I needn't do that. I do nothing that is not legal. My only feeling about the business is a very natural one." He turned to O'Leary. "You yourself can understand the principle—" His attitude proclaimed a doubt as to the policeman's ability to see anything in the line of economics, but he went on, "An overproduction of anything lowers prices. It is in my interest—and Raf's and my sister's—to keep the sale of emeralds down to a specified time limit."

"Three days," Raf muttered. "Which means a competitor either breaks the law or sells to my brother. And my brother," he said to the room at large, "*is* the law in our little home."

There was silence. It was so still in the room that the ever-present hum and throb of New York became an audible murmur.

Finally the captain said, "Will you take that ring, Miss Lacy? It seems to belong to you. Now then, try again to think where your fiancé might be. I must see him, you know. The sooner the better. I'm sure you realize that."

"I don't know. He said he had to see a doctor—"

220

O'Leary permitted himself a very small smile. "You should know that we have necessarily put out inquiries here and there. We have even gone so far as to send his description and the name he uses—his own name, I mean—to agents of the government at various airports. He admitted having a passport. Or," he said, "passports." He looked at Lacy very seriously. "Mr. Blake insists that he has a most demanding government job, but we cannot discover what it is. He really must confirm this by telling us just what his department is."

Raf's eyes gleamed. "Secret service, you mean?"

The captain looked annoyed, though only slightly. "I didn't say that. Miss Lacy, as I remember from what you told us the day Rose Mendez was murdered, she was not very specific about which husband she was afraid of. As you understood it then, it was possibly the former one. Not the present husband."

Carlos bristled, his pale eyes glittering. Yolanda took off the other pump. Inez and Jessie could have been sisters, each sitting very erect in exactly the same way.

Lacy searched back in her memory for the scattered accusations Rose had made. "I thought she meant Carlos. But she may have meant the present husband. She had a notion that he married her for the money she appeared to have. However, I'm not sure. Mrs. Llamas knew all about it and told you that Rose knew that her allowance would be cut off when the former husband—"

"You mean Mr. Carlos Mendez," the captain said.

Carlos didn't steam like a volcano giving warning, but the effect was the same.

Lacy said helplessly, "I can't be sure of anything now! I'm sorry. But when you came to her house I told you every single word I could remember. I'm pretty sure I did."

"You were upset," O'Leary said. "Now, I am going to see your friend Mr. Smith. Will you please come with us, Miss Lacy?"

There was nothing for her to say but yes. Hiram would

have accompanied them; Raf also made a gesture of attending them, too. But O'Leary said, "Just you, Miss Wales."

The New York precinct officer somehow managed to get to the hall door ahead of Lacy and O'Leary. The captain had a firm grip on her elbow. Led away to be arrested? Lacy thought wildly. But no. O'Leary looked back at young Hobie and said positively, "Stay here. We'll be back."

He politely assisted her out of the door and into the backseat of the police car at the curb. The precinct officer took the wheel. All those familiar sights: the Lexington Avenue traffic, the traffic lights, red and amber and green, as they went north on Park Avenue, everything incredibly the same. The captain did not say a word. Lacy was vaguely thankful that she had given her hair a good brushing before going to meet Hiram in the park. Buddha wouldn't like this uninvited visitation.

The earlier call the police had made must have caused considerable talk among the various doormen, the elevator men and in general the entire staff of Buddha Smith's very proper, very dignified, indeed very luxurious apartment house.

The doorman may have recognized officialdom in Captain O'Leary or the neatly clad precinct officer himself because he showed them in without a word. The elevator man eyed them curiously and stopped at Buddha's floor without being told.

Buddha himself opened the door. "Come in—come in."

"You were expecting us," O'Leary said.

"Why, naturally," Buddha said, "there is a house phone down at the door, you know. Callers are always announced." He gave his whispering little chuckle. "Whether invited or not. Surely you don't think you could have arrived here at my door without my being told. But I didn't expect you, Lacy. However, do sit down. Tell me what's on your mind."

Lacy sat down on the chair he offered. O'Leary took another. His cohort refused and stood before the door rather as if he might have to block Buddha's exit.

"I'll not bother you long," O'Leary said. "I realize this is an intrusion, but you see—"

"Oh, I do see." Buddha smiled. "You must perform what you have to perform. Is there any news? Anything," he added mildly, "that you can tell me? Nothing confidential, of course."

"I'm not sure." O'Leary adjusted a crease in his trousers. "I only wanted your opinion as to whether the former husband of Mrs. Mendez—"

"Carlos," said Buddha helpfully.

"Whether Mrs. Rose referred to him really when she told Miss Wales that she was afraid of either her former or her new husband."

Buddha glanced at Lacy and lifted his eyebrows. "Surely Miss Wales told you everything Rose Mendez said to her."

Lacy cried, "I'm not sure what I told them! I was so confused and shocked and I just blurted out every single word, everything! But now—I'm not sure of anything!"

Buddha nodded. "Forgive me, Captain O'Leary, but I'm afraid Miss Wales was not in a state to tell precisely all that she had seen or heard."

"What do you know about it?" O'Leary said quietly. Buddha eyed the notebook in O'Leary's hand, and he adjusted his bulk quietly in the enormous chair. "Why, there you have me. I'll have to think— Why, yes, *you* told me. The first time we met." He almost bowed in O'Leary's direction. O'Leary's face did not alter.

Buddha beamed. "You told me! It was her former husband she was afraid of. Why, Lacy, you told the police that as soon as they came to her house. So the police knew it and asked me about it. Of course, I knew nothing myself."

Lacy leaned forward earnestly. "Captain, I said I was upset when you first came. I am still not sure what I told you—"

O'Leary's gaze said mutely, *I'm* sure.

She went on. "Rose wasn't herself. Somehow I did get the

notion that Carlos, her former husband, had cut off her allowance and that the present one had believed she had a great deal of money. I suppose—well, remembering Rose, I can imagine that she spent everything Carlos gave her, lavishly—"

Captain O'Leary interrupted her. "Giving an impression of being a very rich woman?"

"Well—yes." Lacy hated saying that: it was like an insult to a woman who had been her friend.

But Buddha shook his head. "You must be mistaken, Lacy. That's not what you told me—"

"I didn't tell you about that—"

"But, Lacy—"

O'Leary said, "I see. *I* told you that, Mr. Smith. I'm afraid I had forgotten." Lacy suspected that he forgot very little.

The captain went on, "We seem to have intruded on you for nothing. By the way, do you happen to know where Miss Wales's fiancé, Richard Blake, is at the moment?"

Buddha glanced at Lacy and shook his head and his chins. "No. Don't you know, Lacy? Oh, of course you'd have told the police. But certainly he may have had to return to wherever the government wants him to go."

"Quite," said O'Leary agreeably. "But you see we cannot find any connection he has with any government bureau. None at all."

The precinct officer at the door stood like a stone endowed with watching eyes and listening ears. Buddha shook his head. "You must have been misinformed, Captain. Oh, by the way—or not by the way at all—you have frightened off my manservant."

"That little guy?" O'Leary did not look at all regretful.

Buddha shook his head sadly. "I'm afraid you did. You see it developed that he is an illegal immigrant, so he gathered up whatever baggage he had and simply disappeared. At least he did have the courage to tell me why, but he couldn't be induced to stay."

"That's too bad," said O'Leary. "When did he leave?"

"I don't know. Sometime during the night—out the back way and the freight elevator, I suppose. I told him I would do my best for him. He couldn't be sure, though. So"— Buddha shrugged—"there you have it. He was really a very good valet-cook—everything."

"Also an illegal immigrant," O'Leary said. "Well, that's all for the moment. Thank you." O'Leary rose. The notebook vanished. The tall figure in the doorway stood aside. O'Leary slid his hand under Lacy's elbow, said again, "Thank you, Mr. Smith," and in no time they were all three in the hall again. The door closed softly, shutting off the sight of Buddha rising politely and all the luxury of the room as well as a drifting faint odor of cigarette smoke. Buddha was far too careful of his own health regime advised by the doctors at the spa he visited now and then (but where he never managed to lose more than a pound or two) to smoke.

O'Leary asked nothing as the elevator swooped them downward.

In the police car, though, going back down Park Avenue, the driver said, "Does your friend Mr. Smith smoke cigarettes, Miss Wales?"

"Never. He's a kind of health freak. So heavy, you know—"

"He certainly is far too fat." That was definite.

"I hope," O'Leary said almost conversationally, "that he is not hiding this Richard Blake. You, Miss Wales," he added, stunning Lacy, "are too pretty a girl. Too nice, too." Suddenly the precinct officer swerved the car to avoid an encounter with a bus. He managed to make the bus keep its distance and turned into Lexington with an air of accomplishment.

Twenty-three

Then the officer spoke over his shoulder, avoiding a taxi this time with an adroit turn of the wheel. "There was a slight odor of cigarette smoke. Stale."

"Right. But couldn't take a look through the place. No search warrant."

"Also, different precinct," the officer said with a sigh. "Take some time to get things shaped up."

O'Leary seemed to sigh, too, before he turned again to Lacy.

"Miss Wales, I have asked you so many questions, but there remains another. Many others perhaps. But for now, *why* did Mr. Mendez divorce your friend, Rose Mendez? Must have been a good reason."

Lacy hesitated, then said tentatively, "I don't really know, unless it had something to do with his present wife, Yolanda."

"As I understand it, they have three children. So she may have brought pressure. But somehow your friend Rose must have given him a *reason* for divorce, although Carlos

Mendez may have simply got tired of her, or given in to Yolanda's demands finally. I don't feel that Mr. Mendez is precisely a gentle or forgiving man. He may not have wished to continue his marriage to Rose but he certainly set a price on her remarriage. I wonder how many people knew that."

"Maria Geno Llamas knew. She told you. And I told you that the day Rose died. I was so shocked, I would have said anything! Especially," said Lacy rather indignantly, "to somebody who had authority and a right to question me. But when you ask me which husband she was afraid of, I'm not, now, really sure. Still, she did think that her current husband would be very angry when he discovered she had no money—I'm sure of that."

They turned toward the Waleses' house.

Hobie came prancing along the sidewalk, leading another prancing figure, Jessica, waving her tail happily. Hobie carried what looked like a small long-handled dustpan. Hobie grinned and waved the dustpan. "Pooper scooper," he yelled. "Law in this town. Whoops, don't run, Jessica! Stay away from that car. Can't you see it's police?"

There was the suspicion of a grin at the corners of O'Leary's eyes.

"Hobie is a sharp kid. I brought him along—purposes of identification," said O'Leary pleasantly. "Go on, please, Officer."

The car surged on. Hobie had certainly enjoyed being so flatteringly close to the police! He and Jessica bounded away. The car reached the cleanly swept steps to Lacy's home.

Another automobile was drawn up at the curb. It was a long, shiny limousine and the driver was in proper uniform. So, Carlos and Yolanda were still there.

"We'll go in the house," O'Leary said to his cohort.

But he took a serious look at the limousine and the driver as they went up the steps. The door was unlocked. Lacy opened it. Instantly Hiram's voice came from where he was

227

standing at the hall telephone. He sounded indignant. "—but I did have a vacation coming up. Can't I take it when I— Oh, I don't care what you tell my father. He can't escape having me as a son, can he. . . . Sorry, Mr. Fitterling, but this is very—oh, all right." He dropped the telephone, turned and saw Lacy and O'Leary and the precinct officer standing there, listening.

Hiram wiped his forehead with his free hand, airily adjusted the sling on his other arm and said, "I forgot to tell him I'd had an accident. I simply forgot— Excuse me—" He caught up the receiver of the telephone, dialed rapidly and as someone answered, said, "Annie? I may not be in the office for"—his eyes went to Lacy—"for a few days, but don't let my father get worked up about it. Tell him I'm still at the hospital. . . . oh, no, that won't work. He'd comb every hospital in the city. No, tell him I'm staying with a friend. He'll phone the club but that's fine. Thanks, Annie. You're a sweetheart." He put down the phone.

"Have any luck?" he asked O'Leary.

"Too early to say," O'Leary responded and led the way into the living room, where, unbelievably, Carlos, Yolanda, Raf, and Jessie sat together. Not even fighting, Lacy thought, surprised. Raf said, "Inez is preparing something for us to eat and drink. Dear Inez! Feed the savage beasts."

Jessie rose, gave Lacy a quiet but friendly glance and went out of the room, moving with nearly the same dignity and grace that Inez had. They couldn't be related, but there must be something in their genes that resulted in a certain likeness.

"Please stay here, Miss Wales," O'Leary said, anticipating her own move kitchenward.

Lacy stayed. Hiram settled himself on a footstool. Carlos had usurped Buddha's chair.

The precinct officer withdrew to a window.

O'Leary coughed a little, eyed Carlos and said politely, "Mr. Mendez, I don't like to question you about your personal affairs but it is part of my job. Why did you divorce Rose Mendez?"

Yolanda's eyes narrowed, like a cat about to pounce. Carlos simply folded his arms.

After a rather deliberate pause, he said frostily, "We were not suited to each other. We had, as the lawyers say, irreconcilable differences."

"It occurred to me that just possibly your former wife was interested in"—O'Leary was at his most polite—"another man—"

"Certainly not!" Carlos said, lifting thinly arched eyebrows. But Yolanda stopped swinging her foot. "Oh, come on, Carlos! You know there was that young pipsqueak always hanging around her. It gave you the only excuse you had for getting rid of her." She smiled. "I never saw him, but I heard and—"

"Stop it!" Carlos's voice was cutting.

"Don't be silly. You divorced her. Well, I knew it would happen."

"You were waiting for it, Yolanda," Raf said not at all agreeably.

The lady's eyes flashed again with something like a wish to murder. Lacy thought it imprudent of Raf to take too many chances with a woman like that. O'Leary had taken out his notebook but slid it back into a pocket—it struck Lacy that he was going to rely on his memory. "However," Raf said in a honeyed, too sympathetic way, "everyone knew about you and Carlos—I mean your extremely long"—Raf paused, selected a word and finished sweetly—"association."

Yolanda's sturdy hands opened and closed, disclosing long red fingernails that seemed to threaten Raf's throat. Carlos said, "Now, Yolanda! Behave yourself, Raf! You are going to get into bad trouble if you keep on!"

O'Leary put up a commanding hand. "Let's go back to the young pipsqueak, if you please, sir. Who was this?"

Carlos leaned back. "Nobody."

Yolanda cried, "You know! Everybody guessed—especially when you divorced Rose. Never could see why you married her in the first place. But I suppose at your age—" (Lacy thought that Carlos winced a trifle at the word "age.") Yolanda went on, "Of course, with you, Carlos, it was merely a case of off-with-the-old and on-with-the-new. But the difference was, the new love demanded too much money. Or got bored with life in *our* country. Then she met somebody else. She had got tired of you—"

Raf said with an obvious pretense of regret, "Family rows again. There must have been a man, Captain. And it does seem that the man was this Richard Blake she married." Raf glanced at Lacy, but continued, "I do assure you that while I met Rose only once and very briefly, I did not get the impression that she would have permitted Carlos a divorce without demanding a good settlement from him. And then too late she discovered that Carlos had put that cautious and, I must say, rather mean clause in his promise of an allowance—this allowance I feel must have been in order to get rid of her. Dear Yolanda! Stop flexing your fingers at my throat—"

"Raf!" Carlos didn't shout; that would have marred his pose of the perfect gentleman. The effect, however, was like the thrust of a razor-sharp icicle. "Shut up! This is none of your affair—"

"Oh, yes, it is," Raf said mildly.

Unexpectedly Hiram joined in. "I rather feel that this whole round of battle is my affair, too. *Did* you try to run me down with your car last night, Mr. Mendez? And if you did, why?"

Carlos drew himself up in his haughtiest attitude. "No!"

There was an abrupt, very thoughtful silence until O'Leary spoke, rather obliquely, "Mrs. Mendez, you speak very good—indeed, very colloquial—English."

"Huh?" Yolanda sat up and stared at him without even

fluttering her long black eyelashes. "Why not? Do you think we are barbarians?"

"No, not at all!" Nothing seemed to disturb O'Leary's exquisite politeness; even if he felt he must get out a dagger, he almost certainly would ask his victim's pardon before he stabbed with it. "Not at all," O'Leary repeated. "I would expect Spanish to be your native tongue—however, that is none of my business."

Carlos said loftily, "Educated in England. Nice family. Many of us in Logonda speak English, our second and, as a matter of fact, more frequently used tongue, except for a few scattered Indian phrases or Spanish among our workmen. That"—he cast a brightly cold glance at Raf—"is why I did not object when my young brother, Rafael, here, chose England for his education. I do now know that he had only started with law in England and then chose to divert to the study of lapidary skills in Antwerp. I take it you did not do very well there, Rafael."

"You know perfectly well that I didn't do very well! How could I—at my age! Your real jewel cutter starts when he is very young." He addressed O'Leary, pleasantly as always, but there were the familiar ruby lights in his eyes. "He is started as a child. Carlos did not permit me to do that. Indeed, he tried to keep me away from his own private—oh, very private—lapidary. I watched whenever I could, so he sent me away to get rid of me. Not to learn law. Besides, British law does not obtain in our country. Carlos is the law there anyway."

"But you didn't stay in Antwerp." Carlos linked his long fingers together.

"No. I couldn't have succeeded! I tried—" Raf shook his head and gave what Lacy believed was a sincerely regretful sigh. "Oh, I tried. After smashing a couple of diamonds because I couldn't study the planes of the stones properly—at least, I didn't know enough for that—I gave up. They gave up on me, too. The diamonds they allowed me to try after a bit of too rapid training, for I hadn't all the time in the world. In any event they let me pay for the two stones I had ruined. They were not large or important ones, of course. Nobody would have trusted me to cut anything like that."

Carlos shrugged and rose. O'Leary put out a hand. "Please don't go just yet. This young pipsqueak your wife mentioned. Did Mrs.—" He hesitated and said, "Did Rose Mendez take to him, so to speak?"

"Yes!" Yolanda cried triumphantly. "She couldn't see enough of him. Head over heels. Everybody told me. I don't see what there could have been about that woman," she added quite seriously as if trying to analyze some quality in Rose that had attracted Carlos and the young pipsqueak.

"Never mind," Carlos said. "Come on, Yolanda."

O'Leary again intervened. "I think you must tell me the name of this young man."

Carlos replied, all dignity. "He was only a dealer, nobody important. I told you before it's the way we do business. Dealers come to us to buy stones. Our best or, at least, our most highly priced stones are emeralds. We also have aquamarines. But the emeralds are the real wealth—" His pale eyes flickered once toward Raf. "I should say our real bread and butter. Too bad we can mine them for only three days—"

"What a lie!" Raf laughed, but his eyes were furious. "You mine them the year round. Carlos, come on, tell us who was the dealer who stole Rose's heart?"

Hiram quite suddenly got himself into the conversation. "Yes. What is his name, Mr. Mendez? There's no secret about it surely."

Carlos again drew himself up to his most unapproachable stance. "Really, my dear fellow. I don't keep a record of the dealers. My bookkeeper does, I believe. I only give them a few moments of courtesy when they arrive. I simply do not remember any names, and if I did, I promise you I would not get anyone into trouble—a nuisance, of course, but still trouble—with any of the jewelers who procure these services. Suggesting that any dealer induced me to divorce my wife! Absurd! Come, Yolanda—"

But just then Inez came into the living room followed by Jessie, who carried a tray of appetizing sandwiches. Suddenly hunger overcame Lacy, and she snatched a sandwich as Jessie came near her. Jessie paused to give her a gentle, friendly smile. "This is chicken. That one is ham—all of them good. I tried the ham myself—"

Raf said, "I'll get drinks for us in a moment, Inez."

"Thank you. Why, Carlos, you're not leaving."

"Yes," Carlos was all arrogant dignity, until his chill gaze fastened on the food, and suddenly it warmed faintly. Yolanda didn't even look at him but dropped back into her chair and slid out of her pumps again.

"There is enough for everybody," Inez said. "Oh, didn't the boy come back with Jessica?"

Hiram said suddenly, "What was your family name, Mrs. Raf?"

Jessie gave a lovely, serene smile. Perhaps, Lacy felt, her tranquillity as well as her beauty had drawn Raf to her.

"Carr," Jessie replied. "At home it is pronounced Kerr. But Raf"—her expression softened as she glanced at her husband, whose expression also softened, "liked me and my name. Little Jessica was mine as a puppy. She's a Hampdon spaniel. It's an odd breed. I rather think it is not well known here. It amused Raf to give her my name, insisting on the Carr. So there she is. Jessi*cah*. I think that boy should have brought her back by now."

Inez was looking worried. Certainly she could feel the beginning of another family quarrel. Lacy took a bite of her sandwich. It was very like Inez to use food and drink to try to induce the semblance of a mere family gathering into an atmosphere of quarreling, suspicion and police inquiry. Hiram drifted over to Lacy and quite neatly and swiftly took the sandwich from her hand. She looked up, startled.

233

He shook his head imperceptibly. But of course: she had taken a drink in that house, her own home, and nearly died from it.

Why, I'm just a fool, she thought. Somebody here loaded that drink yesterday. Somebody hit me over the head out in the garden. Somebody ran down Hiram with what he could only describe as a big and speeding car.

Did Carlos drive his own car? He could certainly drive. He must own any number of fine and expensive cars. Although in what was to him a foreign city, wouldn't he be obliged to hire a car and a driver? Yes, he had forbidden Yolanda's use of it earlier. And no chauffeur would possibly be induced to run down anybody; he'd have to settle not only with the New York police but also with his employer. From the hall Hobie shouted, "Come on Jessica. . . . Say, Mrs. Wales, here's the bag of shit!"

Hobie stood in the doorway beaming happily as if expecting congratulations. Talk about the boy who brought the news from Aix to Ghent! But Hobie did not drop dead at anybody's feet; he merely looked around the room, grinning.

It was far too appropriate, in its way. Hiram gave a sudden choke of laughter. Raf gave a loud whoop. There was even a spark of light in Inez's eyes. Carlos looked his haughtiest. Yolanda was puzzled, "What's funny about that?" Her English-speaking ability did not seem to include American slang. Lacy got up quickly and said to Hobie, "I'll see to it."

Hobie thrust the long-handled dustpan at her, and she departed with it toward the tiny entry hall near the back door and disposed of the waste. When she returned, Raf was at the liquor cabinet in the dining room. He placed glasses and bottles on a tray and followed Lacy back to the living room. Hobie eyed the glasses rather wistfully. "Guess I can't. Not now, anyway. I'm eighteen, though." He shot a glance at O'Leary, received no encouragement and said, "But thank you. That's a nice little dog of yours. Ready to go home, Captain?"

"Perhaps." Captain O'Leary spoke soberly, very gravely. The whole atmosphere of the room instantly changed. It was as if everybody in it had jerked upright, pulled by an ominous string. He nodded at his New York City precinct cohort. O'Leary paused in the doorway, said "Thank you," and bowed neatly to include all of them. Raf stared. "Now, what did he mean by that?"

"Nothing," Carlos said shortly. "Damned interfering yokel. Busybody. Farmyard mechanic."

Hobie had paused to give Jessica a farewell pat and overheard. "Oh, I wouldn't say that, sir. He's— Well, good-bye, all."

Jessica gave a little yelp after him as he left.

Hiram said thoughtfully, "I feel that Captain O'Leary is a very, very smart man." He forgot his admonition to Lacy and helped himself to not only one sandwich but two.

Twenty-four

Carlos gave Yolanda an icy look, which had in it something that impelled her to put down her drink, squeeze her feet into her pumps and pull herself up, one bejeweled hand on the chair. There was only the sound of a car starting up in the street and swiftly diminishing. Oddly (or maybe not so oddly), everybody stopped chewing to listen. Then Jessie looked at her watch. "If I'm to stay here, Inez, I must gather up my clothes at the hotel and—"

"And I must pay your bill." Raf helped himself to another sandwich.

Carlos said, "Good night, Inez—come along, Yolanda." He needn't have spoken, for Yolanda was already in the hall, her lovely silk suit rustling with the speed of her departure.

Carlos, however, evidently felt it necessary to show some degree of courtesy, for he kissed Inez's cheek—coldly, Lacy was sure—and, since he had to pass Lacy, took her hand, kissed the air above her fingers in an elegant gesture and departed. Lacy glanced down at her fingers—everyone of them still there! What an idea! At least Carlos could be polite when it suited him.

Again there was silence in the room as all of them listened for the departure of Carlos's car. There was a swift but low-toned and powerful throb of the engine, then nothing.

Inez sighed. "Do any of you really think that Captain O'Leary has got some definite ideas in his head?"

Raf replied, "Oh, yes, I should think so—"

The telephone pealed shrilly. Hiram was closest to it.

"Shall I?" he asked Inez, who nodded.

Again nobody talked, nobody chewed, nobody drank; everyone listened. Hiram said, "Sure . . . sure . . . But I can't just now. . . . Oh, you wouldn't do that. . . . But it's only about seven. . . . What if it is dark? I can find my way really, sir. . . . Oh, you wouldn't do that! Please, I tell you I'm fine." There was a long, long pause. Lacy guessed that it was Hiram's father telling him off in no uncertain terms. At last Hiram said, "Oh, all right, just for a few moments. . . . Well, I can't help it! I've got something . . . Oh, all right."

He put down the telephone with a bang that must have nearly shattered it and came back to the living room.

"I've got to leave—just for a little while," he said to Inez and then turned to Lacy. "That was—"

"Your father," Lacy said.

"Yes. He's making a big fuss about my arm and the car that ran me down. He told my mother, and she—" He looked at Inez for understanding and back to Lacy. "You see, she gets upset."

"Yes," Inez said.

Hiram looked cross and worried. "That ploy of theirs— my mother and my father, you know—they use it all the time. If I do anything one of them doesn't like, then that one says I am upsetting the other and I must come home at once. I know it's a conspiracy. They know it, too, but all the same it bothers me. They have an excuse this time, my run-in with that car. I can't help being annoyed, but I love them, you know. So, I've got to report in. Their town place is only in the Seventies. I'll be back"—he turned to Lacy again and then to Inez—"if you don't mind, Mrs. Wales?"

"Of course not, Hiram. Certainly you must go. Reassure your mother."

Hiram gave Lacy a long look, which said almost in so many words: Now, be careful; don't eat or drink anything.

Too late, for she had already munched on a sandwich. But Inez and Jessie had prepared them. She said, "I know—yes, Hiram—"

He gave Jessica an absent pat and went away. The street door banged after him before Inez said thoughtfully, "His mother, Mrs. Bascom, is not faking anything, you know. She really is a bit on the invalid side, I've heard. She'll be all right once she sees that Hiram is safe. Another sandwich, anybody?"

The telephone rang again, loudly and demandingly. This time Raf answered it and came back at once.

"For you, Lacy. A man," he said, his dark eyes alert. She knew it must be Richard and it was. "Lacy, I have to see you."

"No."

"Lacy, please. I've got to tell you—"

"No!"

He went on quickly. "You've got to be fair to me. That's the least you can do for anybody. *You know* that I didn't murder Rose. So give me a chance to— Oh, Lacy, anybody is supposed to be innocent until he is proven guilty."

She started to put down the telephone, but Richard's voice came through just the same. "Lacy, it isn't in you to be cruel and unfair. *You know* I didn't murder her. But I think I know who did! I must tell you. For your own good—"

She couldn't believe it. "For your good, you mean."

"Doesn't it matter to you about that murder?"

A coin dropped into a slot with a clatter. He was speaking from a pay telephone.

"Where are you?"

"Not far—over on Second Avenue. How about—the park? I'll be at the Lexington Avenue gate. Believe me, Lacy, I am in trouble. I'm not a witness but— I really must see you and tell you what I do know—but only you. Nobody else. You know you are safe with me. I told you I didn't kill Rose!"

The coin must not have been the right one, for the telephone clicked.

"Richard—" she cried, "Richard—" The telephone was completely silent.

She stood at the telephone table for a long moment. Hiram had told her not to venture out alone. Also, Hiram had said she was a fool and not worth his trouble. Yet she would have to listen to Richard. He must know something—some evidence about Rose's murder! He would tell her if only to save himself. But she wouldn't go alone. As she debated, Raf and Jessie, with Jessica on her leash, came into the hall.

"Back soon," Raf said cheerfully and waved to her. "Jessie's clothes."

Inez was still in the living room. Lacy's handbag with the key to the park in it stood on a table near the door, precisely the place where she had been warned never to leave it because its being there was an open temptation to burglary. Never mind; the key was there, and she could follow Raf and Jessie all the way while taking care not to attract their notice, for Raf would certainly want to know why she was going to the park. The reason for going seemed sensible to her but even Inez probably would not agree.

She must hurry; she could walk near enough Raf and Jessie to be safe, she reminded herself, and glanced into the living room, where Inez was bent over the sandwich tray. It was nothing for Lacy to glide past the open door, snatch her handbag and ease herself out the street door. She did so with sufficient care so neither Raf nor Jessie heard her close the door and go very softly down the steps. Once Jessica looked back but merely gave a friendly tail wag in Lacy's direction.

She walked behind them, keeping close enough so that if she needed to call for help, they would hear her.

She reached the gate and saw Richard standing a little in the shadow of some of the thick shrubbery, a distance from the streetlight. Across the street Raf and Jessie were coaxing Jessica to enter the hotel.

"Got the key?" Richard said from the shadows.

"Yes."

"It can be used on both gates, as I remember. Let me—" He emerged from the shrubbery, took the key from her hand and opened the gate quietly. "Oh, Lacy, you are wonderful! I was afraid you'd never come—I've got to tell you—well, I've got to tell you everything. Where shall we sit? Is anybody in the park now?"

"At this hour? I don't see a soul."

Richard peered around and selected a bench beside another heavy clump of shrubbery where the shadows were deep. Richard abruptly swept her into his arms, held her, kissed her—and really, Lacy thought fleetingly, it was again too ardent, too nearly like the close of a romantic play.

She pulled away and sat down on the bench.

"Lacy, I've got things to tell you. I'll spit it out. I did marry Rose."

"But you said—" she began.

Richard put his handsome head in his hands and muttered, "You don't understand. I had to marry her, I had to say what I said. But I swear to you I never killed her!"

The night was warm and rather humid, so there were little wreaths of fog around the scattered lamps. She thought that Richard had uttered a sob behind his hands.

"You said you hadn't married her—"

"That's part of what I must tell you. Just give me a minute

or two, Lacy. I can see now that I was a great fool. But I really thought I had to—"

"Had to marry Rose?" An odd kind of chill was stealing over her. She wished that she had snatched up a sweater.

"I tell you, I had to!" He lifted his face. He was handsome even in distress. The light from a distant lamp fell softly on the face that had once been dear to her.

"So you admit your marriage to Rose."

"I told you I had to. Orders."

"Nobody could have ordered you to marry somebody!"

"But he did. I mean they did. It was something Rose knew about, and it was believed that if I kept seeing her, acting devoted—well, you know. Rose did seem to like me. At least she liked to have me around. They really pressed about it. Don't ask me why, we never know just why we are told to do anything. Then the marriage—but I was told it would be instantly annulled. Instantly, that is, as soon as I could get the information Rose had. They were sure she had it."

"The police still insist you are not associated with any government bureau."

Richard gave a rather harsh laugh. "Of course they were told that. You know, Lacy, that much of their—I should say our—concerns are very, shall I say, sub-rosa. That's the truth. Certainly nobody would tell even the police anything about my work or my job." He turned to her; even in the soft light she could see or at least feel the earnestness in his gaze. "Can't you understand, Lacy? There are just things I can't do. When we became engaged, I didn't know that I would be required to enter into this false marriage to Rose Mendez."

"It wasn't exactly false. After all, I did see the marriage certificate."

"I mean, it wasn't a real marriage. Can't you understand?"

"I don't—no!"

His hand came down over her own. "You must try. I

didn't even like her. She—well, she liked me, yes. But she liked a dozen other young fellows, I suppose. However, when I talked of marriage—Lacy, can't you believe me?"

She didn't even stop to think. Perhaps Raf had given her such a course of lies that she was able to detect another one immediately; Richard was too eager to be believed, too glib.

"No!"

"But, Lacy—I'm *me*. Richard—"

The deep instinct persisted in her. "Rose gave the impression of having money. A great deal of money—" Richard put his face down in his hands again. She went on. "You needed money, you thought she had it—"

He made an odd kind of feeble defense by accusing Rose. "She flashed it around. Spent like everything. Everybody thought—"

"*You* thought she had money! *You* were the husband she was afraid of!"

A light breeze had sprung up and rustled the shrubbery a little.

"*No!*" Richard cried through his hands. "Lacy, you don't understand. Yes! I had to have some money. I didn't realize—I didn't know—but I didn't kill her! I *didn't*—"

She was steely calm. "You owe so much money?"

"Yes—"

"Wait, Richard, stop lying. You and that emerald—why, you knew Carlos Mendez before!"

He jerked up his head. "What do you mean? How could I have known Mendez?"

"By going to him, as a dealer perhaps. That's where you got my emerald. Then you took it from me and gave it to Rose."

"That emerald, yes. I slipped it off your finger. You didn't notice. I had to give something to Rose, I had to make her believe in me—"

"As you made me believe in you." She was cold and lucid—not heartbroken.

"I did *not* kill her, Lacy. I told you I was under orders—"

"No." She had to finish. "You are still lying! I believed you, like a fool, in the beginning. So did Inez. You were very convincing. And very good-looking and easy in your manners and—oh, very believable. Now, what is the evidence of Rose's murder you promised?"

"I'll tell you. But first you've got to believe me. I owe money, yes. But you know that I didn't kill Rose—"

"It must have been a shock to you to find that she lost all her money when she married again." Lacy wasn't even being vindictive; she was only facing the truth of her own conclusions.

"She never told me that would happen. I thought—"

A grim determination gripped Lacy. "You act like a child who expected Christmas presents and didn't get any. How could you have been such a fool! Telling us all those stories of being in the foreign service! You know Carlos."

"Why, *how*—"

"I know it now! I wondered why you were so unfriendly when you met and were both very careful not even to look at each other. I noticed that. I've been the fool! You were both afraid of letting it be known that you knew each other. How did you get away with all that money you owe?"

"Oh, Lacy, try to understand. I was having such a bad time. There were all those jewels Carlos wanted to dispose of secretly. So I—I just took a few—"

Her common sense took a great leap. "You smuggled them for him."

"But—

"How did you get them through customs?"

For an instant a slight smugness came into his handsome face. He shrugged. "Easy. I simply walked through customs with my pockets full. Well, not full exactly but well supplied. Nobody even questioned me. Of course," he added, "Carlos had everything arranged, so it was perfectly legal."

"Carlos knew all about that."

"Certainly. Up to getting the gems into the country. After that—I disposed of them."

"You told me that the emerald you gave me—and Rose—you found in a pawnshop. You simply stole it from Carlos."

"I gave you a choice one," he said feebly.

Twenty-five

She didn't even have to grope for his meaning. "The rest you sold somehow, wherever you could, but you never paid Carlos. And then he began to be suspicious when he didn't hear from you. So—why, yes! He came here to find you, to talk to Rose, to ask her what she knew of you." All at once a whole fabric of deceit made itself clear. "Why, you were the man Yolanda said came to see Carlos and ended by paying such attention to Rose that she agreed to the divorce."

There was again the slightest smugness in his thin smile, as if to say how could any woman resist me!

"You are disgusting," Lacy said clearly. "Now, where is the evidence you promised me?"

He evaded, still trying to justify himself. "I had to fight for my life. So much money and no way to get it and then—then Rose didn't have any money. How was I to know that?" Childish resentment, as if he had been cheated, came into his voice. "Carlos's agent—Maria Geno Something—told the police all she knew. Carlos told her to do so. I think Rose learned from her that Carlos's allowance had been cut off."

"How did you know that?"

"I—I didn't—"

"So when she died you knew you would get no money. So as soon as you came to the police you denied having married her. How did you know she had died? And what did you do with the money you got from the emeralds?"

He hesitated for a moment and finally said, "I used the money and did not report the sales to Carlos and, of course—"

"Of course, he guessed about your stealing."

"Don't call it that. A loan merely. I only wanted to make money—"

"What did you do with it?"

"If you must know—there's one way to make a quick profit—"

"You gambled! With Carlos's money! That you got from underground sales—"

"Not underground. Only—well, I didn't report the sales I made to Carlos. I realized that I couldn't go on with this. Carlos is no fool."

"No," she said bleakly. "I was the fool." She took a long breath and had to continue. "Where did you get all that money you needed to replace the money you must have spent, stolen really from Carlos? Who provided you with money? So much that your only hope was Rose's murder so you would inherit her money—that she didn't have? How did you—oh, Richard, *how* did you kill her? Tell me the truth."

"I didn't—that is—only some evidence clearing me. I want you to know that—"

"*Stop* lying!" She was very tired now; there was no anger or resentment left, only a sense of self-blame. How could she have so deceived herself! All for a something no better than a handsome doll, ready to be sold.

She was as great a fool as Richard. Suddenly she felt something menacing in the shadowy park—the man beside her? She started to rise. He caught her arm and pulled her back to the bench.

"You won't even try to understand. I keep telling you. Carlos went against his own law. He secretly mined emeralds seven days a week and was delighted to find a way to get them out of his little country without incurring the wrath of other mine owners. The money I got from the sales went through my fingers. All right, I gambled. But I was unlucky. The money went almost as fast as I could get it, so I borrowed, and when I couldn't pay off my debt— But you know that I didn't kill Rose."

"You did kill her! But how?" she said. "It happened at a time when you must have arranged a real alibi." She felt chilly. The cold breath of a breeze touched her.

Richard said, "I can't stop to talk any longer now. I've got to get to my government job—"

"You have no government job. And you only kept in touch with me and Inez because of her connection with Carlos. And the emeralds. You didn't know of the family quarrel. You needed us as an alternate choice for some contact with Carlos. But then, you married Rose. Somehow you murdered—"

"And *you* saw someone leave her house!" a voice said over her shoulder. Swiftly, like a lizard, Richard slid away from her into the darkness of the bushes and trees. A shadow swooped forward from the shrubbery behind her. A black blanket—a man's heavy overcoat—descended over her head. She fought it off, tried to get her breath and screamed, but the scream was cut off by hands around her throat.

"At last," she heard dimly, from far away. She was losing her breath and her senses.

Suddenly the grip of those hands relaxed a little. So, she thought, so play possum! Be very, very quiet. She held her breath. She let her head drop back. It was painful, but she had wriggled down on the bench; the barest corner of the stifling cover had slid away, too. She overheard some revealing words.

"Get out! Don't come to me for help again! Here's some cash if you keep your mouth shut . . . .

"No—no— Listen, Blake, I know all about you. Do you think I'd lend you money without investigating first. That story of a rich uncle! Your uncle had a tiny little jewelry store in San Francisco. After he died you sold it and had barely enough money to go to a school of mines. You knew enough from him about dealers in jewelry. You learned about Carlos Mendez and—naturally must have forged papers recommending you to him as a dealer. You were simply born crooked. And you're not as well-bred as you pretend to be!

"I expected to get my money back from your rich wife. You didn't have the guts to kill her yourself. I saw to it that you had an alibi. And you thought you'd still get a girl who had some connection with the Mendez family. You—oh, go on, get out! You've got a passport. I'll see to the girl's body."

The girl? She knew what girl.

She heard Richard give a cry of pain, as if he'd been struck. She tried to pull the small opening further apart so she could get some air. There was a scurry of feet on the path.

Richard had gone.

Yet not quite gone. He cried shrilly from a distance, "You failed twice! You could fail again! You even missed killing that lawyer, Bascom!"

"He knows too much. I'm sure of that. I'll take care of him later. The girl comes first. She's no fool. She saw that scared rat of a Spook, so I had to get rid of him. Eventually she'll tell the police and that will lead them to me. She likes me, so she wouldn't believe that Spook acted on my orders. But she can't go on believing that forever. She's loyal but not"— there was a chuckle—"*that* loyal, I'm afraid. Sometime she will accuse me and the police would probably believe her. *Now get out!*"

There was another quick scramble of feet on the path and a slight rasp of the opposite gate.

Richard had her key. He had gone forever. The hands came back to her throat.

There was a faint puffing sound of breathing near her, too near. There was another scramble; she was slipping down into the blackness but fighting her way, kicking, and her foot must have met some object, for somebody swore, in a muffled way. The hands on her throat tightened.

She thought she heard the nearer gate rasp slightly and the sound of feet running along the path. Then she was sure of nothing except fresh air on her face.

"Lacy! Lacy, breathe! Sit up. No, lie still!" That was Hiram. This was Hiram's arm supporting her. Suddenly there were two more figures. Jessie came out of the nightmarish world and caught Lacy in her arms.

Raf cried, "He's gotten away—"

"I'll put her on her back and pump air into her—" That again was Hiram. "Raf, go to the hotel, fast, call the police—"

There was again the sound of feet running now along the path. Jessie and Hiram were urging Lacy to lie down flat on the grass. Hiram pumped at her diaphragm with both hands, his black sling flung aside.

"Oh, stop, Hiram! You'll break my ribs."

Hiram's face was marble-hard and clear in the light from a strong flashlight, behind which Jessie seemed to be examining Lacy very carefully.

"You look better. Can you stand? I'll help."

"I'm all right. I can stand up." But she couldn't. Something more than lack of breath made her legs feel like jelly.

Jessie said calmly, "A good thing I had this flashlight. Got it so I could keep Jessica in sight. There's Raf."

He came running up, shouting, "They are on the way!"

Hiram cried, "She's got to go home. She's got to be safe. Wherever he is— God, Raf! Don't you realize—"

"Sure. Come on, Lacy. This is no time to linger around in the park. I was told that it is a private park, but the gate was open when we came in."

Lacy tried to explain something but her voice was husky. "He—Richard—has the key. When we came in, he put out his hand. It seemed just a gesture of courtesy to me, so I gave it to him. He opened the gate. He kept the key—"

It had all been part of setting the scene, setting the stage for murder. A silent murder. She said, "I want to go home."

Raf and Jessie each took an arm. Hiram went behind them, a rear guard. Lacy struggled to believe what she had to believe.

On the street sounds of frantic high-pitched barking came from the hotel. Hiram called, "Shut up, Jessica—"

But Jessica took this as an insult and howled—E above high C this time.

Two bellboys ran out. The desk clerk emerged behind them and shouted, "Take your dog, Mr. Mendez, I can't have this—"

Jessie released Lacy's arm, ran back, untied Jessica from one of the posts supporting the hotel's porte cochere, snatched up a large suitcase and ran back with Jessica still yelping, although in a disgruntled way now, at having been not only left alone but actually tied up.

So they hurried on, all together, across the street, along the sidewalk approaching the steps of Lacy's own home.

A police car, flashing lights, drew up at the door ahead of them. Inez came down the steps. Hiram said, "It can't be the police already—"

O'Leary shot out of the car followed by his cohort and, unbelievably, again by Hobie whose eyes sparkled: the time of his life, he might as well have said. O'Leary strode up to them.

"Where is your friend Smith?"

Nobody could speak for an instant; then everybody spoke in a chorus; at last Lacy alone told him.

O'Leary listened. "So he got away? The New York police will search the park. But it'll be no good, now."

Hiram was the first to understand. "You stayed over in the city to question him. You have been—"

"Sure. At his apartment. Talking to everybody. Doorman admitted that Smith had left, driving his own big car, taking some baggage with him. Nobody knew anything about the little guy who worked for him. . . . You'd better get Miss Wales in the house. We can finish this inside."

Once they were all seated in the living room, O'Leary continued, "Miss Wales, you know it was your good friend, your Mr. Smith. I am sorry to say that I gave him some information I ought to have had sense enough not to reveal." His tone held a quality of self-disgust. "I told him that you had seen a figure, or a shadow, or something move away from Rose's house. He didn't know you needed glasses, so he thought you had seen his man, Spook, sneaking into the woods, but he counted on your love and loyalty for a while. I also told him that Rose Mendez's allowance had been stopped. I'm not always such a fool, please believe me! Yet I didn't like Smith's answers. I didn't like—something or other about him, something—call it a hunch—that makes a policeman listen very hard and possibly doubt. So I investigated."

Hobie was at O'Leary's elbow; he tugged it urgently but respectfully. "Please, sir, how did he get to Mrs. Rose's house and leave the candy there before Miss Wales arrived?"

O'Leary looked at him with kind eyes. "He didn't. His man, this Spook, as we see it, had the key to the house, which Rose Mendez must have given to Blake. He got the candy into the house originally. The day she died, Smith had sent him back by another route to Mrs. Rose's house to secretly check on her condition. Spook slid into the kitchen, wily as a rat. I think he must have been there, Miss Lacy, when at Mrs. Rose's request you got out the whiskey. He was still there waiting for you to leave when he realized that she had died; he snatched the half-empty candy box and made for the woods and the car he had left not far from your onetime school, Miss Wales, and drove into New York to report to his employer. You caught a glimpse of him, but Smith appears not to have known about your distance lenses. He trusted to frightening this little guy Spook—as he did later—and to your love and loyalty for him. You see he had to hurry up his murder plan before Carlos and his wife and also you"—he looked hard at Raf—"arrived. Mr. Mendez's agent, this Maria Llamas—we talked to her again. She is a serious and I think very honest woman. She told somebody over the phone—probably Blake—just when all three members of the Mendez family were to arrive. So Smith had to work fast. He had worked out the alibi for Blake by getting him out of town. Spook—sometime we will know his real name; you say he was an illegal alien—"

Lacy nodded.

"Well, somehow little Spook was so frightened that he dropped the candy box and back-door key in the woods when he fled."

Hobie interrupted, saying adoringly, "I'm going to be a policeman someday."

O'Leary shook his head and put a kind hand on Hobie's shoulder. "Not if you've got the sense God gave a goose, son. It's a hard life. This only happened to break. Sometimes it takes months—years even. Remember there is no statute of limitations for murder."

Hobie, remarkably for him, quoted, "A policeman's lot is not a happy one!"

Raf gave a little hoot of laughter. But Hiram said soberly, "It's been such a short time really, Captain. How did you find out about Mr. Smith's financial activities?"

"Oh, we have ways. Banks don't tell much about their clients. Brokers are very secretive, too, but sometimes a question can catch them off balance and what it sums up to is I discovered that he was in the habit of lending money. Charged a good interest for it, too. Then your Richard Blake—he was a little easier to investigate because he had got himself into debt and had cheated Carlos Mendez. I began to feel it very likely that he was indeed the Blake who had in fact married Mrs. Rose Mendez and that since she—as you told me, Miss Wales—*was* afraid of one of her two husbands, it seemed probable the new husband was the one she was afraid of. So naturally I began to think it possible Smith and Blake had some understanding. Remember that smell of stale cigarette smoke in Smith's apartment? Almost certainly, Blake had been hiding there. Smith thought, I believe, that you purposely refused to identify Spook—and then Smith, Miss Wales, because of your loyalty to him."

"I never dreamed—" Lacy began.

"And, of course, when Blake came the first time to see me, someone had already told him the truth about Rose's money. So the rather elaborate plan for Blake to get some money obviously had failed. You heard Blake deny his marriage to Rose. So who informed him of the true situation? Certainly, someone who was in cahoots with him—who had perhaps planned the whole affair. Oh yes, your fine and loyal friend. A money lender on a big and vastly remunerative scale. Then by that time we had established Blake's debts—the usual, races, gambling, buying but not paying back anything. He had been selling smuggled emeralds for Mr. Carlos Mendez but never paid him.

"When Carlos finally became suspicious he decided he had to investigate. He got Rose Mendez's address from Mrs. Llamas hoping that would lead him to her new husband, Blake." He broke off as the wail of a siren sounded outside in the street. "Excuse me, that should be more of our New York friends." He went out of the room and out the front door.

"That's all there is to it," Raf said. "Richard didn't kill Rose after all. Your Buddha had lent him money. He wanted it back. So Richard married a rich wife. Buddha planned it all. He'd get rid of Rose. Richard would get her money, Richard would repay Buddha. All very simple yet wily planning on Buddha's part. But Richard had stolen from Carlos—kept the money he got for Carlos's emeralds. Carlos got suspicious. Meanwhile good Maria had already phoned Carlos and me and, unsuspicious of a friendly voice, had inadvertently given away news of our arrival to Blake. So Smith had to rush on with the scheme. Blake's alibi was planned and in order. Later O'Leary blamed himself for letting Smith know that there was, after all, no money to be had after Rose's murder. O'Leary, in my opinion, was acting as a very good investigator. He shouldn't blame himself. Obviously then Smith had time to warn Blake. No money. Don't admit your marriage. Well—there it is," Raf said.

Inez soberly said, "When things started going wrong, Buddha must have had his passport ready for—I suppose for anyplace. But he always said he went to a sanitarium somewhere—in Switzerland? I'm not sure where—"

Raf said, "We ought to have guessed how anybody got a supply of that hypnotic. O'Leary will get that all spelled out. There's Interpol—"

"I suppose we ought to tell Carlos about this," Inez said.

Raf thought and shook his head, then nodded. "I suppose so." A flash of mischief came into his eyes. "He'll not like it. Trusting that guy, I mean your—this Richard."

Inez sighed. "So Carlos went to see Rose. He had to find out if she could tell him where this—"

"Yolanda called him a pipsqueak," Raf offered.

"He put up a fine front," Jessie said. "Even I could see that."

Raf laughed. "Well, Yolanda knew of Blake only as her rival's lover. Doubt if she ever saw him. Now, Lacy, about this Hiram—"

Hiram, at the door, turned as he heard his name. "O'Leary says they've combed the park, didn't find anything but a doll and one roller skate."

Raf broke in sardonically, "I don't think your Buddha would attempt an escape on one roller skate."

Hiram said, "I very much doubt we'll ever see Richard— or Smith again. Do you mind very much, Lacy?"

"How can you ask!" Lacy began.

There came a certain spark in Inez's eyes. "Come on, Raf. Jessie. We'll let them talk alone—upstairs. Please—"

Even the little dog obeyed.

Hiram came to Lacy's side. "This is not the right time. That is, you must be totally done in— But if you'll think it over and all that and—"

As it turned out, Carlos had almost the last word, for the telephone rang and Lacy automatically, in spite of a happily pounding heart, went to answer it. Carlos's voice said, "Inez? Oh, good—Lacy! It is easier to talk to you than to Inez or Raf. Will you tell them that I am taking steps to restore all their holdings in the mine—"

Hiram, listening with an ear pressed close to Lacy's, said, "He may be brought back as a material witness—"

Carlos heard Hiram. "Only my duty. If and when. You see, I guessed most of it after I talked to Maria Geno and saw Blake, and now—"He seemed to sigh but said, "Tell them all that I must stick to my own law. Three days for emeralds. To all of you *Vaya con Dios.*"

The telephone clicked. Hiram said, "As I was saying, I can't ask you to make up your mind just now but as soon as—"

Raf came leaping down the stairs. "I heard all that on the extension phone upstairs! Good Maria! She struck the conscience of the king." He stopped, then gave them one bright look and said, "I heard you, too, Hiram. Lacy looks as if she made up her mind quite a long time ago. So—" His sharp

255

eyes caught a sudden gleam. "That emerald ring? How about it?"

Hiram said, "For Jessie?"

Raf laughed happily. "Sure. All in the family. I never thought I'd quote Carlos, but I will now. *Vaya con Dios,* my friend. For always."

About the Author

MIGNON G. EBERHART'S name has become a guarantee of excellence in the mystery and suspense field. Her work has been translated into sixteen languages, and has been serialized in many magazines and adapted for radio, television and motion pictures.

For many years Mrs. Eberhart traveled extensively abroad and in the United States. Now she lives in Greenwich, Connecticut.

In the seventies the Mystery Writers of America gave Mrs. Eberhart their Grand Master Award, in recognition of her sustained excellence as a suspense writer, and she also served as president of that organization. She recently celebrated the fiftieth anniversary of the publication of her first novel, *The Patient in Room 18.*